"Why do I feel like
she crunched down

D0357134

Jachin ignored her comment and gave her a curt nod. "Turn around."

Ariel dug her teeth into the apple and did as he asked. As soon as her rear settled on the floor, he gripped her waist and pulled her between his opened legs. "You need to move closer."

Ariel stiffened at their intimate position. Her rear and hips were cradled by his groin, her back against his muscular chest. When his warm breath swept across the back of her neck, she gasped and froze.

"Wh-what are you doing?" she asked, her voice barely a whisper.

"I'm closing your wound," he said in a husky whisper right before his warm tongue swept across her exposed flesh. "You must trust me."

His heat enveloped her. Tingling flooded through her, slamming into her in aching waves of desire.

This wasn't happening. She didn't want this.

I don't want him. He's a vampire.

Books by Patrice Michelle

Silhouette Nocturne

Scions: Resurrection #31

*Scions

PATRICE MICHELLE

Born and raised in the Southeast, Patrice Michelle gave up her financial calculator for a keyboard and never looked back. Thanks to an open-minded family who taught her that life isn't as black and white as we're conditioned to believe, she pens her novels with the belief that various shades of gray are a lot more interesting. She's a natural with a point-and-shoot camera, likes to fiddle with graphic design and, to the relief of her family, strums her guitar to an audience of one.

Visit Patrice's Web site at http://www.patricemichelle.net to learn about her upcoming books, read excerpts and join her newsletter.

SCIONS: RESURRECTION

PATRICE MICHELLE

Silhouette® Books

nocturne™

If you purchased this book without a cover you should be aware that this book is stolen property. It was reported as "unsold and destroyed" to the publisher, and neither the author nor the publisher has received any payment for this "stripped book."

 SILHOUETTE BOOKS

ISBN-13: 978-0-373-61778-4
ISBN-10:   0-373-61778-X

SCIONS: RESURRECTION

Copyright © 2008 by Patrice Michelle

All rights reserved. Except for use in any review, the reproduction or utilization of this work in whole or in part in any form by any electronic, mechanical or other means, now known or hereafter invented, including xerography, photocopying and recording, or in any information storage or retrieval system, is forbidden without the written permission of the editorial office, Silhouette Books, 233 Broadway, New York, NY 10279 U.S.A.

This is a work of fiction. Names, characters, places and incidents are either the product of the author's imagination or are used fictitiously, and any resemblance to actual persons, living or dead, business establishments, events or locales is entirely coincidental.

This edition published by arrangement with Harlequin Books S.A.

® and TM are trademarks of Harlequin Books S.A., used under license. Trademarks indicated with ® are registered in the United States Patent and Trademark Office, the Canadian Trade Marks Office and in other countries.

www.silhouettenocturne.com

Printed in U.S.A.

Dear Reader,

I'm often asked where I get the ideas for my stories. My answers have ranged from a song, to an event, to, yes, even a ring! But the idea behind *Scions: Resurrection*, the first book in my SCIONS trilogy, is a little more unique than my past novels. Many of the scenes and events that you'll read in Chapter One of *Scions: Resurrection* came directly from a dream. Imagine being kidnapped by a vampire, chased by gunmen and thrown through a...well, you'll see.

While this book is chock-full of adventure, I've incorporated an emotional, heart-tugging romance alongside the nonstop action. The entire SCIONS trilogy was built around my inspiring dream, while incorporating a concept that has always intrigued me about paranormal stories—my own spin on the origins of the lore we embrace when we read books or watch movies about vampires, werewolves and other paranormal creatures.

I hope you enjoy *Scions: Resurrection* and that you'll follow each of the Scions as they embark on their own romantic journeys.

All the best,

Patrice

I dedicate this book to my family. I love you all for listening to every new idea with avid interest and for supporting me and my crazy writing schedule.

To my readers, thank you for your continued support. It means so much to me.

Acknowledgments

I wanted to thank my amazing agent Deidre Knight for believing in my writing and finding a home for my books, and my editor Ann Leslie Tuttle for her astute editorial input and endless enthusiasm.

Thank you to my critique partners Cheyenne McCray and Rhyannon Byrd for helping me during every stage of this novel's creation. You ladies rock!

Chapter 1

A death for a life.

Jachin leaned against the rain-slicked brick building in New York City's theater district and stared at the name written in red ink on the five-thousand-dollar bill in his hand. Such a wasteful use of obsolete paper money indicated either his client's sheer wealth or his complete disregard for preserving items of the past. Jachin didn't care which. His client paid, he did his job.

He crushed the bill in a tight fist, mentally sending heat to his palm. Damp, cool summer air blew in the alley between the theater and the warehouse, bringing with it faint scents of car exhaust and day-old trash from a nearby alley. Jachin uncurled his fingers and ashes floated from his hand, dispersing in the wind. No trace, exactly the way he preferred to operate.

How many kills had he made over the past decade? He'd stopped keeping track after fifty. Dealing in death had become his means to live, yet doing so had darkened his soul.

A sound in the dark recesses of the alley drew his attention, and his shoulders tensed. He slowed his breathing to one breath every thirty seconds. His heart rate followed suit while he harnessed his energy to enhance his sight. Anger lashed through him, and his sharp gaze narrowed on the culprit. He'd ignored the hunger pains for four days longer than he should have. No one would screw with this deal.

Small, vivid green eyes stared back at him in the alley's darkness before the cat hissed then fled.

The low rumble of voices exiting the front of the building told him the show was over. His gaze dropped to the old-fashioned watch on his wrist. It was more accurate since it didn't depend on a consistent pulse rate to power it. When it came to his job, timing was everything. Thomas Ramos's security would be escorting the senator out of the building in forty-five seconds.

Jachin slid his hand under his lightweight black leather trench coat, his muscles tensing again as he pulled his pulser weapon from its holder at his lower back. As the weapon powered up, he reveled in the high-frequency zing and the knowledge the weapon was a detached extension of himself. He could easily kill Ramos and his security detail with his bare hands, but this was business, not an act of vengeance.

Bright light flicked on above the theater's back door, bathing the dark alley in a circular glow.

The door began to open and Jachin's fingers flexed as

he gripped his gun. A female voice had him stepping back behind a stack of crates.

Damn. A woman.

He ground his teeth at the unexpected complication and ran his thumb up the weapon's dial, moving the power from kill to stun.

Four people spilled out of the Wesley Theater's back exit. A tall security guard and a short, thick-necked guard preceded a blond woman and Ramos. Expensive perfume, spicy cologne, hyped-up testosterone and the scent of sex surrounded them as the woman giggled at the senator.

She gave Ramos a quick kiss on the cheek, short curls bouncing around her laughing expression. "Honestly, Tommy, how was I supposed to keep my mind on the play with your hands doing their own kind of entertainment?"

Jachin stepped out of the shadows and pegged the woman with his stun burst.

She crumpled to the ground amid yells from the men. Jachin mentally slammed the theater door shut before the men could retreat inside. Instincts on high, he dove out of the way of a pulse burst that missed his chest by a couple of inches.

"Sonofabitch!" The tall man fired constant bursts while using his body as a shield to back the senator toward the Dumpster at the end of the alley.

Squawks from a comm unit echoed in the narrow space. The short, bald guard spoke into a communicator attached to his wrist. "He moves like an animal, so fast I can't get a make on him. Gotta be Slayer. We need backup now!"

No one would come. Jachin had already taken out the security detail sitting in the car outside the front of the theater.

He advanced with rapid speed, using the alley's brick walls as springboards. The security guards yelled, and pulser fire exploded around him, leaving singe holes in the brick wall one step behind him. With each leap he edged forward, corralling the three men.

When one of them nicked his jacket, the close call made Jachin's heart beat faster, heightened his senses. Predatory excitement grew within him. His mouth watered and his gums tingled as he forced the men behind the Dumpster in the back of the alley. The inevitability of the kill was almost upon him.

Jachin leapt over the Dumpster to land in front of the tall security guard.

Before his quarry got one shot off, Jachin grabbed the man's scrawny neck and squeezed, his primal instincts taking over. The dead man's body dropped to the ground with a heavy thump.

Holstering his gun, Jachin flexed his leg muscles and vaulted in the air. He landed in front of the last two men, blocking their path to the door.

The security agent's weapon discharged, and surprising, excruciating pain ripped through Jachin's upper arm. The burning sensation spread down his bicep as if his arm were being burned from the inside out.

Jachin bit back an unholy roar of pain and fisted the senator's lapel in a tight grip at the same time he hammered his other hand against the security guard's barrel-like chest.

When the guard's lifeless body fell to the ground, the senator's jowls quivered as he stared up at Jachin. Stunned shock briefly replaced the fright in his eyes. His gaze flicked to his attacker's elongated canines. "You're a vampire? But…but we thought you were extinct."

"Isn't that a helluva rub?" Jachin leaned close to him. "My race was made by humans, condemned by humans, yet humans have no problem hiring one of us to do their dirty work."

Ramos's rapid heart rate stuttered and a look of pain crossed his face. Sweat trickled down his temples as he crushed Jachin's coat with his meaty hands and gasped for breath. "You can't."

"Watch me." Jachin pulled the man close and sank his teeth deep into his thick jugular. Rage made Jachin's chest constrict. As Thomas let out a low scream, flashes of Jachin's Sanguinas clan members suffering from the humans' torturous testing, dying before their time, flew through his mind. Decades of vengeful instincts demanded he rip the human's throat out.

Taking deep breaths through his nose, Jachin fought the urge to inflict pain.

This was business.

Instead, he merely swallowed the warm blood. Thomas's low scream dwindled to a hoarse whimper a few seconds before the corrupt Senator's heart jerked to a halt.

Jachin had only taken two swallows when the familiar nausea slammed into him, twisting his insides. Disgusted, he retracted his fangs, swiped his tongue over the bite wound and dropped the dead man on the damp asphalt.

Not a single ounce of remorse entered his thoughts as he pulled his gun from the holster, adjusted its setting back to kill mode and put two pulse bursts into the senator's chest. After he reholstered his weapon, he picked up the unconscious woman and set her inside the theater door.

Wiping the remnants of blood from his mouth, Jachin turned away from the carnage and never looked back.

A short time later, Jachin stood in an upscale gardened courtyard on the Upper East Side, banging on Roach's door.

"Hold yer horses, for God's sake," Roach said from behind the thick, intricately carved wood.

When the old man opened the door, Jachin barely held on to his consciousness. He stumbled through the threshold and fell on the tiled kitchen floor.

"Six pints," he said in a hoarse voice.

"Damn it, don't you die in my house!" Roach stamped his foot on the floor in irritation.

As the geezer bent and ran his hand through his spiky gray hair, scowling at him, the smell of aftershave wafted his way. Jachin would forever associate that strong spicy scent with irritating yet necessary salvation.

Roach's pale green eyes narrowed. "Payment first. Ten thousand."

Jachin gritted his teeth. Ten thousand was half his take. "Extortionist! Dim the lights," he growled, then tossed the bastard his payment.

"Bloodsucker." Roach's bony fingers gripped the slim card Jachin threw his way. Once Roach ran the card through a handheld scanner he'd pulled from his robe pocket, he nodded his approval and slid his finger across the touch pad on the wall to lower the lights. Before he left the room, he tossed Jachin his card back and grumbled, "Don't you bleed on my new floor."

In order to remain conscious, Jachin slid his card into his coat pocket and focused on the newly remodeled kitchen with its contemporary black cabinets and stainless-steel appliances. The hard white tile beneath him felt surprisingly warm. Heated tile. Roach had spared no expense on his new kitchen. How ironic, considering Jachin sought out the man for his ability to concoct a palatable meal—a mcal from a lab, not a kitchen. He didn't know how Roach was able to make human blood viable for him. All he knew was the man was a retired chemist.

Jachin lay very still. Every sound echoed in his throbbing head. Even the soft glow of indoor lights made him want to puke…if he had anything in his belly to toss. He'd already retched up the senator's foul blood on the way to Roach's.

The grating shuffle of shoes announced Roach's return. Several pints of blood smacked on the floor next to Jachin. He winced at the deafening noise reverberating in his head and grabbed the pouches.

Holding three bags together, he ripped the plastic corners with his teeth and sucked down the pints in two large swallows before he reached for the next set.

A chair scraped the floor. "Who bought it tonight?"

Annoyed that his hand shook, Jachin ignored Roach's question and lifted three more full bags to his lips.

"Serves you right for attempting to take tainted human blood." Roach snorted while lowering himself into the chair.

Once Jachin downed his sixth pint, the cramping in his stomach abated somewhat. He elevated himself on his elbow and focused on Roach. "I should've drained you dry. Keep upping your prices and see if I don't one day."

Roach laughed out loud and ran his gnarled fingers across the old scar on his neck. "Just like all humans, my blood is still poison to you. Can't you come up with any new threats? I feel slighted that you don't make the effort to be original with me."

A lingering pain slashed through him, stealing Jachin's breath. Doubling over with pain, he growled while flipping off Roach.

"Eh, that's what *you* need—a good lay." The crotchety man thrummed his fingers on the table.

While the sterilized blood spread through his system, Jachin took a deep, inhaling breath. He shuddered at the sheer power and nutrients it provided, the awakening of his senses. The rush was almost arousing.

Almost.

"I don't need sex. I need sleep." He glanced past the hole in his jacket and touched the burn on his arm. At least the partially healed wound had begun to close. It would fully heal. There was only one scar he cared about.

Roach slid his gaze to the empty plastic bags littering his floor. "You wouldn't need so much if you didn't continue to believe in the ramblings of an old vampire on his deathbed."

Jachin stood to his six-foot-four-inch height and narrowed his gaze on Roach. "The prophecy is true." *It has to be. It's the only thing that keeps me going,* he mentally finished. He turned to leave, and dizziness made him grab the back of the kitchen chair.

Roach let out a heavy sigh. Pulling two more pints of blood out of his plush terry robe's pocket, he handed them to Jachin. "On the house."

"Your generosity overwhelms me," Jachin said, taking the plastic pouches.

Roach snorted at his sarcasm. "I have to keep my income source in fit condition."

Jachin turned to leave, calling over his shoulder, "Friggin' opportunist."

"Don't let the door slam you in the ass on your way out, bloodsucker."

Once he'd tucked the two pints of blood into his coat's inside pocket, Jachin took the subway to the Lower East Side. Jamie's Pub was within a couple of miles of his home. As he walked inside the pub and sat down at the bar, the scent of burnt almonds, peanuts, smoke, sweat and free-flowing alcohol slammed into him. The place was packed with men staring at the curvaceous blond newscaster currently displayed on the large projector screen along the far wall.

"We interrupt tonight's sports event to bring you breaking news," she said, eliciting groans from the men, who were obviously there to watch the tournament game while they downed a few beers. "Senator Ramos and his entire security team were murdered tonight in what appears to be a brutal assassination. The only survivor of the crime was a female theatergoer, but she was knocked unconscious before she could see the assassins. We'll keep you informed once autopsies have been conducted."

As the newscaster cut to another journalist on the scene, Jachin scanned the room. He caught a whiff of Landon's scent before he saw the man with short, light-brown hair get up from a table at the back of the room and begin to weave his way around the tables.

"Your drink, sir." Kip set the imported whiskey down in front of Jachin. Jachin picked up the double shot and inhaled the alcohol's strong aroma.

"Know anything about that deal tonight?" Landon narrowed his green eyes on him before he turned a deliberate gaze to the thin man sitting on the stool next to Jachin. Jerking his head toward the main room, he addressed the man. "There's a better view of the game out there."

Landon's broad-shouldered stance, his entire dominating presence, demanded respect.

"Fine," the man slurred. He cast bleary, bloodshot eyes Jachin's way before he swiped up his drink and slid off the stool to stumble to a nearby table.

Landon ran his hand across the cleft in his chin and assessed Jachin with shrewd frankness before he sat on the stool next to him and signaled for the bartender.

Jachin threw back his entire drink in one swallow. While the alcohol did its magic, burning all the way down to his belly, he deliberately eyed the smashed bullet plug dangling from the silver chain around Landon's neck. The small piece of metal stood out against his black T-shirt. He knew what that bullet meant to Landon and where the man's loyalties lay.

"You asking in an official capacity?"

Landon cut his gaze from the beer Kip just set down in front of him back to Jachin. Picking up his cold longneck, he took a deep swig. "Do I need to?"

Jachin noted the rise in Landon's heartbeat, the increase in his musky, primal scent. He was tensing, preparing to fight if need be. Jachin knew he could probably take Landon. Hell, in the past he could've overpowered him with one hand tied behind his back. But he was done with his share of violence for the night.

"Just out for a stroll and a drink before calling it a night."

Jachin tapped the wood surface to let Kip know he wanted another round.

"You look half-dead."

Jachin glanced at the wall-length mirror behind the bar. Whereas Landon's face appeared tanned underneath his scruffy, several days' growth of beard, Jachin's clean-shaven, angular face looked haggard and pale, his high cheekbones sharper and more defined than usual. "Shit happens," he said after the bartender replaced his drink and walked away to help a customer at the other end of the bar.

"Nice and clean. Smells like a pulser burn to me."

Landon's comment jerked Jachin's gaze back to him, but the man's line of sight was focused on Jachin's arm.

Glancing down at his coat sleeve, Jachin's gut tightened. He'd forgotten about being hit earlier. "It rained tonight. Your senses are off, my friend." Jachin lifted his drink and gulped it back, then met Landon's gaze with a steady, challenging one.

Friends they weren't, but wary adversaries caught up in similar circumstances. Those circumstances had made for an interesting if uneasy truce between them over the past few years.

"He had a wife and a family." Landon looked at the projector as he took another swallow of his beer.

Jachin considered the blonde he had seen hanging on the senator, remembering the smell of sex that surrounded the two. He snorted. "Life's a bitch. I'll venture a guess that his family is better off."

"You're a coldhearted sonofabitch," Landon snarled in a low tone, swinging his gaze back to Jachin. His hold on the beer bottle was so rigid, his knuckles turned white. "You call this surviving? You've lost your humanity."

Fury swept through Jachin at Landon's comment, knotting his stomach. "Humanity is who made me what I am. You've been rubbing shoulders with them so long you've lost sight of the fact they'd hunt you down if they knew what you really are. Maybe you should spend more time with your own kind."

Landon's eyes narrowed for a long second before his gaze swept the room. "They're not *all* your enemies, Jachin. Some have the capacity to understand and the willingness to embrace all kinds."

Jachin took in the people in the room as he addressed Landon's optimistic view of humans. "They are weak, pathetic, short-lived shells of what they could be."

Landon grabbed Jachin's forearm and dug his fingers into the muscle. "The man I listened to, the one I came to trust six years ago, was a philosopher, an idealist with a will to live. How can you believe in this prophecy you mentioned and spout that bullshit at the same time?"

The man's words hit home and Jachin's chest constricted. He should never have told Landon what Ezra said before he died, but Jachin had figured he might need an ally in the Lupreda world to fulfill the dying vampire's prophecy.

He jerked his arm out of the man's grasp. Landon was right. He couldn't go on living like this.

Stepping down from the stool, Jachin stared at the projector screen, where pictures of Ramos flashed on the news. "We all get what we deserve."

Landon clenched his jaw before he spoke. "One day Slayer will screw up. The NYPD will call me to hunt you down."

Jachin gave him a curt nod. "Fair enough."

A heavy weight spread across Jachin's shoulders as he left the pub. He knew his tenuous truce with Landon had shifted tonight. He didn't miss the irony—that a werewolf descended from a petri dish, had more humanity in him than he did, a vampire born of man.

Jachin's boots echoed in the dark, narrow street as he made his way toward the building that housed his loft apartment. Car exhaust, rodent droppings, human food remnants from sour cheese to various nutty smells, all mixed with the polluted rain hanging in the air, bombarding his senses.

As a backdrop to the smells, human and animal heartbeats pounded in various stages, from excitement to slumber. Every sound and scent penetrated his consciousness. Shaking his head to try and block them all, he vowed to never go so long without food again.

Not only did the lack of nutrients wreak havoc with his ability to adjust his senses, it also slowed his reflexes. At least the money from this latest hit should sustain him for a good three weeks.

Unfortunately, the specialized blood Roach provided only lasted forty-eight hours once the bags were exposed to air and light, which meant he had to see Roach in a couple of days to retrieve more food.

He despised depending on anyone.

At this point, with the money he had left he could go two more weeks before he'd have to kill again. He had a list of clients waiting on him to be hungry enough to work.

When Jachin reached the end of the road, he ignored the

bright yellow *Caution, Dangerous Chemicals* plastic tape crisscrossed in front of the six-foot tall industrial-grade metal fencing and building.

Jachin sensed nothing but quiet peacefulness as he entered his loft apartment and shrugged out of his trench coat. Once he pulled the pints out of his coat's deep pockets, he tossed the coat on a side chair in his entryway and poured the contents of a bag of blood into a martini glass he retrieved from the kitchen.

With a wave of his hand he used his mental powers to turn on the projector and sound system. While soft jazz music filtered through the surround sound in the two-thousand-square-foot loft apartment, Jachin picked up his drink and sat down in his butter-soft black leather chair.

Sipping his drink, he savored the taste as it slid down his throat. It had been so long since he'd tasted untainted human blood he couldn't describe the flavor if he had to. And yet, as he took another sip, he knew this blood was missing something. The spice of life was glaringly absent.

It was the *essence* that made blood distinctive to a specific person, that made human blood irresistible to his kind. The human's smell, the person's flavor, their very soul resided in their blood, giving it an added zing. All the blood he'd bought from Roach tasted the same—bland. Nothing to sink his fangs into.

But with it he survived.

His gaze scanned past the shuttered windows that lined the entire exterior wall and landed on the side wall with built-in bookshelves. They were packed with books, leather-bound originals in many cases. The library had cost him a small fortune to collect over the years.

Raising his glass in salute to the wall of books, Jachin said, "I'm not the uncivilized, uncultured man you think I am, Landon," as he stood and approached his collection. Surveying the section related to psychic phenomenon, telepathy and harnessing one's mental powers, he smirked. His studies had their uses. He'd been able to expand his abilities over the past decade.

Now a thick layer of dust claimed the books' surfaces. He used to clean them like clockwork once a week. In the past, the sight of dust would irritate him, but today he felt nothing.

Angry with himself for losing the simple joy of reading, he downed the rest of his dinner and turned out the lights. Exhaustion weighed heavily on him. He lifted his hand to mentally turn off the music, and the same blond newscaster from earlier came on the screen. Turning up the projector's sound, he waited to see if there were any new updates on the Ramos story.

"Good evening. Here's the latest report on Senator Ramos's murder. It is now believed that the assassination was done by one person. The female witness does remember seeing a man standing in the shadows as they exited the theater, but she never saw his face. Stay tuned for the midnight news, where we'll interview the witness. And be sure to tune in for tomorrow night's special guest. We'll be sitting down with debut novelist Ariel Swanson and her controversial book about vampires that's causing quite a stir."

A human writing about vampires? The thought intrigued him.

Landon's comment that he'd lost his humanity echoed in Jachin's head. He cast his gaze to his library once more. It'd been at least three years since he'd bothered to open a book.

Jachin walked over to his desk and switched on his laptop. Why not see what a human has to say about vampires? Once he typed in "Ariel Swanson" on the Internet, he was surprised to find hundreds of reviews of the woman's book already posted on the Web store's review site.

Jachin chuckled as he purchased the e-book version of Ms. Swanson's novel. *The Vampires' Return* might make for some entertaining reading tomorrow.

After he'd downloaded the e-book and opened the file to make sure he'd gotten the right version, he was about to shut down the laptop when his gaze landed on the quote at the bottom of the book's cover page.

They thought vampires were extinct. In truth, the vampires were only waiting to fulfill the prophecy.

Jachin's entire body tensed. This human female wrote about vampires…and a prophecy?

Pulling out his chair, he sat, then scrolled down to chapter one of *The Vampires' Return.*

He didn't believe in coincidences.

Chapter 2

"Sitting at number eight on the *Sentinel Daily*'s list after its first week of sales, Ariel Swanson's debut novel, entitled *The Vampires' Return*, has stirred up quite a controversy."

Ariel took a deep, calming breath and folded her hands in her lap as the blond reporter, Sandy Myers, held up her paperback book for the cameraman. "While it's true that vampires have been extinct for twenty-five years, many still remember the creatures' terrifying nightly reign that lasted for a decade. For those too young to have experienced it, we have plenty of history books to remind us. Miss Swanson's novel might be a fictional tale, but it brings back many a scary memory and, with them, some of the fear."

Lowering the book to her lap, the reporter smiled at Ariel sitting across from her in the studio. "Miss Swanson, what possessed you to write a book about vampires? I understand you never experienced their terror firsthand, but you mentioned losing a family member to an attack. With your access to library records, you must be well versed in our history with vampires."

Ariel's chest tensed at the newscaster's obvious delight in the fact her book had stirred up such strong sentiments. The woman damn well made sure to bring up her past. Ariel had only mentioned one family member's experience to the woman off the record in a preinterview conversation so the reporter would know she didn't take humankind's past with the vampires lightly.

Smiling to overcome her anger at the newscaster's casual comment, she cast her gaze to the huge glass window behind them where people held up Ban the Book picket signs before she met Sandy's expectant gaze. She refused to let the reporter dredge up her past. "As you know, I work in a library. Being surrounded by books, I guess it was a natural progression that one day I would write one."

"Yes." Sandy glanced at her notes. "But you didn't write just any book. You wrote a book depicting a race of vampires thought extinct but who really never died out." Gleeful excitement filled Sandy's voice as she picked up Ariel's book once more and flipped to the final page. "In the last paragraph you wrote of a prophecy that could lead to the vampire clan's return. And I quote, 'A human will speak of our demise. Her purity and intelligence will help us survive. A mate she becomes to the leader of vampires, joining our races, fulfilling our ultimate desire.'"

Once Sandy finished reading, she set down the paperback and her piercing gaze locked on Ariel. "Your story might be a work of fiction, but needless to say, this book has scared a lot of people."

Her ominous tone had Ariel's heart thudding at a hummingbird rate. She'd heard the same comments from her agent and editor, but they had taken a different slant: people were willing to pay to be frightened and entertained.

Ariel jumped at the sudden slamming thud behind her. One of the picketers had gotten past the wall of security guards and flattened his picket sign against the glass. Camera flashes lit up the night sky outside, illuminating the script he'd printed on the surface.

Vampire Lover, it read.

Vampire lover? That couldn't be further from the truth. I'm just trying to move on with my life, to learn to live without fear, Ariel thought with a wry twist of her lips until the man turned the sign around and she read the rest of his message.

Die!

The camera crew panned over to the sign and Sandy expelled a nervous laugh. "Some people apparently feel *very* strongly."

Ariel squared her shoulders. Pushing her long, white-blond hair away from her face, she said in an unaffected tone, "Like you said, it's a work of fiction. This story is in my head, needing to be told. It's a journey of sorts." *A journey that I hope will free me,* she finished mentally.

"And a very successful journey, too, I might add." Sandy held the book up again. "I understand this first book will be part of a trilogy and it's selling so well that your editors have moved up the release date of the next book by four months." Leaning forward, she lowered her voice just a little. "Come on. Give us a hint as to what happens next. What's this prophecy about? You really left us hanging at the end of *The Vampires' Return*."

Ariel laughed in sheer bemusement. *I wish I knew what comes next.* "I don't know yet."

The reporter's blue eyes went wide in surprise. "What? You don't know what happens, yet your publisher wants this next book earlier than was originally planned?"

Ariel smiled at the genuine look of confusion on the woman's face. *'Bout time I stumped Miss Know-All-Her-Facts.* She shook her head. "No, I don't."

Leaning back, Sandy let out an exasperated, "Wow!" She faced the camera and continued, "You heard it here on UBNY News, everyone. Ariel Swanson doesn't know what'll happen next." Her calculating gaze shifted to Ariel. "I guess that means we'll have to have you back on the program right before your next book is released, right, Miss Swanson?

Lovely. If she tries to bring up my family's past again, I'll lambaste the woman. Ariel gave a sweet smile. "We'll see."

Sandy turned back to the camera. "Well, that's all for now, everyone. Tune in tomorrow night when we'll interview Zadie Morrow and talk about her debut rock video, 'Moon Shadows.'"

Ariel let out a silent sigh of relief once the camera's red light went out. Sandy stood and Ariel followed suit.

"Thanks so much for coming down to the station tonight, Ariel." Sandy cast a quick look at the glass window behind them, then waved to a couple guards standing off the set. "Security will escort you to your car."

Ariel nodded her appreciation for the escort and followed the tall, dark-headed guard, while a shorter blond man wearing the same security uniform stepped into place behind her.

As soon as the guard opened the studio's side door, the deafening roar of the crowd rushed forth. Ariel resisted the urge to cover her ears at the loud noise—some cheers, some hateful slurs. The slurs seemed the loudest.

Cameras' bright lights flashed repeatedly, and the smell of the earlier rainstorm hung thick and heavy in the night air. Ariel's insides rocked at the crush of people surrounding them. She moved closer to the guard in front of her as the large man shouldered his way through the crowd, yelling, "Back up, people!"

A woman stepped out from the crowd to Ariel's right, her mike held in front of her. "Miss Swanson, obviously you've stirred some mixed emotions with your novel. Care to make any comments?"

Ariel started to respond when someone in a long black coat landed in a crouched position on the asphalt to her left.

Along with her intake of breath, a collective gasp moved over the crowd at the stranger's appearance. Before Ariel had time to react, the man stood and grabbed her left arm. When the first security guard turned his gun on him, the stranger shot the guard in the thigh using a pulser gun.

Ariel let out a horrified scream as the man went down. She tried to pull her arm free, but the intruder shoved her behind him right before a series of traditional gunshots exploded, pinging against the asphalt next to them.

Screams of terror rose from the mob, and the second security guard went down, murdered by the spray of gunfire coming from above. It happened so fast; Ariel turned to see a bullet hole oozing blood near the man's heart as he stared sightlessly into the night sky.

Panic swept through her, closing her windpipe. She shrieked and ripped at the firm grip on her upper arm, trying to get away. The dark-haired stranger's vise lock around her arm tightened, while the people around her scattered in every direction.

A new round of gunshots resounded above them, and the man holding her murmured, "Damn it to hell," right before he turned and dipped, throwing her over his shoulder as if she weighed nothing more than a bag of feathers.

Air whooshed from her lungs with her hard landing on his shoulder. Dizziness swept her mind, disorienting her while he vaulted up the hood of a car, then across its roof, before jumping onto a metal awning above Frederico's Restaurant.

Ariel finally regained her breath and her ability to focus only to gulp in terror at the sight of the street a good fifteen feet below her. As the man leapt once more, this time to the rooftop of a low building on the same side of the street, she grabbed his waist and closed her eyes briefly against the vertigo that gripped her.

My God, he just jumped at least two stories as easily as if he were taking a stroll in a park. Ariel forced air in and out of her nostrils. Cinching her arms around the man's muscular stomach, she pressed her cheek against his soft coat. The leather smell was rich and strong against her nose. No matter how frightened she was, she refused to pass out and lose her grip. Otherwise, with his next jump she'd go sailing straight to the cement below.

He ran across the rooftop and the jarring and jerking

caused her stomach to roil. She made the mistake of opening her eyes. A high-pitched screech erupted as they leapt from one building top to another. Bile rose in her throat, bringing with it a flood of spit.

You have to calm down so you can keep screaming, stupid, she told herself as she swallowed several times to keep from puking. The gunfire around them told her someone other than police officers were trying to save her from the kidnapper.

The NYPD and the military were the only groups licensed to carry pulser guns. Handguns were still the weapon of choice among the criminals. At this point, she didn't care who was trying to save her, just that someone was. Hope made her tight chest loosen a bit and she began to scream once more.

Long and loud.

"Enough!"

Her kidnapper's curt tone penetrated her screams as he tightened his grip on her hips. She fell silent while helplessness wrapped around her like a thick, oppressive blanket. Her kidnapper had a pulser weapon. When had the order of things—good guys carrying pulsers and bad guys carrying handguns—been turned over on its head?

No matter. While he moved several stories above the pavement, she kept her lips buttoned. She didn't need to provoke her captor any more than necessary; he might decide to drop her!

Once they stopped moving, Ariel let out of a sigh of relief. The man tensed and then turned one way and then the other in rapid movements as if he were looking for an unseen assailant.

Another gunshot ricocheted a split second before a sudden burning sensation ripped through her shoulder. *Use your night goggles, you idiots,* she mentally wailed as she realized she'd been hit by friendly fire.

Without warning, her kidnapper jumped off the building. His black leather coat flapped against her face, muffling her shriek of terror as they flew toward the street below.

As he landed in a partial squat, her arms instinctively covered her head to protect it, while her hip bone jarred against the man's shoulder. Shooting pain radiated down her spine and a low moan escaped her lips at the impact. He didn't miss a beat. Instead he immediately jolted into a brisk run.

Bullets continued to pepper the pavement around them as he moved around a building, then ran underneath it into a dimly lit parking garage.

When he stopped next to a small black car and the trunk popped open, Ariel began to scream once more. She kicked her legs at the same time she pounded on his back and butt with her fists.

Pain splintered across her shoulder from her actions, but she was fighting for her life. Adrenaline had to be the only way she was staying conscious.

"Keep your mouth shut or I'll knock you out," he ground out in a cold tone right before he rolled her from his shoulder into his compact trunk. The parking lot's yellow lights glowed behind his head, casting his face in shadows. She had just enough time to curl her legs inside the small space before he slammed the lid down.

Newly shampooed carpet invaded her nostrils as Ariel moaned at the pain in her shoulder. She knew her injury had gotten worse from being tossed in the trunk. The engine revved and wheels squealed. As the car backed up, she jerked sideways. Ariel bit her lip to keep from screaming out at the fire spreading across her shoulder. She lay in the darkness, whispering over and over again, "You must stay conscious. Breathe easy. In and out."

She heard him talking in a low tone, but she couldn't make out what he said over the sound of the car's engine. They rode for a while, and she had to force herself to keep her eyes open in the pitch dark. The pain in her shoulder burned so much her body begged to succumb to the darkness surrounding her.

The car finally stopped and she heard birds squawking. A foghorn blew in the distance. They must be around or near the river docks, she thought just as the trunk opened.

The interior light shone in her eyes, and Ariel blinked against the brightness, trying to see her captor's face.

He grabbed a fistful of her linen shirt, and the sound of fabric tearing echoed between them as he used the shirt to stand her upright on the ground beside him. Ariel winced at the pain that speared through her shoulder when he released her.

Her stomach churned in queasy fits and her feet turned to lead blocks. Her anxious gaze traveled the man's towering frame. He had to be at least nine inches taller than her own five feet seven inches.

He gripped her upper arm, his penetrating eyes narrowing as his dark eyebrows drew down in a frown. "I have a pickup to make. You will behave."

His eyes were so black they appeared bottomless. *No— soulless,* she mentally corrected. The five-o'clock shadow across his angular jaw and the thin scar that ran down the side of his neck only magnified his deadly persona. She scanned his tall physique, looking for something distinctive. He appeared human, but no human could leap across buildings as easily as if he were jumping cracks on a sidewalk. *He could be a vampire.* The thought echoed quietly in her head, but she refused to acknowledge it. Vampires were extinct.

When her gaze returned to his face, his mouth was set in a hard line, apparently waiting for her response. Her stomach knotted and her shoulder stung as if it were being attacked by an army of fire ants. She quickly nodded her agreement. What the hell else could she do?

Her captor tugged her up a ramp that led into a wood-planked three-story building. The warehouse sat on wooden pillars that disappeared into the Hudson River below. Before they walked inside she noted the sign marker on the side of the building: Pier #48.

When they stepped off the wide ramp, she saw that the deserted floor of the building had cement columns supporting the weight of the floor above it. Glancing back at the reinforced ramp they'd just walked up, she realized this floor must be some kind of parking garage. Why hadn't he parked inside? And why had he brought her here?

The man didn't give her time to ponder her surroundings or his actions. He hauled her beside him over to a stairwell door along the building's side wall. Once he pulled open the heavy metal exit door, he flipped on the light, and they began to climb the stairs. With each step she took apprehension dug in her gut like termites slowly eating their way through.

Their shoes rang on the metal stairs beneath their feet, and Ariel's heart thumped at an erratic rate. She'd never been more frightened in her life, but if they met someone along the way, she wanted to stay focused so she could somehow let the person know she wasn't there of her own free will. Glancing at her torn thin tan jacket and white linen blouse underneath, she saw she was covered in black carpet lint.

Blood had to have seeped from her shirt through the back of her jacket. Every move she made caused the shirt to peel away and then restick to her skin. Someone only had to see her disheveled, bloody appearance to know she needed help. At least she hoped that was all it would take.

When they reached the third floor, he opened the stairwell door and drew her close to his side as he entered the long hall. The man's booted feet echoed on the scratched-up hardwood floor as they walked down the hall toward a closed door.

His firm grip never loosened on her arm while he knocked three times and waited.

A bearded man with messy red hair answered the door and glared at them. The snake tattoo on his bicep, exposed by his wife-beater tank shirt, seemed to hiss at her. Somehow she didn't think this person was the Good Samaritan type. Disappointment set a twenty-pound weight on her chest.

The man's brown gaze darted briefly to Ariel. "I don't like this short notice."

"Where's my merchandise?" her kidnapper said in a clipped tone.

He sighed and backed up, opening the door wide to let them in.

As they walked past him, the smell of lukin weed and sweat slammed into Ariel. The bearded man reeked of the powerfully addictive hallucinogenic drug as if he'd been bathing in it, yet no smoke filled the room. *He must just do his drug business here,* she thought as a sudden secondary concern rushed to the forefront of her mind.

Oh, no! My kidnapper is a junkie. Maybe that's why he took chances as though he had superhuman strength, though she couldn't explain his ability to jump from buildings without a scratch. Bitter anger welled within her as an image of her brother Peter, whacked out on lukin, materialized in her mind. Peter hadn't survived his jump—but then, she didn't think he'd planned to.

Her chest tightened and her heart rate sped up as they walked farther into the open room that spanned the entire top floor of the building. Huge-paned windows lined the far wall all the way across, giving a view of dock lights reflecting off the dark water below.

The fluorescent lights above them shone on the dealer's bushy hair as he preceded them, heading toward a long table near the windows. Other than a few shipping crates scattered throughout the room, the wobbly, scarred wooden table was the only piece of furniture.

After the man walked around behind the table, he popped open a small silver briefcase sitting on the surface. They approached and he turned the three-by-twelve-inch case toward them. "Fourteen grand."

A dozen slender vials of clear liquid nestled in the foam lining inside the case. She didn't know lukin weed could be used in liquid form. But she did know the case held *a lot* of drugs. What did any of this have to do with her?

"We agreed on eight."

At her captor's deadly tone, Ariel's gaze snapped to his.

"The last time we talked, price was a casual mention, not set in stone." The drug dealer shrugged and tilted his head, a curious expression on his face. "What are you going to do with all this stuff anyway? It's useless in this form."

The man stepped forward, dragging her with him. His movements slow and precise, he shut the case and snapped the hinges closed. "Eight grand."

A high-pitched whining sound drew Ariel's attention back to the redhead. "You're more reasonable when we deal in weapons. I said, fourteen." He held a pulser gun aimed at the tall man's chest, a stubborn look on his face.

Her kidnapper's unreadable expression never changed, but his fingers cinched tighter around her arm. *Damn, this can't be good.*

The bearded man licked his dry, cracked lips. "So what's it gonna be—" He stumbled back and fell, screaming out in pain as he grabbed his upper arm.

"That's for trying to gouge me." Her captor kept his own pulser gun trained on the redhead.

The man scrambled to his feet, his face contorted in rage. "Sonofabitch! I'm going to kill you—" he yelled as he lifted his weapon toward them and fired off a shot that whizzed in their direction.

Without losing his grip on her, her captor turned his shoulder. Moving at lightning speed, he'd avoided the shot that would've hit him in his chest.

Shocked at the near miss, she returned her gaze to the drug dealer and saw a black singe dot between the man's eyes. He crumpled to the floor like a discarded marionette doll.

"That's for trying to kill me," her kidnapper bit out. He released her arm, then lifted the slim briefcase from the table and set it down beside his feet on the floor.

Ariel looked away from the dead man's beady, accusing eyes staring back at her. Her heart seized and she swallowed the lump in her throat. Death surrounded her tonight.

Was she next?

Pulse thrumming, she pivoted and started to run toward the entrance. She'd only taken a couple of steps when fingers dug into her upper arm and she was jerked to a halting stop. Pain lanced up and down her arm, spreading to the wound in her back.

Her vision blurred, but she refused to go down easily. She tried to jerk free of his vise hold. "Let. Me. Go!"

When he aimed his gun at the windows, Ariel's eyes widened in confusion. Her jaw dropped as he rapidly pinged off bursts from his gun in a circular pattern toward the huge glass panes. She'd never seen anyone move as fast as he did.

Before she could utter a word, he cut his gaze to the door as if he were waiting for someone and placed himself between her and the entrance.

"Take a deep breath." His tone was low and intense, yet his focus remained locked on the doorway they'd just come through a few minutes before.

Ariel's "What?" came out more like "Whaaaaat" when he jerked her arm with a strong, ripping force.

She didn't have a chance to fathom his intent as her body flew across the room toward the wall of glass. Shrieking, she crossed her arms in front of her face right before her body slammed against the fragile surface.

The window gave with the impact, and she burst

through, her heart rate stuttering. Ariel flailed her arms in a pathetic attempt to save herself, but gravity took over where momentum left off. Her screams of terror turned to frantic pleas for survival.

I don't want to die.

Pulser and traditional gunfire ricocheted inside the building above her right before a huge explosion sent a heat wave full of bits of wood and shards of glass shooting down around her as she barreled toward the water.

She hit the surface a few seconds before something big displaced the water beside her. Ariel's vision pixelated to hazy fuzz and then went totally black.

Chapter 3

Swaying movement jarred Ariel awake. Someone was carrying her. The person smelled of water and outdoors and something she couldn't place…an elusive, exotic, indescribable scent.

Pain wracked her body and she whimpered at the sharpness ravaging her. Wet clothes clung to her skin. Her shoulder burned as if someone had set a hot iron to it. She wanted to moan, even heard the sound in her head, but she didn't have the energy to make the noise.

"Shhhh, you're safe." She rolled closer to the man's comforting voice, inhaling that appealing scent. When her nose came into contact with soft, wet leather, the distinctive scent brought everything rushing back.

She hadn't dreamed a horrible nightmare. She'd lived it.

Fear took over her mind, a cloud of suffocating black

smoke. Her skin prickled and her sluggish pulse began to race. She stiffened and immediately regretted her action as fresh pain lashed through her.

An involuntary moan escaped. She tried to open her eyes, but her lids wouldn't obey. "Hurt. So tired." She rasped the stilted words.

"Weak, pathetic and vulnerable." The judgmental words slid from her captor's lips in a low rumble before he said, "Sleep, Ariel," and blessed blackness washed over her once more.

Jachin carried Ariel's limp body over to his bed and laid her on it. Her long white-blond hair clumped in a wet mass under her head. He spread the damp strands against his navy pillow case. Glass cuts sprinkled her fair skin, while her long lashes lay against the dark shadows under her eyes, making her look even more waiflike.

He picked up her limp arm and encircled the thin wrist with his fingers. "So tiny and fragile. How are you to be Braeden's mate?" he murmured as he let her arm slide out of his fingers to fall to the bed.

Jachin knew he needed to look at her shoulder. He was afraid he might have dislocated it when he sent her through the window.

Grasping Ariel's wrist once more, he held her arm out, feeling around her shoulder. Yes, he'd dislocated it, damn it to hell.

With a quick yank on her arm he reset her shoulder. Her body jerked from pain, but he was glad she didn't waken.

Working at an efficient pace, Jachin began to remove her torn, bloody clothes. He wanted to know just how much damage she'd sustained. She needed to be fit to travel as soon as possible.

The Sanguinas had apparently learned about her book. His vampire clan members would be relentless in their pursuit of Miss Swanson. They'd hunted him and Ariel from the news station to the warehouse. He knew he was on borrowed time.

Once he'd removed Ariel's clothes and moved closer to assess the extent of her injuries, her appealing scent of peaches and sugary almonds washed over him. Jachin quickly backed away and focused on her on a business level. Fortunately she didn't appear to have any glass imbedded in her wounds, but she had a ton of cuts that needed to be closed.

He sat down beside her on the bed and stuck his index finger in his mouth, then ran the wet tip across the gash on her arm. The tension knotting his shoulders eased when his saliva stopped the bleeding and the wound began to close.

Jachin continued until all the small wounds on her front side had begun to heal. Gritting his teeth against the erection pressing against his wet pants, he wouldn't allow himself to acknowledge how soft her skin felt underneath his fingertips or how long he'd been without a woman.

When he rolled her limp body over and saw the crusted bullet wound, Jachin set his jaw, angry with himself for not noticing she'd been hit earlier. He tried to heal the wound on her shoulder the same way he had her others, but the gash was too wide. It had started to bleed again. If he didn't close it soon, she'd lose too much blood.

Stilling himself, he lifted her upper body across his lap and leaned close to sweep his tongue against her cool, pebbled wet skin.

The taste of dried and fresh blood made his body tense in agonized response.

Life—the zing he'd been missing.

Instantly his fangs unsheathed, ready to devour.

Jachin turned his head away and ground his fangs against his lower lip, hoping the pain would help him regain control over his primal need to feed. He wasn't done yet. Her wound was deep.

Tensing his gut, he prepared for the poison to grip his belly in painful knots as he pulled her close and ran his tongue over her wound once more. Fresh blood rushed forth, coating his tongue.

His stomach twinged, but nausea didn't overwhelm him. He was a bit stunned but thankful he'd been able to finish his task without poisoning himself. He slowly swiped his tongue along the open wound one last time.

This time her flavor tasted sweet and nutty, full of erotic promise.

Heat swept through him, gripping his groin in agonizing waves so strong they rushed over him in throbbing pulses of need.

Surprised at how good she'd tasted, Jachin rested his chin against her temple and squeezed his eyes shut at the thought that this human's blood might not be poisoned like all the others. But then, he shouldn't be surprised. He'd been right to take her.

Something about her *was* different. The prophecy would be fulfilled and he'd regain his rightful position among the Sanguinas.

When he opened his eyes, it unsettled him to see he'd instinctively pulled Ariel's naked body across his lap. The goose bumps he'd felt on her skin earlier had disappeared, turning her flesh smooth and silky underneath his palms.

Shaking his head at the possessive hold he had on the woman, he straightened his spine and slowly uncurled his fingers from her body. He glanced at her wound, satisfied to see it had begun to close. As he laid her gently on her back, his heart thumped uncharacteristically at a rapid pace.

Adrenaline due to tonight's events, he told himself as he stood beside the bed and pulled the thick covers over her shoulders.

The journey would begin as soon as she woke.

Ariel awoke to the sound of Sandy Myers's voice. She kept her eyes shut and listened to the news that had to be coming from a nearby projector.

"The shootout that led to the kidnapping of debut author Ariel Swanson has stumped law enforcement. Due to the skills the kidnapper possessed, there is speculation that Miss Swanson's book was more than a work of fiction but indeed based on some truth—that vampires aren't extinct. From the speed with which he moved to his ability to leap to the top of a building, her kidnapper's actions were more supernatural in nature."

Ariel's heart jerked at the news. Was Sandy right? Was the man who'd kidnapped her a vampire? Terror gripped her chest, and her throat burned from the stomach acid that quickly rose to the surface.

No. Her book was supposed to be cathartic. Writing from a bird's-eye view within the vampire world was supposed to help her see them as more than monsters, a kind of self-help therapy. It wasn't supposed to lead a vampire wannabe right to her.

What have I done?

Ariel slit her eyes open and started to sit up when she realized she had no clothes on underneath the soft comforter covering her. Worry made her tremble all over. She gingerly lifted and moved her legs under the covers until she confirmed she felt no pain between her thighs. As far as she could tell, he hadn't violated her.

He sat with his back to her, watching the projector screen. Her pulse racing, she put one foot on the floor and started to slowly inch her way out of the bed. The bedside lamplight reflected on something shiny on the foot of the bed. She paused.

A pair of scissors.

Her heart leapt in fear and then elation. She had a weapon. When she leaned forward and gripped the scissors, she was surprised her shoulder only throbbed a little.

"Cut it." The man's low voice floated across the room.

A soft gasp escaped her lips at the knowledge he hadn't even turned yet knew she was awake. "Wh-what do you mean?"

He stood and turned to face her. "Cut your hair or I'll do it myself."

Ariel didn't know what she'd expected her kidnapper to look like, but seeing his face in full light for the first time stunned her.

With his tall height, broad shoulders surrounded by a black T-shirt and jeans hugging trim hips, the man looked imposing, but he didn't appear the monster she expected. Instead his clean-shaven angular features and short wavy hair made him look just as human as she. Only the jagged scar on the side of his neck gave an appearance of roguishness.

He might look handsome in a dangerous, bad-boy sort of way, but she knew different. The man had kidnapped her and he'd assassinated that drug dealer. He was a murderer, even if he didn't look the part.

She swallowed the knot in her throat, but she had to know what he really was. "Are you a vampire?"

His gaze narrowed. "What do you think?"

"The things you did were…inhuman." She paused, then continued, her voice stronger than she felt, "Vampires are extinct."

"Are they?" A deadly smile spread across his face.

The sight of his fangs sent a cold chill down her spine, spurring her into action. Heedless of her naked state, she leapt from the bed and bolted across the room, heading for the only door she'd seen.

When she glanced back to see if he'd pursued her and couldn't locate him, her heart rate doubled. Where had he gone? She quickly returned her gaze to her destination only to find the man now stood in her path.

Ariel was moving so fast she didn't have time to stop herself. She ran right into her captor.

Her heart stuttered and her stomach roiled. Such close proximity to a vicious, bloodsucking vampire made her shudder in fear, but she refused to be murdered like her family.

Ariel lifted the scissors, ready to jam them into the man's jugular.

He gripped her wrist at the same time his other arm went around her waist, holding her naked body prisoner against him.

"Why am I here?" She'd never been more terrified in her life.

His intense gaze searched her face. "Because you wrote a book."

Even though relief spread through her when his fangs receded, Ariel's eyes still widened at his comment. "It's a work of fiction, nothing more."

His dark gaze narrowed. "The characters may be fictional, but the rest is very real, from the truth that vampires aren't extinct down to the prophecy at the end of your novel."

Horror spread through her, light-headedness its swift companion. She blinked to keep from passing out. "Are you saying the vampires will be returning?"

"Tell me the prophecy, word for word."

She bit her lip, hesitating. The man was delusional.

"Tell me," he roared, his fangs extending once more in his anger.

Ariel's voice quivered as she recited the verses she'd written at the end of her book. Verses that had popped into her head as she had written the story.

"'A human will speak of our demise. Her purity and intelligence will help us survive. A mate she becomes to the leader of vampires, joining our races, fulfilling our ultimate desire.'"

When her voice trailed off, his jaw tensed and his grip tightened around her. "I want to know the rest of it."

She licked her dry lips, then spoke the next line. "'The hunted becomes the hunter, no longer the prey. An enemy—'"

"'In your midst is less dark, more gray,'" he interrupted, finishing the rest of the line for her.

Ariel's eyes widened in shock, but sheer curiosity had

her continuing the next line, her voice growing stronger. "'Examine your failures and there you will find…'" She paused and waited to see if he knew the rest.

"'The answer to all your questions in time.'" He completed the line with a satisfied expression on his face.

"You—you read my mind," she insisted, her entire body trembling against him. It wasn't possible for him to know what even her editor hadn't seen.

His grip loosened on her wrist and he ran his thumb along her rampant pulse. "No. It is as you stated…every word. Only the man who prophesied this died before he could finish the last part of prophecy. I need to know the rest."

Ariel shook her head. "I don't know."

His hold on her wrist tightened and his dark gaze blazed. "Lies!"

For a few brief seconds Ariel had tried to convince herself she was talking to a human man, but the truth was…a horrific monster—one that had likely participated in forging a murderous path among humans twenty-five years ago—simmered just below the surface. She had to remember that. Her entire body began to quake.

Shaking her head in frantic jerks, she tried to keep the terror from her voice. She knew vampires got off on humans' fear, could smell it like a cloying cologne. "I…truly don't know. I wasn't lying to that newscaster. The next story hasn't come to me yet…and neither has the last part of the prophecy."

"You must—" the man began, then cut himself off and tilted his head as if listening. Snarling, he ripped the scissors from her hand and threw them across the room, where they embedded deep in a far wall.

Ariel jumped at his mercurial show of rage, but she didn't have time to react. The man grabbed her upper arm and snapped out orders at the same time an elevatorlike sound seemed to be heading toward them, resounding in the quiet room.

"Gather your clothes. We have to move now."

She stood her ground, pulling against his hold. "You threw me through a window, for cripe's sake. I'll take the chance the police have finally found me. I'm not coming with you."

He jerked her close, his cold, dark eyes locking with hers, the odd blackness mesmerizing her.

"Your book has stirred the sleeping beast. You're being hunted, Ariel. I'm the least of your worries. Get your clothes and move!"

His ferocity spurred her into action. Ariel gathered her dry, tattered clothes from the chair near the bed, then turned to the man for direction.

He already had a backpack slung across his shoulder and was standing in front of the bookshelves. He pressed a button, and the entire bookcase slid out of the way to reveal an old, narrow, gated elevator.

As he lifted the gate, Ariel decided to trust her instincts. He might've thrown her through a window, but she'd heard pulser fire and gunfire as she'd fallen toward the water. Had he tossed her through the window to protect her? The man could've killed her while she slept, but he hadn't. No doubt he could murder with deadly accuracy, but right now *this* enemy she knew.

She glanced toward the closed doorway in front of her, chest heaving. Without looking back again, she ran toward her captor, who stood in the gated elevator with a menacing look.

As soon as she stepped into the elevator, he slammed the gate down. The bookcase door started to close at the same time their elevator began to descend.

Ariel dropped her clothes, then stepped into her underwear and pants with jerky movements. It wasn't as though she had time to worry about modesty when her life was on the line, not to mention the man had already seen her completely naked.

Pushing *that* unnerving thought away from her mind, she ignored her bra for brevity's sake and tugged on her shirt, quickly buttoning it. Once she slipped her arms into her jacket, she jammed her feet into her loafers. When she finished dressing, she shoved her bra in her jacket pocket and glanced at the man beside her, realizing she had nothing to fear modesty-wise. He'd turned his back to her, his gaze focused on the closed door above their heads.

An explosive boom jarred the elevator car so hard she fell to the floor. A wave of heat and fire rushed above their heads right before an ominous snapping sound punctuated the air.

Two seconds later, the elevator jolted, then jerked as the cable above them broke. As the elevator plummeted toward the ground floor, a scream lodged in her throat.

The man let out a deafening roar. "Stay down." He moved with lightning speed that became a blur, hammering his fists against the cage's sidewalls. Left, then right, then left, then right.

While they built speed and momentum, his massive hits dented the metal frame, buckling the cage against the walls.

Ariel covered her ears against the metal-against-metal's

ear-piercing, jaw-locking sound. In her squatted position, she shuffled her feet, moving closer to the middle of the elevator as sparks began to fly through the air.

When the elevator finally came to a screeching, jarring stop at a tilted angle, she was slammed to the hard floor.

Swallowing the huge lump in her throat, Ariel resisted the overwhelming urge to throw up at her most recent near-death experience.

She took a deep breath and stood on shaky legs, thankful her shoes had rubber soles to keep her from sliding into her kidnapper as he pulled the damaged gate open with his bare hands.

"We're stuck between floors. We'll have to take the stairs from here," he said as he stood on his toes to pry open the metal elevator doors a couple feet above them.

Ariel's feet wouldn't move. She shook her head and whispered, "I can't do it."

His mouth tightened and his jaw ticced before he gripped her shoulders and turned her toward the open elevator doors. Grabbing her waist from behind, he said, "You will," in a tone that brooked no argument as he lifted her in the air toward the opening.

Suspended in the air, Ariel had little choice but to comply. Taking a calming breath, she gripped the floor above her. Her shoulders felt weaker than they normally did and her biceps strained as she tried to pull herself up. He gripped her rear and pushed her from behind, giving her the lift she needed.

Ariel landed on the floor above with a loud *umph*. Realizing she had a couple of seconds of freedom before he followed her up, she stood and turned to bolt down the long, dark hall to her right.

He grabbed her jacket and shirt from behind and hauled her back against his hard chest none too gently. "Going somewhere?" he growled in her ear.

"Just out for a stroll," she mumbled, feeling defeated.

"We don't have time for this," he hissed, and a familiar firm grip slid around her upper arm.

Pivoting to the left, he pulled her along beside him. She grimaced. *Lord save me from my poor sense of direction.*

When they entered the stairwell and began to descend the metal stairs, gunfire echoed in the stairwell. Ariel screamed as cement-block powder rained down on their heads. Adrenaline spiked her breathing to heavy gusts.

"Stay low and move!" He shoved her away from the guardrail and pulled a pulser gun from the holster strapped across his shoulder and chest.

While he returned fire, she did as she was told. Heart pounding, she took the stairs as fast as her legs would allow. When she hit the last stair, her thighs burned and she panted so hard she thought her lungs were going to explode. *So much for all that exercising to keep myself in shape.* Then again, she never expected to have to run down several flights of stairs at a superhuman pace. Placing her hands on her knees, she took deep breaths to keep from hyperventilating.

"Weak human," the vampire grumbled as he lifted her bent-over frame and tossed her across his shoulder. After pulling the door open, he entered a garage and shut the door behind them. Firing his pulser gun several times against the door handle, he melted the metal to the frame.

Only outside lampposts lit their path as he ran toward his vehicle. When he reached the back of a car, it beeped to indicate he'd unlocked it. Ariel had regained her breath enough to struggle against his shoulder. "You're *not* shoving me in that trunk again."

"Should've cut your hair. The color stands out." He lifted the trunk lid and dumped her inside in an unceremonious heap.

"Bastard!" Ariel quickly recovered. She struggled to climb out of the trunk, but he put his hand on her head and shoved her down right before he closed the lid on her once more.

As he started the engine and she hammered against the trunk lid, she realized the last time she was in his trunk she had been in a world of hurt. Her hand automatically moved to her shoulder, and she gently massaged the area where she could have sworn she'd had a nasty gash in her flesh from a stray bullet. Her fingers met firm skin. Bewildered, she wondered just how long she'd been knocked out.

The car's wheels squealed and she jerked hard against the back of the trunk as he made a quick turn. "Ow!" she yelled and then put her hands on the trunk lid to brace herself.

After a good fifteen minutes had passed, the car went over a bump and her head slammed into the metal trunk floor. Gritting her teeth, Ariel decided she'd had enough. Determination fueling her actions, she hammered her fists against the metal above her.

A few minutes later the car stopped and she thought she heard the car door open. Fear made her throat work, but no sounds came out. Ariel gritted her teeth at the paralyzing terror that gripped her. She had to get out of this trunk. Maybe her kidnapper had stopped somewhere public and there were people who might hear her.

She began to bang on the roof of the trunk as hard as

she could. "Help me! Someone please help me get out!" she screamed at the top of her lungs.

A few seconds later a loud sound pounded on the top of the trunk.

She gasped at the noise and paused.

"Stop!" the man barked, then continued in an even tone, "You need to take a nap."

Sudden exhaustion washed over her, making her limbs heavy. Ariel fought the darkness beckoning her, but her fists fell to her sides and her voice gave out, turning to a tired whisper.

Shaking her head, she tried to recover, but she finally succumbed to the blackness enveloping her in a blanket of secure, sleepy warmth.

Once Ariel finally settled, Jachin glanced up and down the dark, quiet street on the Upper East Side of town to make sure no one was about.

Knowing he didn't have a lot of time before the other vampires caught up with them, he dashed to the back of Roach's house. The trip to the mountains shouldn't take them long by car, but if something went wrong, he wanted to make sure he was covered for food while he traveled with the human. The more blood he lost in battle, the quicker his need for sustenance would return.

He started to hammer his fist on the heavy wooden door, but it creaked open under his first blow.

The hackles on Jachin's neck rose. Roach always locked up.

Broken glass crunched under his boots as he stepped into the entryway of the kitchen. A couple of the chairs were splintered into small pieces, and the heavy wooden table was turned on its side. Every single cabinet in the kitchen stood open, a couple only hanging by one hinge.

He drew his weapon and stepped farther into the kitchen.

A bloody handprint streaked the doorjamb leading into the rest of the house. Removing the safety on his gun, he pushed open the door that led to the supply of blood Roach kept.

Blood caked the handle of the small stainless steel refrigerator underneath the cabinet.

Jachin jerked open the fridge to see no more blood remained. Only broken racks were left behind.

Shit! No food. He stepped forward and glanced into the living room.

Nothing.

No one and no sign of trouble.

The furniture in the living room appeared to be undisturbed. Jachin listened, and when he couldn't detect a human heartbeat or hear anyone breathing, he knew.

Roach was gone.

Jachin slammed the refrigerator shut in frustration and kicked a dent in it.

What had happened to Roach?

Angry for wasting precious time, he gritted his teeth and rammed his fist through the door separating the kitchen from the living room.

Shoving the broken door out of his way, Jachin left Roach's house, his body tightly wound. He refused to acknowledge his concern for what might've happened to Roach…just as he refused to listen to the hunger in his gut whenever he looked at Ariel.

Jachin opened the car door and slid into the front seat.

Starting the engine, he put the car in gear and hit the gas
pedal, ready to put as much distance between himself and
the other Sanguinas as the sports car would allow.

Ariel opened her eyes to pitch black, along with the
rocking motion and the sound of a moving car underneath
her. She had no idea how long she'd been out, but she
refused to stay locked in the trunk's confined space.

Sliding her hands over the roof toward the back of the
car, she felt blindly for a handle or a lever. When her fingers
came into contact with a thin cloth strap, she pulled and
smiled in satisfaction as the back of the trunk fell away,
exposing the car's backseat. *Sheesh, why didn't I think of
this sooner?*

Once she'd climbed into the car's tiny backseat, she was
surprised to see it was still nighttime as she quietly shut the
seat back. Placing her chin on the back of the driver seat,
she asked in a casual tone as the vampire took the sports
car to its full speed up a winding road, "Are you ever going
to tell me your name? And where are you taking me?"

At the sound of her voice his shoulders tensed. That was
the only indication she'd taken him by surprise. In the dim
interior, she met his narrowed gaze in the rearview mirror
with a raised eyebrow, challenging him to deny her freedom.

"My name is Jachin Black. Get in the front and put on
your seat belt," he growled as he turned onto a road that
led to the Shawangunk mountain range.

Ariel shrugged out of her jacket and moved to the front
passenger seat. Jachin didn't say a word or even glance her
way once she'd snapped the seat belt closed around her.

Turning on the light in the car so she could see him

better, she refused to be ignored. She didn't give a damn if he was flooring the hell out of the vehicle. She wanted to know where he was taking her.

"I said, *where are you taking me?*" she repeated in a slow monotone while manipulating her fingers in gibberish sign language. She finished with her middle finger straight up.

"To fulfill the prophecy," he said, cutting his gaze her way.

Chapter 4

At the sight of Ariel flipping him the bird, Jachin couldn't help the amusement that teased the corners of his lips upward. He turned off the light and returned his gaze to the road.

"You're certifiable," she said, lowering her hands. "Did you forget to take your pills today?"

His gaze snapped to hers. "Your spunk and sarcastic attitude will either keep you alive or assure you a quick death. Bravado isn't enough. You reek of fear."

Her brow furrowed. "What human doesn't fear vampires?"

"You wrote a book about them," he countered. At first he thought her fear was due to everything that had happened to her the last few hours, but the alarm he smelled went deeper, perplexing him.

"Because I had to," she shot back.

He met her gaze, suspicion kicking in. "Explain."

She folded her arms and settled in her seat, her mouth set in a stubborn line.

Anger rippled through him when she refused to speak. He gripped the steering wheel so tight the round frame took on the indention of his fingers.

"Does this have to do with the prophecy? Tell me, Ariel!" he ordered.

Tension hung in the air between them like storm clouds churning in the sky, ready to let loose the gale building inside.

A loud boom resounded, quickly followed by a bright flash.

The road shook as it exploded in front of them, the asphalt buckling.

Jachin's chest tightened in fury at the sight. Avoiding the flash of fire and the new hole in the road, he jerked the car in the only direction he could—to his left and into the mountainside. Turning right would have taken them straight down a sheer canyon.

Upon impact, his head slammed against the car's door frame. White spots floated before his eyes. His groggy, disoriented mind vaguely wondered if Ariel had magically tampered with his side air bag, disabling it, before he lost consciousness.

Ariel trembled when the car stopped shaking. She glanced at Jachin to see if he was hurt. His forehead was bleeding and he appeared to be unconscious. She leaned over and had just felt his slow pulse when a car pulled up behind them. Sobbing her thanks to the heavens for Good

Samaritans, she unbuckled her seat belt and got out of the car.

Her first thought was to ask the people to call an ambulance for Jachin, but reason returned as a blond-headed man flipped on his car's interior light and rolled down the passenger window. "The road's a mess. What happened?"

Ariel blinked back stinging tears and coughed at the smoke in the air. "I don't know. Please, I need your help." She pointed to Jachin's car. "That man kidnapped me. I need to get to the police department in town right away. Can you take me there?"

The man glanced at Jachin's crumpled vehicle, then got out of his car. "Is he dead?"

Her heart hammered as she followed his probing gaze. "No…I—I don't know. He's knocked out, I think."

Without a word, he motioned to his driver. The tall, dark-haired man with small, beady eyes got out of the car at the same time a black sedan with three more men pulled up behind their car.

Something wasn't right. A sudden sick sensation bottomed out in her stomach.

Instinct told her to run. Run like hell!

She turned to bolt away, but the blond man grabbed her arm and yanked her against his thin frame. "You're not going anywhere," he said, then turned to the dark-haired driver. "Get rid of it, Thad."

She began to struggle against her new captor's tight hold. "No, you can't! He's still inside."

He turned a cold smile her way. "I know."

The car lights behind her illuminated the pure evil in the man's smile. Excitement reflected in his eyes, making her skin crawl.

Disbelief washed over her as Thad proceeded to push Jachin's car all the way across the road, pieces of crumpled headlight glass crunching under the tires. He lifted Jachin's car up on its side and her throat closed. He'd done it without help, as if the vehicle weighed no more than a bicycle.

That could only mean one thing.

"You're all vampires." Ariel's gaze snapped back to the man holding her arm. Her breathing ceased and she watched in horror as his incisors elongated.

He gave her a pleased smile. "Now we'll be the ones turning you over to Braeden."

Was this Braeden a vampire? She had to assume he was. Is that what Jachin had planned? To hand her off to another vampire? Panic rippled through her, knocking the breath from her lungs. "No," she croaked, renewing her struggles with more vigor. She growled in frustration when the tip of her shoe bounced off the man's shin as if she'd kicked him with cotton.

The dark-haired man gave Jachin's car one last shove and the vehicle rolled over the mountain edge. Her stomach pitched with each sickening crunch of metal and breaking glass as the car tumbled down the ravine. There was no way Jachin would survive, yet she couldn't help but scream his name. "Jachin!"

The futility of her situation overwhelmed her. But she knew she'd be a fool to stop fighting. If she were going to die, it was better on the mountain road then as some vampire's torture toy.

"Let me go!" She yanked hard, trying to pull free, but the man's grip only constricted around her upper arm.

"Stop your whining, you pathetic human." He shook her so hard dizziness soon followed. Ariel ceased her struggles and took deep breaths to regain her equilibrium.

When the earth shook and the night sky lit up from an explosion in the ravine below, she jerked around. Tears streamed down her face. The one man who could've saved her was gone.

Two of the three vampires from the black sedan stood at the edge of the road. One of them had a grenade launcher on his shoulder and was pointing it toward the ravine. She realized that the car hadn't exploded yet—that the bastards were trying to nuke it.

"Leave him in peace!" Fury made a rush of adrenaline sweep over her, and she managed to break free of the blond vampire's tight grip. She'd only taken a couple of steps before he grabbed her around the waist and clamped his teeth on the side of her neck from behind.

The terrifying sensation of his bite holding her in place, fangs ready to plunge deep, conjured images of her grandmother's scarred throat in Ariel's mind.

She froze her movements and began to pant, her heart thumping at a rapid pace.

The man removed his teeth and nuzzled her throat. "That's my girl," he whispered in her ear. "You'd better keep in mind who owns you now."

A deafening rumble woke him. Jachin shook his head to clear it and realized two certainties before he opened his eyes: he was upside down, and the smell of leaking fuel meant he had mere seconds to get the hell out of the car.

His head throbbed from the wreck and smoke burned

his eyes, blocking his view. He listened for Ariel's heart-beat and inhaled to detect her scent.

Nothing.

She wasn't in the car, nor was she in the close vicinity. He'd sense her if she was.

He pushed his seat-belt latch and grunted in anger when the damn thing didn't release. Gripping the strap tight, he braced against the smashed car frame to keep from falling and yanked the seat belt.

Metal ground and creaked as the latch gave way. Breathing hard, Jachin locked one leg and continued to brace himself while using his booted foot to kick the crumpled door's broken glass completely out.

Smoke burned his throat as he pushed himself through the opening. Glass shards cut into his hands while he used the ground for leverage to pull the rest of his body out of the car. As soon as his feet hit the ground, Jachin squatted and catapulted his body into the air as far away from the car as he could.

He landed with a heavy thud and started to run, but an explosion behind him slammed him to the ground like a giant's hand squishing a bug flat. Heat and glass flew over him as he tried to regain his breath. While his lungs heaved, his sight blurred and his hearing disappeared for several seconds.

Once his vision cleared and his ability to hear returned, he forced himself to stand on unsteady legs and stumbled farther away from the wreckage.

Another explosion slammed him to his side on the ground. Pain shot up his hip and spine from the impact. Jachin jerked his suspicious gaze up the ravine in time to see two men standing at the top with a grenade launcher.

He recognized Vlad and Aaron from his clan. Car wheels squealed as a vehicle near the men drove off.

His stomach burned with fury. He knew they'd taken Ariel. The moment his gaze met Vlad's and Aaron's, the vampires disappeared from the side of the road.

Letting out a battle roar, Jachin curled his fingers into the grass and dirt before he took off up the hill. He had no clue if his weapons had survived the crash, but he didn't care. If those pricks touched Ariel…

He clenched his fists, pissed at himself for caring so strongly for the human's safety. His thoughts about Ariel had somehow turned more possessive in nature, going way beyond the prophecy.

On his way up the hill he caught sight of his black backpack lying on top of a clump of weeds. A deadly calm washed over him as he swiped the bag and slung it over his shoulder without interrupting his fast gait.

Once Jachin reached the road, he crossed it, pulled his backpack on both shoulders and grabbed hold of the rocks and shrubbery on the side of the mountain. Determination fueled his climb, his movements fast and assured.

Jachin was gone. Ariel sat between the two vampires in the front seat of their car as they drove up the mountain road, her heart hammering. They'd driven for a few minutes when Thad stared past Ariel and addressed the blond vampire. "We don't have a lot of time before sunrise, Sethen. Where to?"

Sethen nodded toward the road. "Another mile up the road there's a turnoff to the left. I've scouted out places we could wait out the daylight if we needed to. There's a cave a few turns up."

Ariel dug her nails into the palms of her hands. She needed something to keep her from shaking all over. Even the tiny bit of pain helped a little to distract her thoughts from what could possibly happen to her once she was alone in a cave with a couple of vicious vampires.

Several minutes later, Thad parked the car at the base of an incline that led to a cave opening. Sethen opened the door and dragged Ariel out of the seat by her arm. When her feet hit the ground, she stumbled and her tattered shirt tore some more.

"Stand up," Sethen growled, jerking her to a standing position.

"If you'd let go, I can walk on my own two feet," she snapped.

The man snorted and spoke to the driver. "Pull the car out of sight of the road. Then meet me in the cave. Vlad, Aaron and David will just have to find another place to hide out until the sun sets."

The cave smelled stale and musty, as if its past critter inhabitants had abandoned it. She couldn't see a thing in the cave's deep recesses, so she jumped and let out a gasp of fear when Sethen's hands landed on her shoulders. He turned her to face him while shuffling shoes approached from behind her.

"This human's too mouthy. Much as I'd like to rip her throat out, this isn't about taking her blood. But we can teach her a lesson."

Thad gave an evil chuckle. "I'm all for that."

Sethen's grip slid to her upper arms and he yanked her

against his bony chest. As he leaned close and ran his fangs along the column of her neck, her heart seized.

Bravado quickly evaporating, Ariel took a breath to scream. When the vampire plunged his fangs deep, excruciating pain flooded her throat. Her vision blurred and a gasp of deep-rooted fear escaped.

Another pain slammed into the back of her neck as Thad sank his teeth into her skin, as well.

Ariel screamed at the same time her knees started to give way. Her heart skipped several beats and her breathing turned frantic. The terror, the pain was just too much. She swayed, on the verge of collapsing, when Thad tensed behind her.

His tight bite slackened and a jolt of heat radiated at her back as if from him. He withdrew his fangs from her neck right before an invisible force pressed her forward and a bright light filled the entire cave.

Sethen released his fangs, his eyes widening in disbelief as he glanced down at his chest. His entire body began to shake, then crack, splintering into a thousand tiny fissures across his skin. Brilliant white light filtered through the cracks as if he were burning from the inside out.

Her stomach pitched at the thought and Ariel jumped away, screeching. A sudden energy pulse and a rush of heat sent her stumbling right before Sethen's body exploded in a flash of fire.

Bits of burning ash lit up the space in front of her, a thousand fireflies floating in the air. She quickly turned to see Thad was gone, as well.

Once the tiny sparks of Sethen's and Thad's ashes settled on the cave floor, dimming to black, she cast her shaky gaze to the cave entrance and tried to blink past her terror.

The dawn's light, barely breaking the sky, outlined a tall man holding a gun aloft.

Before she could speak, he shoved his gun in a holder at his waist and closed the distance between them. "We must move deeper into the cave or I'll end up nothing but ash, too."

Ariel's heart leapt at the sound of Jachin's voice and the reality of her situation kicked in. Her legs gave out and her vision began to blur. The vampire caught her before she hit the floor, sweeping her up into his arms.

"I didn't know pulser weapons could make a person combust like that." Her voice trembled as she stared at the ash remains on the ground.

"Only with a specific body chemistry and the right catalyst."

Indirect sunlight began to filter into the shadowed recesses of the cave, filling the space with dim light. As Jachin carried her farther into the cave, she noted the partially healed gash on his forehead. She was amazed he'd survived rolling down a mountain in a crushed car, even with a vampire's ability to heal.

Relief at being rescued slowed her breathing to an even keel, yet she couldn't get Sethen's comment about taking her to Braeden out of her head. Jachin might've just saved her, but he'd said he intended to "fulfill the prophecy." He had kidnapped her with the same intent—to take her to this other vampire.

She narrowed her gaze on Jachin. "When I get my equilibrium back, I'm dragging your sorry ass into the sunlight."

"That mouth will most *assuredly* be the death of you."

He gave a low chuckle and set her on the ground, then slid his backpack to the cave's dusty floor.

Her entire body continued to shake in the aftermath. Even though she was pissed at him, Ariel found herself inching as close to Jachin as she could without touching him. She had to be in shock, she told herself. Why else would she stand in a vampire's personal space after what she'd just experienced?

Shivering, she closed her eyes against the memories of the two vampires' vicious bites, but the trickling sensation of her blood rolling down her neck wouldn't let her lock the memory safely away.

She reached up to touch one of her wounds, but Jachin grabbed her wrist before her fingers could connect with her skin.

"Sit. We need to tend to your injuries."

Her gaze locked with his hooded one. His face was shrouded in darkness, so she couldn't gauge his mood...or his sincerity. His voice told her nothing. It was devoid of emotion. Apparently that was his norm.

"Do I get a choice in the matter?" she asked.

"No," came his stoic response.

She sighed, and apprehension tightened her chest as she lowered herself to a seated position on the hard ground in front of him.

Jachin unzipped his pack and withdrew a red apple. He held it out, and his voice was gruff when he said, "Eat."

Terror still flowed through her. Food was the last thing on her mind. She started to shake her head. "I'm not hungry—"

Jachin's dark gaze narrowed and his jaw tensed. Ariel's heart jerked at his fierce look. He obviously wasn't taking no for an answer. She took the apple and bit into it. The flavor exploded over her tongue, making her mouth water. As she crunched the sweet fruit, she asked, "Why do I feel like Adam?"

He ignored her comment and gave her a curt nod. "Turn around."

Ariel dug her teeth into the red peel for another chunk of fruit and did as he asked. As soon as her rear settled on the floor, he gripped her waist and pulled her between his opened legs. "You need to move closer."

She stiffened and gasped at their intimate position, almost choking as she swallowed a large piece of apple. Her rear and hips were cradled by his groin, her back against his muscular chest. Heat radiated from his hard body, seeping into her skin through her clothes. The smell of smoke mixed with his exotic masculine scent made her pulse race.

"Relax, Ariel." His low voice ran over her as the slow rhythm of his heartbeat thumped against her back. The combination had an unexpected and immediate calming effect on her frazzled nerves.

Her stomach rumbled, hunger finally kicking in after her first couple of bites. She bit off another chunk of apple and chewed as she waited for him to pull some bandages from his backpack.

When his warm breath swept across the back of her neck, she gasped and froze, panic ramming in her chest.

"Wh-what are you doing?" She gripped the apple, her voice barely a whisper.

His arm moved around her waist, holding her still as his other hand swept her hair away from her torn skin.

Ariel quickly pulled her hair down the side of her neck, covering the birthmark that resided right below her hairline on the back of her neck. It was such an odd crescent-moon shape people had always commented when she'd pulled her hair up in a ponytail as a child—and she'd become self-conscious about it.

"I'm closing your wound," he said in a husky tone right before his warm tongue swept across her exposed flesh.

Chill bumps formed on the surface of her skin and her belly tightened at the strange sensation. Her grip on her hair relaxed and she forgot about being self-conscious when the skittering and fluttering in her stomach grew stronger. The history books never mentioned vampires closing wounds, just causing them.

As if he'd read her thoughts, Jachin said, "My saliva has a healing agent in it. How do you think you recovered from all your other injuries so quickly?"

"I haven't had time to wonder," she lied, resisting a shudder at his comment. He must've closed her wounds while she'd been unconscious. Heat flushed her cheeks, and she swallowed hard at the thought of all the places he had to have run his tongue across her naked body to heal her. He could've bitten her then.

"You must trust me." His voice sounded almost hypnotic.

"Said Eve to Adam," she said in an unsteady tone.

"Are you saying I'm in league with the devil?" His tongue ran across her wound once more, this time in a slower, leisurely sweep. Before she could respond, he turned her in his arms so her back leaned across his biceps. "I'm not in league, Ariel, but it's in your best interest to remember everyone has an agenda."

His gaze locked with hers and for a second she thought she saw his pupils dilate. How was that possible for her to see? His eyes were as black as his pupils, weren't they? She blinked, and as if she'd imagined it, the imagery was gone. His stare was as dark as sin once more.

Ariel's breath caught as he lowered his head to her throat. His clean-shaven cheek brushed hers, silently telling her to give him access to her neck.

Her heart thundered and her pulse raced as she gripped his arm. The man was pure muscle, a murderous killer. She'd never felt more vulnerable in her life. Yet, if it weren't for him, she probably wouldn't have survived her biggest fear: being attacked by a vampire. Make that two vampires.

She closed her eyes and held her breath as she tilted her head back and waited in tense silence.

His heat enveloped her while his musky, seductive scent surrounded her. Anticipation curled in her stomach as his warm breath bathed her neck.

She held back a gasp when his tongue slid up her neck. He applied pressure along with another swipe of his tongue and the tension within her changed. Tingling flooded through her, slamming into her sex in aching waves of desire.

Her reaction shocked her, causing her heart rate to jump-start in excitement. She held herself perfectly still, refusing to acknowledge her swelling breasts or her hard nipples. This wasn't happening. She didn't want this.

I don't want him. He's a vampire.

His hand slid up her waist until his thumb came to a stop between her breasts. "You must breathe or my efforts will be fruitless, Ariel."

She released her pent-up breath in a quick gust and then held it again at the sharp desire that coursed through her.

His fingers tightened around her ribs as he ran his tongue along her wound once more. He couldn't be feeling what she felt—aching, unbidden arousal.

Right now he should feel ill.

"Won't my blood make you sick?" she asked, hoping to redirect her physical response.

She'd claw his eyes out if she knew what he was thinking. That he wanted to sink his fangs deep and savor her sweet blood. How much he wanted to taste her body, to run his tongue along every single inch of it, even down to that deep red crescent-moon birthmark on the back of her neck.

Ariel's wit made her an intriguing creature, while her ethereal package of flowing white-blond hair, defined cheekbones and full lips made him ache. He'd never been more turned on in his life. Jachin set his jaw and met her gaze, his grip tight on her waist. "It's not enough blood to kill me. My goal is to keep you safe."

She pulled out of his hold and crab-crawled away from him. "So you can deliver me to another vampire named Braeden, right? Who is he? Your leader?"

His jaw hardened at her accusing tone. "Where did you hear that?"

She continued backward until she leaned against the cave's stone wall opposite him. The apple forgotten on the ground, she pulled her knees against her chest and crossed her arms over them. "From your two vampire buddies who thought I'd make a good gnawing post." She tilted her head to the side, her eyes slitting in suspicion. "And why would your own kind want you dead?"

Jachin let out a deep sigh, both regretful and thankful the sexual tension between them was broken. He refused to go down the same road that put him in this living hell in the first place. He'd learned a long time ago—a good sexfest wasn't worth it.

"What did Sethen and Thad tell you?" He contemplated how much to divulge to her about the Sanguinas vampires' pasts. She was a necessary piece of the puzzle, but she didn't need to know all the bits that put her there.

"Why does this Braeden want me?" she countered.

He noted the set of her mouth and realized she wasn't answering his question until she got answers of her own. Stubborn woman. "Braeden is the Sanguinas leader. I told you before. You wrote a book."

Her eyes widened in disbelief. "Give me a break! I'm not buying the fact that I put pen to paper as the reason I managed to draw the short straw."

Jachin suppressed a smile. He liked her quick wit. It would serve her well as Braeden's mate. Braeden might be inflexible at times, but he'd believed in the prophecy as much as Jachin had.

"There's more to it than that. You fulfill other parts of the prophecy."

She let out a frustrated breath. "Let's just say I believe this fairy-tale stuff you're feeding me. What makes you think I'd do anything to help the bloodthirsty creatures—" her words hitched before she continued "—come back to terrorize my people?"

"Because we're your people, too," he shot back in a

biting tone. He didn't give a rat's ass if he shocked her. She wanted the truth. Let her stew on that one.

Her eyes widened for a couple seconds and then narrowed. "You're all inhuman."

"Who do you think created us?" His voice cut across the narrow space between them, harsh and unforgiving.

"You're lying!" She jumped to her feet, her hands fisted at her sides. "There is nothing in the history books about vampires being created by humans. Nothing!"

"Why *would* the government admit to genetic tampering on human subjects?" he challenged, his dark eyebrows drawing together. "It was illegal. They broke every code in the book of ethics without batting a lash…all in the name of scientific advances."

She ran shaky hands through her disheveled hair, disbelief in her expression. "Why would our government create creatures that preyed on their own kind? It doesn't make any sense."

"They began the Scions project sixty years ago in an effort to create the ultimate superhuman. With the past biological attack on the paper monetary system, the government might've moved to a credit system to appease the general public's fears of a potential repeat attack, but National Security had been secretly working on the Scions project for decades. They knew that biological warfare had been used repeatedly throughout history for a reason— enemies would see it as the swiftest method with the most devastating results."

When he saw Ariel start to shake her head in denial, he said, "The word scion has two meanings. The first one is descendant. And the second one is a shoot or sprout of a plant used in grafting. The vampires are both in a way, hence the name of the government project."

As an inkling of understanding dawned in her expression, he rubbed his hand on the back of his neck and continued, "The project's goal was to create humans who could resist disease. They created us with greater strength, the ability to heal quickly and, as a side benefit, we age much slower." His gaze locked with hers. "We were bred to be survivors. Our fangs were a surprising genetic anomaly they hadn't anticipated, but they made sure to give us a weakness, too. Just in case."

"Vampires' aversion to sunlight," she murmured, supplying the answer.

He gave a curt nod. "They were playing God until the very end—and they royally screwed up."

Ariel sank down to her knees, her shoulders hunched. Something in his tone must've told her he spoke the truth. "Why would these superhumans attack their own kind then? Why bite the hand that fed you?"

Jachin smiled, allowing her to see his fangs before he retracted them back to their normal size. "There was a first generation—human turned vampire due to genetic alteration. The offspring were pure vampire. We were physically stronger than the first generation and we developed at a rapid pace until we reached adulthood, where we aged like our parents—much slower than humans. We were a new, developing race."

The optimism in his voice disappeared and his expression hardened. "Not only did the scientists breed us to survive, they bred us to do so no matter the cost. Their tests were cruel and vindictive. They treated us like creatures without souls. We had no life but the one they designed us for, even for those who wanted something more."

His tone turned flat. "But someone high up decided to shut the project down, which meant get rid of all the evidence. A revolt was an inevitable outcome. The vampires eliminated all the scientists running the program and destroyed the facility, too."

Ariel shook her head in disbelief. "That doesn't explain why the program subjects attacked innocent humans once the facility was destroyed."

"At first, it was just revenge against all humanity, plain and simple. Then, over time, things started to change. Many vampires wanted a life…or at least one as similar to humans' as possible." His gut knotted at the memory of the infighting that went on between the vampires, the splintering of ranks with varied views. "Many had begun to move forward, to back off from the severe violence against humans, when suddenly dozens of our kind got very sick and began to die."

"Pity for you," she smirked, her gaze unsympathetic. "According to history, when humans realized their blood was poisoning the vampires, they thought it was nature's way of taking care of the problem…kind of a defensive evolution."

Jachin knew different, but he refused to debate the subject. Ariel didn't need the whole sordid past. She thought they were monsters already. There was no need to fuel the fire of her prejudice.

His tone went cold. "I told you this so you would understand that there is another side of the story."

"Do you think your explanation justifies what the vampires have done to—" She set her lips in a firm line, crossed her arms and sat down against the wall once more. "Think again."

Ariel had paused in what she was going to say. Did her vehement prejudice spring from something personal? The need to know drove him. "Then why write about such 'horrific beasts,' Ariel? Why give us our own history, create characters with life issues that humans might actually identify and sympathize with?"

She gave an indifferent shrug. "It's fiction. If I wrote about you the way you really were, no one would want to read the book."

It was a logical answer, but his instincts told him that was just a surface response. "You're not telling me everything."

They stared across the cave, each challenging the other with slitted, distrustful gazes.

"When you decide to tell me the truth about your book, we'll talk more. Now get some rest. We'll head out as soon as it's dark." He pulled the gun from its holster and set it on the ground next to him, then straightened his legs and crossed his ankles. Opening his backpack, he withdrew the silver case and retrieved another vial of lukin.

Ariel scowled at the vampire. He never did tell her why his own kind were trying to kill him. Her intuition told her Jachin had relayed the truth about the vampires' past, but she meant what she'd said—the past didn't excuse their brutal treatment of the human population for ten years.

Nor would she ever forget the vampires' role in the devastation of her family.

Did he really think she'd let him take her to his leader to fulfill some prophecy she'd made up in a book? Sheesh, the man seemed smarter than that. So what if he'd finished her lines while she'd recited the prophecy? Maybe she'd mumbled them while she'd slept at his house.

As angry as she was with him, she couldn't help her curiosity as she watched him open a chamber on the side of his gun and insert the vial. Apparently he wasn't a drug addict. "What does the lukin do when added to your pulser gun?"

He closed the chamber on the gun and glanced at her. "It creates a concentrated dose of UV light."

"That's the catalyst you mentioned." Smart vampire. If only the government-sanctioned vampire hunters known as the Garotters had had that weapon to use against vampires a few decades ago, she might not ever have had to learn what it felt like to be so alone, always looking over her shoulder…wondering when she was going to be attacked.

Fury knotted her stomach over a past she couldn't change. She needed space, not to mention her cramping stomach made the need to urinate that much stronger.

When she stood up, his gaze followed. "Where are you going?"

Ariel rolled her eyes. "To pee, if you don't mind."

He jerked his head toward the back of the cave. "Go back there and relieve yourself."

She curled her lip in disdain. "I'm *not* going in the same place I have to stay. Forget it!"

He set the gun down next to him. Folding his muscular

arms over his chest, he leaned against the stone wall and closed his eyes. "Then don't go. It's your choice."

Jachin heard Ariel sit down with an exasperated huff. He needed sleep to help his wounds heal. The additional loss of blood from the wreck didn't help his lack-of-food situation. He knew he could go a couple more days without blood as long as he didn't sustain any more wounds. But soon he'd need to eat or his strength would diminish—not an option when facing Sanguinas like Vlad and Aaron and any other vampire out there hunting them. They wouldn't give up their pursuit of Ariel.

The Sanguinas might be weaker than him, due to his steady diet of sterilized human blood, but they sure as hell outnumbered him. When he was cast out from the clan a decade ago, the Sanguinas' population stood at one hundred and twenty-five strong. How many were there now?

Ariel squirmed around as if she really had to go. Jachin took deep breaths and focused on her. *You're tired. Sleep now. When you awake you can relieve yourself.*

Through a hooded gaze he watched her eyes begin to droop. When she jerked her head up to try to keep herself awake, he pushed on her consciousness harder. *Sleep, Ariel.* She finally yawned, then stretched out on her side, closing her eyes. Satisfaction rippled through him.

He stared at her fey face for several minutes, unable to look away. She was definitely attractive…for a human. Her willful personality made it easy for him to forget she was only thirty or so. He might look and feel as though he was in his mid thirties, but Jachin was a good twenty-five years older.

A long time ago he'd made it a personal policy never to take blood from humans so much younger than him. He knew Mira had been a driving factor. Her youthful blue eyes, normally full of wonder and excitement, had stared at him with deep sadness when he left the Sanguinas. Her well-being had weighed heavily on his conscience these past ten years.

Yet now, even with his hunger at bay, he stared at Ariel like a man starved. It disturbed him how much he ached to feel the texture of her blood on his tongue and her warm, soft body underneath him while she moaned in ecstasy.

He dug his shoulders against the rocks' rough texture behind him, needing the pinch of pain to clear his head. He stared at her with narrowed eyes, reminding himself of his long-established disdain of her kind.

Humans should never be trusted.

Jachin closed his eyes and sought a healing sleep.

Ariel came fully awake with the need to urinate. The sensation was so strong her stomach cramped. She cast her gaze in Jachin's direction, relieved to hear his breathing deep and even in sleep, and crept out of the cave.

Once she'd relieved herself behind some bushes on the side of the road, she cast her gaze to the sinking sun and tried to decipher the time, since the river had ruined her watch. Her best guess was that she had about an hour of sunlight left, maybe less. That wouldn't be enough time to get back to Manhattan, but she should be able to make it to a smaller town along the way if she could find the car.

Her adrenaline pumped as she walked around the outside of the cave, looking for the vehicle Sethen had told

Thad to hide. When she spied the car's deep blue finish shining through some foliage, her heart raced in relief. She quickly pulled the tree limbs back to uncover the car, while she hoped and prayed the keys were still in the ignition.

Tossing the branches aside, her hands shook as she pulled open the driver's-side door. When she didn't see the keys in the ignition, disappointment rushed through her, making her stomach knot.

"Too bad hot-wiring a car wasn't part of Home Economics 101," she mumbled as she sat down in the driver's seat and opened the glove compartment.

No keys.

Saying a silent prayer, she flipped down the visor and jerked in surprise when a set of keys landed in her lap with a quick jingle. Hope swelled, overcoming her tense stomach.

As her fingers curled around the keys, someone yelled, "Ari-el!"

The booming male voice came from the direction of the cave. Ariel jumped and clutched the keys to her chest. She pulled the door shut, then jammed the keys into the ignition.

Locking the doors, she tried to put on a seat belt, but the car didn't have one. Hands shaking, she put the car in reverse, backed out of the hidden spot and turned the car onto the main road.

Gripping the steering wheel tight, she gunned the engine. The tires squealed, leaving the smell of burned rubber in her wake as the car shot forward.

Ariel cast a brief glance toward the cave's entrance as she drove past. Jachin stood just out of the sunlight's beams, watching her.

I'm done playing nice. His deep voice reverberated in her mind.

She shook her head to clear it as she returned her gaze to the road. The vampire had really gotten to her if she was hearing him speak in her thoughts.

A shudder rushed through her at the idea he'd make her pay if he ever caught up with her. Straightening her spine, she slammed the gas pedal to the floor.

Chapter 5

As Ariel drove down the mountain's curving road, the tension in her shoulders began to ease with the bright afternoon sun warming her face.

Now that she wasn't threatened by vampires, she focused on steering the car around the hole in the road. Once she maneuvered past the broken up road, she pressed the pedal down and considered what she'd learned.

Humankind had created the vampires.

If what Jachin told her was true, what would the general public think if they knew their government was responsible for unleashing the vicious monsters on humanity?

Jachin had said that some of the vampires, the Sanguinas, were determined to move toward a different life when many of them became ill. Maybe all vampires weren't menaces.

Gusts of wind accompanied the sunlight's sudden disappearance, drawing her gaze to the sky. Dark clouds accumulated with rapid speed, blocking out the sun. Ariel's heart jerked as the summer storm brewed overhead. She gripped the wheel tighter, mumbling, "This can't be happening."

From what she remembered in the history books…as long as the sunlight was blocked, vampires could come out.

As Ariel navigated the narrow, winding road for ten minutes, increasing paranoia wound her body into a tangled mass of nerves. Her neck ached and a tight knot had formed between her shoulder blades. Frantic for any sign of civilization, her gaze zeroed in on a new road sign up ahead.

Fifteen miles to New Paltz.

Almost there.

Ariel forced herself to relax, rationalizing that Jachin was on foot. Exhaling, she rolled her head from shoulder to shoulder to relieve the pent-up tension. New Paltz was a small town, but at least there was population around. She could call the NY police from there.

While she considered what she would say, an alarming thought occurred. What if the police didn't believe her? As far as she knew, no one had seen proof that her kidnapper was a vampire. It would be just her luck if law enforcement discounted her story as some kind of publicity stunt to increase sales of her current and future books.

Her car's sudden jarring and the sound of metal crunching metal yanked her out of her concerned musings. Ariel's head snapped backward at the impact. Something had rammed into her car from behind.

Heart hammering, she tightened her damp hands around the steering wheel and jerked her gaze to the rearview mirror.

Three men were in a black sedan behind her. The blond vampire who'd launched the rocket on Jachin's car was at the steering wheel. Her red brake lights accentuated the pure malice in his expression as he sped up and rammed into the back of her car once more.

Chest tight, her foot riding the brake, she bit back a scream and concentrated on the bend in the road ahead. Keeping the wheel as steady as she could, she maneuvered the curve, rounding the mountain and straightening out her car only to have it lurch forward again. Scraping metal and broken glass groaned and crashed in her ears.

She hunched her shoulders, wishing she could block out the horrific sounds, when something landed with a heavy thud on the hood of her car.

Her blood pressure skyrocketed at the sight of a man turning toward her windshield. He balanced on the car's hood as easily as if he were riding a surfboard.

Ariel quickly glanced back toward the car behind her to discover the passenger was missing. A hysterical scream ripped from her throat as the sedan rode her bumper. While he forced her forward in a squeal of protesting brakes, burning rubber's acrid smoke seeped into her enclosed car, stinging her nose and eyes.

The man on her car put one knee on the hood and smashed his fist straight through her windshield. She squeezed her eyes shut against the bits of flying glass that peppered her face with sharp stings.

Ariel opened her eyes too late to dodge the man's

groping hand. His fingers wrapped around her hair on top of her head, yanking hard. Tears blurred her vision and she screamed out at the excruciating pain.

"Pull over, bitch!"

Even as she sobbed, self-preservation kicked in. Jerking her car to the right toward the mountainside, she hoped the impact would knock the vampire off her car.

The side fender hit a jutting rock first. Metal crunched and creaked as the fender crumpled and the passenger door frame dented inward. Broken bits of rock and shrubbery exploded, cracking the side window, but the impact only caused the vampire to cinch his hand even tighter in her hair while he slammed his other fist through her driver's-side window.

She turned her head to avoid more flying glass, causing shocking, white-blinding pain to lance through her skull where his fist remained. Ariel's vision spotted and she wailed as she worked hard to keep the wheels on the road.

When her screams changed to silent cries, she blinked to try and refocus. Approaching another curve ahead in the road, she glanced past the vampire's body. Her heart jerked at the thought he'd fly off her hood with the turn, pulling her full against the steering wheel and possibly tugging her through the windshield if she took the curve at her current speed.

She laid hard on the brakes. This time the pedal went all the way to the floor with ease. The resistance was completely gone.

God, no!

When her car rounded the curve, the wheels squealed and the vehicle elevated slightly on the two left tires. The vampire let out an infuriated growl. He bent low, his bloodshot brown eyes narrowing in hate. The wind blew his black spiky hair toward his head. "It would take very little effort to snap your puny neck right now. Do as I said or die." His mouth twisted in a cruel sneer and he yanked her hair once more.

This time some strands ripped from her skull. "I can't stop!" she yelped, pumping the useless brake pedal up and down to show him.

Realization that she was telling the truth dawned on the vampire's face right before a heavy thump landed on the top of her car, denting the metal.

Ariel's heart jerked at the sound. Damn it! Was it another vampire?

A loud pop preceded the squeal of tires sliding across asphalt. Ariel glanced past the vampire's arm to the corner of her bent rearview mirror in time to see the car behind her swerve away, blown tire bits flying through the air.

The sedan veered out of control toward the edge of the road. The vehicle's front bumper hopped against the guardrail while the driver tried to regain control. Sparks and an eerie fingernails-down-a-chalkboard screech announced its scraping path against the metal barrier before it sailed over the edge and straight down the side of the mountain.

Ariel breathed in gulps of air and kept her grip tight on the wheel, trying to keep her car from following the same fate, which wasn't an easy task. The vampire holding her appeared to be trying to grab the person on the top of her car, and each time he did so, he used his hold on her head for additional leverage.

Pain engulfed her. She knew it centered on her head, but she felt it all over in the series of hot and cold flashes. She blinked back her tears to see past the vampire to the road ahead of her, just as the hand on her head started to shake.

Veins of bright light lined the vampire's cheeks and forehead, and she realized he was about to explode in a ball of fire just as the other vampires had back in the cave. As the brilliant light disintegrating his body from within rushed down his arm toward her head, panic reached an all-time high, making her light-headed.

"No, no, no, no, no!" Ariel screamed. She gripped the steering wheel with one hand and frantically slapped at the vampire's hand still fisted in her hair in an effort to keep the flame from reaching her.

When the light became too bright, she held her breath, squeezed her eyes shut and grabbed hold of the steering wheel with both hands, praying she was on a straight length of road. Sudden warmth infused her face right before the tight grip on her hair disappeared.

Ariel jerked her eyes open as bits of warm, dark ash landed on her face and lips. *Ewwww!* A shiver of sheer disgust rippled up and down her spine at the gross realization the man's cremated body was settling on her. She spit to dislodge the flakes of ash from her lips only to hear Jachin's angry voice above her.

"Quit screwing around. Hit the brakes, woman!"

Ariel jumped at the sound of irritation lacing his tone. She wasn't surprised it was Jachin, due to what happened to the vampire on her hood, but she resented his implication she was out for a joyride. *Ooh, what I wouldn't give to be able to slam these stupid brakes right now,* she thought, but the sight of the curve ahead of her had her screaming instead. "The brakes are gone!"

Her heart leapt to her throat as she barreled toward the sharp curve, going faster and faster. She repositioned her hands on the wheel even though she knew she wasn't going to be able to control the car around this curve. A screeching sound vibrated in her left ear as the driver's-side door frame ripped from its hinges.

Before she could fathom what Jachin was doing, he reached inside, grabbed her left arm and jerked her out of the car. As Jachin and the vehicle careened over the road's edge, Ariel landed on the roadside gravel—hard—momentum rolling her toward the steep drop-off.

Survival instincts on high, she grasped at bits of grass, dirt, rocks—anything to stop her fall. The smell of earth, asphalt, grass and blood flooded her senses, while her heightened emotions crammed her throat closed.

But her momentum worked against her.

She pitched sideways over the edge. Her body instantly shifted to a horrifying headfirst position straight toward the rocks and trees below.

Only then did an unholy shriek erupt from her throat.

Unwilling to witness her impending death, Ariel squeezed her eyes shut at the same time something yanked at her ankle, halting her descent.

At the sensation of fingers squeezing the bones in her ankle, her eyes snapped open. Jachin's pulser gun flew past her. The weapon bounced off a rock, then tumbled a hundred more feet before shattering against a bed of rocks below.

Her stomach clenched at the sight of the gun exploding on impact and the car continuing its rolling path down the mountain, metal and glass crunching and shattering. And she was being held up over this steep drop by nothing more than a tight grip around her ankle!

Her scream's pitch elevated to glass-shattering levels.

Stop screaming, Jachin's command sounded as if it'd come from inside her head.

She gulped to take in much-needed air. Her heart slammed out of control, while blood rushed to her head in dizzying waves of pressure. "Pull me up!" she yelled.

"You *will* behave."

He wanted to dictate her cooperation now? "Are you out of your ever-lovin' mind?"

"Quite. Now answer."

The dark sky above them chose that moment to open up, dumping its contents on them in cool, driving sheets. As her clothes quickly soaked through, she agreed in desperation, "Whatever you want."

His fingers cinched in a bone-crushing vise. "Mean it," he called above the pouring rain and claps of thunder.

She jerked when lightning flashed. "Fine. Just pull me up, you sadist!"

"You're going to have to help me," Jachin directed. "Reach up with your left hand and grasp as high up my forearm as you can. As soon as you do so, I'll release your ankle and grasp your forearm in turn."

The blood rushing to her head was starting to get to her, making her woozy. "I'm about to pass out and you want me to do yoga moves? No way. You'll drop me!"

Trust me, Ariel. Listen only to my voice and focus on me, nothing else. The sensation of Jachin's voice in her mind was so strong she wondered if she was on the verge of losing her sanity. Yet a surreal calmness washed over her at his words, along with a deep sense of certainty.

Ariel snorted the dripping rain out of her nose as she twisted and turned, using stomach muscles she didn't know she had in order to reach Jachin's wrist.

"Ready?" His dark eyes locked with hers.

She nodded at his calm tone, then let out a small yelp when the tight sensation around her ankle suddenly released.

Releasing a shallow breath of relief that Jachin now had a tight hold on her forearm, Ariel made the mistake of looking upward past Jachin. Anxiety made her chest constrict and her pulse ramp even higher. They were a good five feet below the road, and Jachin was holding on to the edge of a rock jutting out from the mountainside, his fingers gripping tight.

As rain pelted her face, she jerked her disbelieving gaze to his. "Please tell me your five fingers aren't the only things holding us both up."

He spoke in a calm tone. "We need to move quickly. My hold won't last long in this rain. I'm going to pull you as high up my body as I can, but you'll have to do the rest of the work."

"What do you want me to do?" she asked as the rain began to slow to a steady, cool drizzle.

"You're going to have to climb up my body until you can wrap your arms around my shoulders and your legs around my waist."

Ariel shook her head at his plan. His arm was slippery from the rain. She had no friction to help her with the task he expected her to do.

His determined gaze drilled into her. "You're well-muscled, Ariel. You can do this."

His intense confidence managed to assure her. Taking a deep breath, she nodded.

Jachin began to pull her upward, hissing out through gritted teeth at the added stress on his fingers holding them up.

Ariel tried not to focus on the strain he was under. Instead she grabbed hold of his belt with her free hand and tried to redistribute some of her weight away from his arm as he pulled her higher.

"Bend your elbow to give you the height you need to reach my shoulder," Jachin said in a strained voice.

With the strength of his hand giving her the leverage she needed, Ariel reached up with her right hand and clasped his shoulder. As soon as her right hand gained purchase, Ariel fisted her left hand into his T-shirt and strained to pull herself upward, hoping like hell the cotton material didn't rip. Slowly she inched herself up his body until she was able to wrap her right arm around his shoulder and neck.

As soon as her legs folded around him, Jachin released her arm and quickly moved his freed hand to cup her rear to support her.

Once she'd wrapped both her arms around his neck, Ariel rested her head against Jachin's shoulder and panted.

"Not bad…for a human," Jachin said right before he released her rear and swung to the left to grab hold of another rock.

Ariel shifted with his movement and let out a scream.

Jachin's shoulders hunched underneath her arms and he

gritted out in obvious irritation, "My hearing is only super-sonic if I still have it."

"Sorry," she whispered, right before he vaulted upward.

With her stomach in her throat, she slowly slit her eyes open to see they were standing on a ledge no wider than Jachin's shoulders. The road's edge was another few feet straight above them. Before she could say a word, Jachin backed up to the ledge as far as his boots would allow, then bent his knees and jumped.

As soon as his feet landed on the graveled roadside, Ariel unhooked her legs from his waist and slid to the ground. Her knees gave way once her feet hit the wet asphalt. She landed hard on the pebbled pavement, panting.

While the rain came down in a slow patter, her chest hurt as if she'd just run a marathon. Blood's metallic flavor bathed her mouth, surprising her. She must've bitten the inside of her cheek in her effort to remain quiet.

Jachin's hand encircled her upper arm in an unforgiving grip. "Let's go."

She lifted tired eyes his way. "Can't we rest for a second?"

Rain dripped off his straight nose, cutting a swift path down his angular cheekbones and making the scar on his neck stand out. His mouth set in an unforgiving hard line as he hauled her to her feet. "You've cost me my only weapon and precious time. You will not disobey me again." His dark gaze bored into hers, challenging her to buck him.

Dusk was upon them as thunder boomed overhead. They stared each other down, each taking stock of the other's mettle. She knew she'd run again if given the chance. He'd be a fool to think otherwise, yet one word she'd never assign to this vampire was *fool*. Without another word, he tugged her behind him as he headed toward the woods along the edge of the road.

From the moment they entered the woods, Jachin took off running. Ariel had little choice but to follow his brutal pace, thankful she'd maintained a strict running schedule every day.

Two hours and several miles higher into the mountains, where Jachin only stopped once to retrieve his backpack, Ariel couldn't take the breakneck speed he'd set any longer. The rain had long stopped and she'd given up trying to pace herself. After the last thirty minutes of a straight uphill trail, she tugged away from Jachin's grip and fell to the moss-covered ground in sheer exhaustion.

He turned and frowned at her, while the moonlight speared through the trees, illuminating his annoyed expression. At the moment, she was too tired to care. Leaning her back against a tall tree no wider than her waist, Ariel took deep breaths of air into her aching lungs. "If I don't rest, you'll be delivering a dead woman to your stupid vampire leader."

Jachin narrowed his eyes on her for several seconds before he set his backpack on the ground. When he tugged his wet T-shirt off his body, Ariel averted her gaze from his gorgeous, well-built chest and ripped abs.

Sheesh, wet or not, wouldn't he need that T-shirt to stay warm? It had been an unusually cool summer and the higher elevation only made it colder. Her attention focused on his hands once he began to shred the black cotton material. What in the world was the vampire up to?

Jachin approached her and squatted down to grip one of her wrists. She tensed and tried to jerk her arm away. "What are you doing?"

He held firm to her wrist and began to wrap a strip of his shirt around it. "You said you needed to rest."

When he turned her knuckles toward the ground and kept his hold on her wrist as he began to move behind the tree, his intent became clear. She tensed and tried to pull her arm free. "You're not tying me!"

Jachin gripped her other arm and tugged it backward, pulling her upper body against the tree with a heavy thump. "I trust my instincts more than your word," he replied while he quickly wrapped the other end of the material around her wrist and tied a knot, locking her to the base of the tree.

Anger formed a lump in her throat. She tugged at her restraints and glared at him after he'd rounded the tree and sat down on the ground a few feet across from her. "Don't think for one minute I was joking about dragging your good-for-nothing ass into the sunlight!"

Jachin bent his knees in front of him. Resting his wrists on his knees in a relaxed pose, he met her gaze with an unconcerned one. "I have no doubt you'll do so given the first opportunity."

As her own heart rate began to slow to a slightly higher than normal beat and her heated body cooled, Ariel stared at the unreadable man before her. Jachin's gaze was so cold, so devoid of emotion, she wondered if he'd ever had any or if feelings had been genetically filtered out when his race was created.

He sat there half-naked, his chest slowly rising and falling as if he'd just woken up from a long nap. Even though the moonlight reflected on his face, she couldn't read his mood. His still pose gave nothing away.

Silence stretched between them for several minutes until

a cool breeze blew through the trees. She shivered in her damp clothes. Jachin's gaze drifted to her chest that was pressed outward in her bound position. She glanced down to see her hard nipples against her thin linen shirt. *Where's my bra?* she wondered, then remembered it was in the pocket of her jacket…in Jachin's blown-up car.

Her pulse racing, she jerked her gaze to his and lifted her knees toward her chest to block her body from his view. Despite the cold wind blowing around her, warmth infused her body at the heated look in his eyes.

As cold as she was, her skin had started to prickle for an entirely different reason once she'd seen his hungry gaze locked on her chest. She cast a quick glance across his broad shoulders and down his muscular arms. Smooth skin flexed over toned sinew. He showed no outward signs of being affected by the cold air or otherwise. Damn him!

"Why do you call me human?" she asked, hoping to distract herself from noticing something so detailed about him.

His gaze slitted in suspicion. "Because that's what you are."

"You said you're human, too. So why refer to me as *human* in such a derogatory way?"

A flash of surprise reflected in his eyes before he masked his reaction behind an unreadable stoic look. "We're on different levels."

Annoyed he refused to acknowledge the irony of his logic, she challenged him. "Why? Because you're a superior human?"

His gaze strayed to the dark woods as if their conversation bored him. "Exactly."

"At least I have *my* humanity."

Jachin's dark eyes snapped to hers. "I seek the same for my people."

"I think you seek retribution." At his narrowed gaze, she continued, "You say you seek a humanlike life, yet you have no problem using violence—"

"I'm a survivor."

She leaned forward, warming to her subject. "Your hatred of a race you claim to be a part of is palpable. You have no compassion, no conscience. You show no emotions. Do you even experience any? Those are the qualities that ultimately make one human, not one's genetic makeup."

His hands fisted on his knees and his lip curled into an angry snarl. "Don't think you know me, because you do not."

Ariel mentally cringed at the furious intensity in his voice, but she refused to let him intimidate her. "I've felt your anger, experienced your disdain, but if you've felt anything else, I've yet to see it. So if we're keeping score in the true humanity category, I'm *far* superior."

While tension ebbed between them like a cobra bobbing back and forth, waiting to strike, her stomach chose that moment to let out a loud rumble.

Jachin raised a dark eyebrow at the obvious sound of hunger. "I hear how superior you are."

His sarcastic jibe knotted her stomach in fury. As he unzipped his backpack, Ariel curled her own lip, wishing her hands were free so she could wipe that smug look off his face. She glanced away, mumbling, "Shut up."

"Such hateful looks from someone who's supposed to be so humane."

Jachin's amused voice sounded as if he were right next to her ear, while his exotic scent seemed to envelop her. When Ariel turned and saw him sitting in front of her, invading her personal space, she sucked in her breath.

He took advantage of her gasp of surprise and slipped a small piece of dried bark past her lips. A plethora of spices exploded in her mouth, invading her senses, making her mouth water.

"Chew," he demanded, a fierce expression creasing his forehead.

Before she could spit out whatever he'd shoved in her mouth, he pressed two fingers over her lips, holding them shut. "You need to eat. This is packed with nutrients. Chew."

She didn't like to be mocked, and this man obviously enjoyed reminding her of her body's weakness. Ariel shook her head, knocking his hand free.

A low growl erupted from his throat as he grasped her chin in a firm grip and pressed his lips against hers.

Chapter 6

Ariel froze, inhaling deeply at the intimate press of his lips against hers.

Jachin's appealing smell of outdoors and musk washed over her in a wave of seductive aromas. As her heart began to thud again at a rabbit's pace, his hands clasped her face and his voice entered her mind. *I won't remove my mouth until you swallow, you stubborn little human.*

He was mocking her again, but she couldn't think with his mouth covering hers and his naked chest mere inches from her own.

His sexual magnetism seduced her unlike any man she'd ever encountered. Shocked at her reaction to his nearness, she began to chew the bit of food in earnest, desperate for him to remove his mouth and his warm, hard body from her personal space. The dried bit of food tasted like mint, cloves and other spices and herbs she couldn't decipher.

When she swallowed, his thumb leisurely followed the food's descent down her throat. His fingers continued downward, massaging the back of her neck in an intimate caress until his thumb rested in the soft hollow at the base of her neck.

He pressed against her skittering pulse, and her breasts swelled and her nipples tingled in response. She ached to brush her curves against his chest, as naked as he. Jachin applied persuasive pressure against her mouth, his lips slanting over hers in dominant demand for entry.

As she opened her mouth and accepted the possessive thrust of his tongue against hers, Ariel became very aware of her vulnerable situation, tied to a tree. His hard thigh pressed against her hip, while his large body towered over hers in complete dominance. And what excited her most: there was nothing she could do to stop him.

Her heart thumped as she realized the out-of-control situation made her hot all over. Maybe it was because her morals couldn't come into play or because the absence of a physical choice allowed her to disregard them.

Ariel arched her neck and twined her tongue with his, responding to Jachin's kiss—a kiss that held a depth of intimacy and passion she didn't think he possessed.

Jachin's fingers feathered down her neck, sliding across her chest until his hand palmed her breast. Following her instincts, their sheer sexual attraction, Ariel strained against her bindings and pressed her breast against his palm, encouraging his touch.

A low growl rumbled in his chest, and he ran his thumb

along her hard nipple before tweaking the responsive tip between his fingers. Delicious pleasure radiated from her nipple, splintering throughout her body.

Ariel heard herself moan as her arousal built to a desperate pitch. Her sex began to throb and she lowered her knee, pressing her thigh against his...asking for more.

When Jachin's hand trailed down her blouse, then skimmed her stomach, taking them down a seductive one-way path, she had to mentally remind herself this man didn't care for her. He wasn't interested in keeping her for his own but in delivering her into the hands of another.

And he was a vampire.

As his fingers slid across the top of her thigh, her sexual desires tried to override her rational thoughts, but reason prevailed.

One thing was certain: this particular vampire didn't scare her as much as her surprising arousal at his touch. She'd never been more turned on. By a vampire, no less.

That frightened her.

Ariel protected herself the only way she could.

When Ariel bit down on his tongue, Jachin pulled back and glared at her. Damn, the woman bit hard. His tongue throbbed as if it'd been cinched in a vise.

She strained against her bindings and leaned as close to him as she could, snapping her teeth together. "Never forget—we *all* have an agenda, Jachin."

Furious at himself for being so thoroughly duped, Jachin fought the desire coursing through him, the beast that urged him to touch her again despite her obvious act of revenge. Was she angry at him for making her want him? He hadn't imagined her elevated heartbeat, her breathlessness or the way she'd leaned into his touch.

She'd wanted him.

He gave her a dark smile, displaying his fangs in all their glory. "Never forget—I bite harder."

Ariel's mocking expression faded and the color of arousal quickly drained from her face. She might not be afraid of him as a man, but she definitely feared his fangs. He almost felt guilty for playing on her fears.

Almost.

Jachin moved to settle himself against a tree across from her once more. In her current position, her perky breasts strained against her soiled linen shirt, the tips showing dark through the wet material.

His cock strained against his pants, an uncomfortable reminder of their unfulfilled passion. Ariel's aroused response to his kiss surprised the hell out of him, but not near as much as his own ravenous reaction to her soft, warm mouth. "Tell me why you wrote your book."

She stared at him for several seconds. "Tell me why your own vampire clan is trying to kill you."

The woman was so willful. "I was banished from the Sanguinas a decade ago."

"Why?"

"For following my emotions." His lips quirked upward at the irony, considering her earlier assumptions about him. "Why did you write a book about vampires?"

Ariel's gaze strayed to his chest as she answered. "I'm terrified of vampires…have been ever since I was a child, when I attended my grandparents' funeral." Tears glistened in her eyes when she returned her gaze to his. "It was a closed-casket ceremony, but I wanted to say goodbye to my grandmother and grandfather. I opened my grandmother's casket." She paused and her voice quivered as she shook her head, her gaze faraway. "I'll never forget the scars on her neck."

"You said your grandparents' funeral?"

"Yes, they were both killed—slaughtered by a vampire."

Shocked disbelief weighed heavily on Jachin's chest. It was unprecedented for a vampire to go after more than one person at a time. "Both your grandparents were attacked?"

"My whole family." She sniffed, trying to hold back tears. "After my grandparents' deaths, my parents moved our family to another side of town, but that only delayed the inevitable. While I was spending the night at a friend's house, my parents were murdered. I wasn't allowed to see their bodies. And my brother Peter…" She trailed off as tears streamed down her cheeks. "A godparent took me in and raised me until I was old enough to be on my own."

He fisted his hands as swift, vengeful anger washed over him at her story. No wonder she had a deep, abiding fear of vampires. "Did a vampire come after you?"

She shook her head. "Not long after I lost my brother, the vampires all started getting sick. I've always dreaded a vampire would come for me, finally finish off my family." Shivering, she blew out a steady breath. "But I told myself vampires were extinct, and if I ever wanted any kind of life, I had to move on. I couldn't live in fear forever. I wrote the book as a kind of therapy. I needed to overcome my phobia, to live my life without constantly looking over my shoulder."

A giddy self-deprecating laugh escaped her lips. "And now look at me. Maybe I should become a psychic."

And I'm going to deliver you to an entire vampire clan. Guilt curled within him, making his stomach burn. He'd hoped she'd written the book because she secretly harbored a desire to be with a vampire. To discover the opposite…

Jachin set his jaw and strengthened his resolve. He refused to give in to the remorse that raged in his gut. Setting the Sanguinas on the right path was his main concern, not the emotional stability of one human.

Even a desirable one.

And, despite his contempt for her race, he did desire her…more than he had any woman.

As another cool breeze whipped through the forest, Ariel's trembling turned to uncontrollable shivers. She closed her eyes and laid her forehead on her knees as if trying to hide the fact she was freezing.

Jachin withdrew his leather coat from his backpack and laid it out on the ground. Without a word, he walked behind the tree and ripped the binding that held Ariel's wrists together. When he came around the tree, her teeth chattered as she wiped her eyes with the wet cloth still attached to her wrists.

A primal need to protect her rose within him, searing a hole in his chest.

Jachin scooped her up in his arms. She tried to protest, but her voice sounded so tired as he walked over to the coat. Lowering to one knee, he laid her on the makeshift bed.

He was glad she refused to meet his gaze. Her emotions were too raw, the relaying of her fears too recent. "Trust me to provide the warmth you need. Rest for now. We'll resume our hike in an hour."

When he lay down behind her and wrapped his arm around her waist, Jachin expected resistance. What he didn't expect was for Ariel to let out an exhausted sigh and press her slight body closer to his, seeking his warmth.

Her display of complete trust in him, despite her family's past, both enchanted and troubled him. Once he'd removed the bindings from her wrists, then settled his head near hers, the intriguing scent of rain, peaches and sweet almonds teased his senses.

The desire to bury his nose in her damp hair was strong, but he didn't want to break the temporary trucelike spell that had settled between them. *She's weak and vulnerable…and so damned feminine,* he thought as he inhaled deeply, reveling in her alluring scent.

His action made him want her all over again. Jachin blew out a harsh breath to tamp down his arousal and reached in the backpack behind him for another piece of hay ash.

Breaking a four-inch-long piece, he handed the food supplement to Ariel. "Rub this across your teeth to clean them, then eat it. Get some food in your belly so you'll feel warmer."

She took the flat piece of dried food from his hand and rubbed it against her teeth before biting off a section. As she slowly chewed, she burrowed closer to his body and mumbled, "This doesn't mean I like you."

His groin reacted to the stimuli, his erection instantly filling with blood. Jachin shut his eyes and gritted his teeth to keep his body from jumping to full-on arousal. Throwing his leg over hers to keep her from squirming, he whispered in her subconscious, *Sleep, my little lioness.*

* * *

She kissed him hard, pressing her tongue deep into his mouth. The sensation of her fangs scraping his lips only made him hotter. Jachin pulled her closer, mumbling against her mouth, "Why do you stay with him, Viv?"

"I'm not with him. I'm with you." Her heated breath brushed across his throat while she ripped his shirt open in one swift tug.

As her fingers dug into his shoulders, his groin tightened, reacting instantly to her aggressive action. Jachin grasped her waist, lifting her body against his until her neck was on the same level as his mouth.

She moaned and wrapped her legs around his hips. Gripping his neck, she yanked his mouth close to her throat and began to gyrate against his stomach.

Jachin palmed her well-rounded ass and sank his fangs deep into her neck. When he began to suck her blood, Vivian mewled and moaned, clutching him closer.

A thundering crash behind him made his heart jerk. Jachin quickly withdrew his fangs from Vivian's neck and turned to see Braeden standing in the library's doorway.

Braeden's hands were fisted by his sides, his expression thunderous. "Put her down, you traitorous bastard."

Jachin looked at Vivian, anticipating some reaction. She averted her eyes as she wiggled for him to release her. When he set her down and she stepped away, refusing to meet his gaze, he realized he wouldn't receive any support from her. Regret made his chest tighten. He didn't want her as a mate, but he did want her to see there were other men who would treat her better than Braeden had.

Turning to face Braeden, he started to speak, but the

vampire lashed out, slashing the side of Jachin's throat with his vampire talons.

Anger blurred Jachin's vision and the tips of his fingers tingled. Before he knew what happened, Braeden held his hand over his left cheek. Blood welled between his fingers and the vampire roared his anger. "You dare to challenge me?"

Jachin moved his fingers back and forth by his side. The wet sensation between them told him his talons dripped with Braeden's blood. "I just returned the favor—"

Braeden launched himself at Jachin, slamming his fist into Jachin's face.

Pain exploded in his head and Jachin flew across the room, crashing against the built-in bookcases.

Vengeance curled in his belly, swiftly rising to his chest, a contained explosion ready to blow. Books were scattered around him as Jachin landed on the stone floor in a predatory crouch.

Braeden flung Jachin's blood from his fingers, the thick red fluid spattering across the floor as he bit out, "You're banished from our clan. Get the hell out of Sanguinas manor."

Jachin narrowed his gaze on the Sanguinas leader. His gut burned in fury at the unjust punishment. "You can't banish me for being with Vivian. She's not your mate."

Braeden's thin upper lip curled in a sneer. "The prophecy might bind me, but Vivian is mine!"

"You use the prophecy as it suits you," Jachin ground out. He knew Braeden never planned to mate with Vivian, prophecy or not. Despite his involvement with Vivian, the man had slept with many willing Sanguinas women.

Braeden's face turned red and a thick vein throbbed on his temple. "You dare to question my belief in the prophecy? I have given up my own personal desires because of it."

Jachin's shoulders tightened as he glared at Braeden. "You don't have the authority to banish me. It must be a unanimous decision by the entire council."

The vampire leader gave a confident smirk. "The council knows I hold the prophecy and the well-being of the Sanguinas in the highest regard."

When Braeden turned and walked out of the room, Vivian followed in his wake. Not once did she glance Jachin's way as she called out to her longtime lover, "I like hearing you say I'm yours. Say it again…."

Jachin jerked awake to crickets sawing their high-pitched songs and frogs croaking. Cool air stirred around them as Ariel slept curled close. She felt so good in his arms, supple and warm.

He was surprised he'd dreamed about his banishment. He hadn't thought about it in at least five years. As he gazed down at Ariel's pert nose, he realized her question as to why his clan members would try to kill him was the cause of his dream.

The Sanguinas didn't want him to return.

He closed his eyes at the unsettling paradox of his situation. She was destined to be Braeden's mate. He couldn't change the prophecy or his unwavering belief in its power to set the Sanguinas on the right path. He'd desired Vivian, nothing more. But this woman—this human—Jachin felt an unprecedented need to protect… and to claim as his.

He lightly ran his finger down Ariel's temple. She sighed in her sleep, turning toward his touch. As she rolled onto her back and her pink lips parted slightly, his cock instantly hardened at the delicate softness of her skin and the desire to feel the press of her lips against his once more.

A hard lump surged in his throat. Maybe it was her sheer vulnerability that called to his inner primordial beast. Or the fact she both feared and trusted him that fueled his desire for her.

Gritting his teeth, he slowly pulled away from her and stood. As his gaze traveled the smooth column of her throat and the gentle swell of her breasts pressing against her wrinkled and dirt-stained shirt, a powerful, wrenching surge of arousal rocked through him. How bitterly ironic to find himself caught in the same untenable situation, desiring a woman he couldn't have.

This time around, the stakes were higher—despite his own personal emotions being involved and battling within him, the whole clan's future depended on his delivery of the one human who could turn their fate around.

As he acknowledged the distinction, Jachin set his jaw. Clenching his fists, he turned and walked away. He needed to remove himself from the temptation that lay sleeping in his "bed" on the forest floor.

Fifteen minutes later, as Jachin turned around to head back to Ariel, something didn't feel right. The hairs on the back of his neck stood up and the air in the forest seemed suddenly still, as if nature were holding an anticipatory breath, waiting.

He'd only taken a couple of steps when a gust of wind carried a very familiar scent his way, a split second before a heavy weight landed on his shoulders, knocking him to the ground.

Jachin's lungs burned with the need for air from the impact, but he ignored the pain and shrugged the person's bulk off his shoulders. Rolling in the forest underbrush to a squatted crouch, Jachin faced his attacker and snarled, "So much for our truce."

Landon stood and brushed dirt from his jeans in unhurried movements. His green gaze narrowed in the darkness. "I told you I'd be asked to hunt you down."

Jachin heard the rustle of footsteps approaching in the woods. His shoulders tensed as he stood to his full height. "Who's with you?"

"I've scouted ahead for the Garotters."

Jachin raised his eyebrow. "The government has pulled the Garotters out of retirement? Did the men have to oil their joints first?" Despite his unaffected tone, Jachin honed his senses and zeroed in on the men. He made out footsteps of eight men approaching from the east—blocking his path back to Ariel. He knew he had very little time before the vampire hunters were within shot range.

"Always the sarcastic one." Landon's smirk held satisfaction. "These men are second-generation Garotters. Many are ex-military. They have far better weaponry than their predecess—"

Jachin didn't let Landon finish. He had to get to Ariel. Fangs extended, he launched across the seven-foot distance between them, jamming his shoulder into the werewolf's stomach and his talons into the man's sides.

A pained grunt escaped Landon as Jachin rammed him into a thick tree trunk a few feet behind him. Snarling in anger, Landon hammered his fist onto Jachin's spine, causing his legs to give way at the bone-jarring impact.

Landon roared in pain as he pulled at Jachin's wrists, trying to dislodge his hold. Jachin only dug his talons deeper into Landon's sides until both men fell to the ground, grunting and snarling at one another.

The werewolf managed a powerful blow to his shoulder before his own nails ripped at Jachin's chest. Excruciating pain lanced through him and Jachin smelled his own blood flowing freely. Moving fast, he slammed the heel of his hand against Landon's chest, sending the werewolf flying backward.

He wasn't going down that easily.

He rolled onto his side, breathing heavily, and tried to stand when he heard several pulser guns charging up at once.

Jachin glanced at the men surrounding him in a full circle, their guns trained on his head.

Landon staggered to stand and moved to lean over him, blocking out the half moon's light. "I told you I could take you."

Despite his throbbing injuries, as his vision blurred, Jachin gritted out, "Only on my worst day."

The werewolf slammed his fist into his jaw, and Landon's low laugh was the last sound Jachin heard.

"Get him loaded quickly." The tall man with light brown hair stood beside Ariel, calling out to the three men dressed in black. The men were carrying Jachin's half-naked, unconscious body up a ramp and into the back of an uncovered cargo truck.

As the men handcuffed Jachin's arms behind his back

to a metal roll bar, Ariel transferred Jachin's backpack to her right hand, then ran her left hand over her dry, rumpled clothes.

The sun was about to peek over the horizon, and she remained tense until the men began to pull a camouflage canvas covering over the whalebone-style frame inside the truck's bed. Why she worried that Jachin was going to be burned to a crisp, she had no idea, but regardless of what the vampire had put her through, she didn't feel he deserved that kind of fate.

"What will happen to him?" she asked, staring at the man who stood beside her.

His steady green gaze met hers. "This is a special task force. I'm not sure how their procedures work."

One of the men jumped out of the Jeep in front of the truck. She focused on the gold capital G and the dagger that formed part of the letter emblazoned on the back of his black jacket, recognizing the symbol from her vampire history books. These men were Garotters, otherwise known as vampire hunters. At least the government must now know vampires still exist, since they'd funded the Garotters in the past. Ariel shivered slightly under the sun's warm rays.

She couldn't believe the nightmare was all over. She'd faced vicious vampires and would live to tell about it… thanks to Jachin. But there was still a strange sense of unfinished business she couldn't quite shake from her psyche. Maybe because Jachin had saved her life she felt the need to help him in turn.

The man beside her was the only person dressed casually in jeans and a long-sleeved dark blue T-shirt. The shirt had holes around his waist that were stained dark with what she could only guess was dried blood. Had he fought with Jachin? From what she could tell, he wasn't bleeding anymore. No fresh blood showed through the tears.

She considered his role among the Garotters. He might be dressed in civilian attire, but they seemed to be keeping him in the loop. Maybe he would have some pull on Jachin's sentencing. "He never hurt me, not really. He— he saved my life several times."

The man shoved his hands in his jeans' pockets, then gave her a sidelong look. "Did he say what possessed him to kidnap you?"

The way he asked the question, as if he were surprised by the vampire's behavior, made her wonder if this man knew Jachin. Ariel nodded. "He said something about ful- filling a prophecy."

His eyebrows shot up. "He spoke of a prophecy? How do you fit—"

"Landon, we're ready to roll," a Garotter called out, giving the man beside her the thumbs-up symbol.

Landon set his mouth in a firm line and addressed her as two men approached carrying pulser guns. "You'll ride in the front of the truck with them." Nodding to indicate the Jeeps parked in front and behind the truck, he contin- ued, "You'll have an escort home. You're in good hands, Miss Swanson."

"This is Jachin's," she said, handing the backpack to Landon before she followed the two armed men to the front of the truck. She knew she should feel relieved that her ordeal was over, but she didn't. Right now she was numb all over.

She was so desensitized it took her a second to realize

the dark-haired man standing beside her had just locked a handcuff on her right wrist and was snapping the other side on her left wrist in front of her.

What's going on? Ariel's heart raced and she jerked her confused gaze to his bug-eyed brown one. "Why did you just put these on me?"

He opened the truck door and made a get-moving motion with his weapon. "Get in, miss."

Grinding her teeth that he'd ignored her question, Ariel stood her ground. "Not until you take these handcuffs off. I'm the victim, not the criminal."

The man's dark eyes narrowed. He pointed his gun at her chest, a high-pitched whine cycling up as it readied to fire. "I said get in."

Ariel considered yelling for Jachin, but he was unconscious and also bound. Not to mention the fact the soldier in front of her could kill her before she got more than two words out.

Her pulse rushed as she climbed inside the truck. Sitting in the middle of the bench seat, sandwiched between two soldiers, helpless fear crushed her chest. At the same time, a surprising realization hit her: five seconds ago she'd almost called for Jachin. Without hesitation.

How had she come to trust a vampire over everyone else?

A humming movement underneath him, rocking his body from side to side, woke Jachin. Dull pain flared in his back and across his shoulders. His hands were bound behind him and he was sitting on some kind of box in the back of a vehicle.

Shaking off the wooziness, Jachin opened his eyes and

Landon's steady gaze came into focus. The Lupreda sat across from him on a black, wooden, military-style trunk. Jachin noted his backpack sat beside the werewolf on the trunk before he assessed the rest of his surroundings in a quick sweep.

He was handcuffed to a metal pole along the edge of a cargo truck's bed. One man sat at attention a few feet away at the back of the truck, and another guard was stationed at the front. Both humans held pulser guns. Sunlight filtered under the canvas flap covering the back of the truck.

Damn.

Reaching out with his senses, Jachin detected Ariel's scent. She was close. Her heartbeat sounded almost frantic, her breathing rapid. He frowned, disturbed by the sound. She'd been saved from the vampire who'd kidnapped her. Shouldn't he be picking up a sense of relief and calmness in her?

"What did you do to her?" he snarled at Landon. The metal handcuffs clanged against a metal pole. He tugged at his handcuffs, rocking the bar behind him, but the pole didn't give way.

"She's safe," Landon responded.

"Liar!" Jachin's entire body tensed. He felt every injury writhing through his system as he growled at Landon like a cornered lion. Under the force of his banked anger, the chain holding the metal cuffs behind his back should've given way, but it didn't budge at all. The Garotters must've used some kind of special metal he'd never encountered. He needed to know what he was up against. Once he had answers, he'd figure out how to get Ariel out of here without frying himself to a crisp in the process.

Landon scowled. "I never lie. Ariel is fine."

Something in Landon's steadfast tone told him the werewolf was telling the truth...as far as he knew it. Jachin slanted his gaze to the two men who still had their weapons aimed at him. Returning his eyes to Landon's, he kept his mental focus on the two men, concentrating on them as he whispered in their minds, *You're tired...so sleepy you can't keep your eyes open.*

The sound of a gun sliding to the truck's metal bed drew Landon's attention. Both men's heads drooped in a heavy sleep. His gaze snapped back to Jachin's. "Impressive. I wasn't aware vampires had such powers."

"Listen to her heart," Jachin snarled in fury.

Landon tilted his head for a few seconds, then inhaled. A deep frown furrowed his brow. "I smell her fear."

"I feel it," Jachin snarled. "Where are they taking us?"

Landon shook his head. "I don't know. They called me to track you after the girl was kidnapped. I believe this new Garotter regime may be privately funded." He gave a sidelong glance to the sleeping men, then leaned toward Jachin. "Ariel said you mentioned the prophecy."

Jachin's shoulders bunched in distrust, but if he had to put his faith in at least one werewolf, he hoped to hell he'd picked the right one. "Your scheme to kill us off through poisoned human blood has failed."

Landon clenched his fists on his knees. "The Lupreda had nothing to do with the humans' blood turning poisonous to vampires."

Jachin clenched his jaw in anger. "Even the Lupredas' blood sickens the Sanguinas. How can you deny your involvement?"

Landon shook his head. "The Lupreda weren't responsible. And if you're so certain of our involvement, tell me how our supposed scheme failed."

Jachin met Landon's steady gaze. "I don't believe Ariel's blood is poisoned."

Landon cocked an eyebrow. "You don't believe? Either her blood is poisoned or it isn't."

Ignoring the were's sarcasm, Jachin continued, "She wrote a story about vampires."

"So?"

Taking a deep breath to help him maintain patience, Jachin continued, "In her fictional story she spoke of a prophecy."

Both Landon's eyebrows rose this time. "You think she's the human who's mentioned in the prophecy you told me about?"

Jachin set his jaw. "I know she is."

"I'm assuming you were in the process of delivering her to your leader when we caught you. I take it Ariel didn't approve of being a vampire's destined mate?"

Jachin clamped his lips in a thin line while conflicting emotions of guilt and duty tugged at his conscience.

"The fact you refuse to respond is all the answer I need." Adopting a closed expression, Landon leaned back against the pole behind him and folded his arms across his thick chest.

"She's in danger." Jachin felt it with every fiber within him.

Landon gave him a condemning look. "Correction. She *was* in danger."

Ariel sat between the two men, her anxiety and heart rate rising with each turn of the truck's wheels. The sound of two rapid gunshots made her jump in her seat.

"What the—sonofabitch!" The man to her right tensed and peered into his rearview mirror. Powering up his weapon, he said to the driver, "Our Jeep in the back just rammed into the mountain!"

Her stomach tensed as more gunfire exploded. The shots were from traditional guns. *Have other vampires found us?* she wondered when the guard sitting in the passenger seat in the Jeep in front of them slumped forward, quickly followed by the driver.

As the driverless Jeep drove right off the side of the mountain road, the man to her right gripped his gun in one hand and cracked open his door, calling to their driver, "I'm on it. Whatever you do, don't stop!"

Rolling down the window, he stood and used the heavy door to shield most of his body as he fired off several rounds of pulse shots toward the cliffs above them. Bullets slammed against the truck's door, making her cringe with each metallic thud.

The Garotter shooting at their attackers suddenly slumped, his upper body slung over the open window to her right.

God, he's been shot, she thought. Tears of frustration ran down her cheeks. She bit her bottom lip, feeling like the helpless cardboard duck set up at a carnival target shoot.

She wished Jachin was conscious. He would get them to safety. Unfortunately, he was vulnerable during this attack…and *vulnerable* wasn't a word she'd ever thought she'd associate with the determined vampire.

A sudden deafening boom rocked the ground underneath the truck. The driver yelled and gripped the wheel tighter, jerking the truck to avoid a boulder that had fallen in the road.

Ariel screamed as a second explosion lifted the vehicle on its two left wheels and toppled the cargo truck on its side.

Chapter 7

The impact tossed Ariel against the driver, cracking the side of her head hard against his. As the truck skidded along the road, splitting pain radiated from her left cheekbone. She screamed until her throat burned.

Sparks flew toward the cracked windshield. She plugged her fingers in her ears against the horrific sound of metal riding against asphalt as best as she could with the damned handcuffs' limitations.

Once the truck came to a shuddering stop, Ariel knew she had precious little time. Whoever was shooting at them would probably come looking to see if there were any survivors and finish her off.

The thought made her stomach churn.

She refused to sit there like a caged animal. Pushing on the driver's shoulder, she turned to speak to him. Blood seeped from his mouth, and his head was tilted toward the window, eyes closed. No breath lifted his chest.

Casting her gaze to her right, she looked to see if the other man had survived the crash. His waist was trapped by the passenger door's weight, his upper body hung upside down against the seat, his head toward her.

She swallowed the need to hurl at the sight of blood coating the bench seat behind his head. He stared with sightless eyes, a bullet hole marring the center of his forehead. Dark, wet streaks slid down the slick fake leather surface toward her. She cringed and pressed herself even harder against the driver under her shoulder to avoid the blood.

Ariel closed her eyes at the picture of death sandwiching her. She willed her stomach to behave. She didn't have time to be sick right now. Unfortunately, as soon as her sight was cut off, her sense of smell took over.

Blood's metallic scent floated in the air, making her head reel. But when the strong stench of gasoline overrode the smell of blood, she quickly opened her eyes and shook her head. *Get a grip, girl. You need to get the hell out of here.*

She stared at the spider cracks across the windshield and cast her gaze frantically throughout the truck's cab, looking for something to knock the safety glass out. The driver's gun was on the floor underneath his legs. Straining against his unmoving body, she leaned down and retrieved the rifle.

After she checked to see that the safety mechanism was on, Ariel rammed the butt of the gun into the windshield as hard as she could.

The sound might draw attention, but with gasoline spreading, she could only worry about one threat to her life at a time. When her pants and the right side of her body began to feel damp, she glanced down to see red blood wicking up the back of her stained and torn shirt.

The need to retch was so strong she swallowed several times to keep her food down. Adrenaline pumped through her veins and she hit the glass with even more force, snarling, "Come on, you freakin' glass."

Time ticked past, and she'd started sliding along the slippery, blood-coated seat when finally the window began to splinter even more.

"Yes!" She breathed out a sigh of relief. One more big impact should do it. Setting the gun to the side, Ariel held on to a cloth strap hanging down from the truck's ceiling and kicked at the glass with all her might. When her feet busted through, she quickly pulled them in and hammered her heels at another area, trying to widen the hole enough so she could squeeze out.

Once the opening was large enough for her body, she lifted the gun and set it on one side of the glass to protect her body while she crawled through.

Heart thumping as her feet hit the ground, she stooped and grabbed the gun. She hoped Jachin had somehow survived the wreck. Why she cared, she didn't know. Maybe it was because he'd been knocked out and unable to defend himself.

Shattered glass crunched underneath her shoes as she made her way toward the back of the truck, sweat trickling to the small of her back. The moment she tried to come around the rear of the truck, a whizzing sound zoomed past her. The bullet barely missed her head.

Ariel bit back a scream. She stumbled back and fell, landing behind the safety of the vehicle.

Ariel.

She heard Jachin's voice over the unrelenting fear pounding in her head.

Bolstered by the knowledge he had survived, she crawled on her hands and knees. Dragging the gun beside her, she ignored the sharp sting of pain shooting through her wounded right hand. She'd cut it climbing out the window.

The camouflage canvas cover had pulled away from the back left side of the truck, enough to shield her from someone watching above. Peering past the thick material, Ariel saw Jachin hanging from a pole. His arms were pulled behind him, rock-hard biceps straining under his weight.

Dried bloody claw marks lined his right shoulder while his muscular chest heaved and his defined abs sucked inward. His booted feet were braced on the upturned floor of the truck in an apparent effort to give his arms some respite from his full weight.

She could tell gravity made his current awkward position very painful. Three men lay unconscious on the bottom of the vehicle. Weapons and other artillery spilled from the broken military trunks scattered around them.

Jachin's grimace briefly changed to relief when he saw her. "I need your help."

She scrambled underneath the flap and stepped around the debris and the unconscious men to reach his side. "What can I do?"

His pained gaze slid to the gun in her hand. "Do you know how to use that?"

She shook her head and held up the gun to slide back the safety. "All I know is that it's a pulser type. I saw the man using it."

"That should work." Jachin took two deep breaths, closed his eyes briefly against the stress engulfing his body, then met her gaze. "Just aim for the chain connecting the handcuffs."

"What if it goes straight through the metal pipe and hits your arm on the other side?" she asked, not at all confident in her shooting skills on such a small target.

"At this point, I don't give a shit," he gritted out.

Ariel eyed the metal pole he strained against for a second. Instead of trying to aim for the chains holding the cuffs together, she had another idea. Setting the butt of the gun against her shoulder, she held on to the weapon as best she could with the handcuffs hindering her movement. "This feels awkward," she said as she aimed at the pole.

"Hold it as steady as you can," he rasped.

Her stomach knotted with fear that she'd grossly miss. "Keep your head down."

"No problem," he replied in a sarcastic tone.

Resisting the urge to wince, she pulled the trigger. The gun whined through the three bursts, but once the pipe glowed red, slashed with laser lines, she figured she'd finally weakened it enough for a vampire to do the rest. "While the metal is soft, use the cuffs to try to slice the rest of the way through the pipe."

Unfortunately, she'd also burned a baseball-size hole through the canvas behind him with that last wild pulser burst. Sunlight poured in, making him growl in pain as it beamed across his shoulder.

His shoulder singeing from the sunlight, Jachin jerked his body to the side to avoid the scalding light as he hitched his feet higher to gain leverage. Using his thigh muscles, he pushed his body upward and yanked hard with the cuff's chain until the chain cut all the way through the pipe. He fell to the floor and instantly rolled over one of the unconscious men in order to get away from the sun.

Ariel stepped over the prone man he'd just steamrolled and waited for Jachin to stand. When he held his hands out behind him, she made sure no one was in the pulser gun's blast path and fired, hoping like hell she didn't shoot his wrist by accident. She blew out a breath of relief when the blast quickly broke the chain holding his handcuffs together.

As soon as he was free, Jachin grabbed her shoulders. "I smell your blood. Where are you injured?" he asked, sliding his hands down her arms, checking for wounds.

Ariel was surprised at the way his touch affected her. Among all this death and imminent danger, she realized with distinct clarity how much she wanted his comfort and protective touch.

No. She craved it.

"I'm fine," she insisted, frightened by her realization. How could she possibly want a vampire? The mere thought betrayed her family. Turning away, her gaze landed on the man who had spoken to her about Jachin. The Garotters had called him Landon. A huge bruise spread across his jaw and blood gushed from a gaping gash on the side of his head.

The amount of blood he was losing made her wince. He probably wouldn't survive. Her heart lurched and a lump formed in her throat. He'd seemed different from the Garotters, more…sympathetic.

"We need to get out of here. Whoever attacked us is still

out there waiting." As soon as she spoke, another boom rocked the ground and the truck underneath them.

Jachin gripped her shoulders so she wouldn't fall to the floor. When the explosion stopped and the truck stilled, a cold expression crossed his face. "Like me, my brethren are trapped by the sunlight. They can only shoot at us from a protected area."

"You're sure it's the Sanguinas?"

He gave her a grim look. "I can sense them."

Feeling trapped, Ariel glanced around the truck. There had to be a way to get them out of the line of fire without exposing Jachin to the sun.

She bit her lip as she scanned every inch of the truck. When an idea came to her, she handed Jachin the gun and held out her hands for him to take care of her handcuffs. "I have a plan."

He shot the chain apart. "What's your idea?"

Ariel rolled her shoulders, relieved to have her freedom of movement back. "Move to the front of the truck."

His jaw ticced and his gaze questioned her. After several long seconds he gave her a curt nod and moved to the front of the truck, only stopping long enough to retrieve his backpack and hitch it over his shoulder.

Ariel took the few steps to the back of the truck and began tugging on the metal clips holding the canvas that served as a door to the top and sides of the truck.

Within thirty seconds she had the makeshift door pulled free. Stepping over scattered weapons and three unconscious men, she headed toward the front of the truck.

As she approached, Jachin squinted at the strong indirect sunlight that poured into the truck from the exposed back.

She stopped in front of him and met his curious gaze. "The gunfire is coming from the mountainside above us. This canvas can provide the cover you need to get to the side of the mountain. We should be shielded from their gunfire there. Once we're there, we can follow the mountainside to the Jeep that slammed into it. The vehicle wrecked right before the truck turned over, so it can't be more than a half mile back. I'm hoping we can get it started again."

"Not bad," he mumbled as she threw the cover over his head.

For a pathetic, weak-willed human, she mentally finished for him. Her lips curved upward at his compliment. It sounded so…grudging.

"How do you propose to get us out of here without becoming Swiss cheese?" he challenged, his voice muffled underneath the tarp.

She tugged the tarp into place, making sure Jachin's exposed skin all the way down to his hands was completely covered. "On a wing and a prayer."

"Wonderful. A half-baked plan," he replied, his tone full of sarcasm.

Reaching under the cover, she retrieved the gun from him. "Watch it, vamp, or one swift tug on this tarp while we're out there and you'll be beyond half-baked, swiftly changing to well-done."

"That mouth *is* going to be the death of you," he shot back at the same time his hand skated out. His fingers laced with hers and he pulled their locked hands underneath the tarp.

When his lips met her knuckles, butterflies scattered in her stomach.

"Lead the way, Rambo."

At his vote of confidence, Ariel squeezed his hand and began to tug him toward the end of the truck. She'd only taken a few steps when he pulled her up short.

She glanced over her shoulder to see Jachin lean down and grab hold of Landon's wrist. "He's not going to make it." She slid her gaze to Landon's mortal wound. The gaping hole in his head had closed considerably. Instead of a gushing valley of blood, only a single streaming trickle slid down his temple. "I don't believe it—" she started to say, her eyes going wide.

"Let's go," Jachin cut her off, his cold, harsh tone back.

Jachin dragged Landon's unconscious body behind him like a dead man to the edge of the truck. Ariel took a deep breath and stepped out of the back of the truck, firing off several pulse bursts toward the cliffs above them.

"I'll follow the sound of your steps. Keep firing and run," Jachin barked.

Ariel didn't have to be told twice. As she bolted toward the safety of the mountain, Jachin and Landon by her side, gunfire was returned from the hidden vampire snipers.

The asphalt behind her took the brunt of the bullets. Each time another bullet whizzed past and slammed into the road, her heart died a little, then rejoiced with a rapid thump.

Her lungs burned by the time she reached the cliff's shelter. She leaned against the rocks to give her shaking thighs a break as she took deep breaths.

When Jachin tugged the unconscious man hard against the wall and she heard a groan, Ariel stared at Landon, amazed at his rapid healing ability. "What is he? Some kind of special vampire who can withstand sunlight?" she asked as she squatted next to Landon and stared at his head wound. It was almost completely closed.

A defiant snort erupted from Landon. His groggy gaze locked with hers. "Bite your tongue, woman."

"We need to keep moving." Jachin said in a terse tone.

She started to stand, when Landon encircled her wrist in a tight grip. "You don't have to go." His voice crackled with pain, but she saw the sheer determination in his expression as he shifted his gaze to Jachin.

"Yes, I do." She tried to pull away, but his fingers cinched harder around her wrist, making the handcuff dig into her skin.

He frowned at the metal ring underneath his fingers.

"The Garotters," she answered the question in his eyes.

"Have an agenda all their own." Jachin finished as he squatted down and lifted the tarp. His face shaded, he met Landon's gaze.

The man nodded in an unspoken agreement with Jachin. "Did any survive?"

Jachin gave him a curt nod. "The two I sent to sleep are both alive."

Firm resolve filled Landon's expression. He sat up against the boulder behind him. "Good. They'll assume you escaped and took Ariel. I'll retrieve the men. Maybe saving their lives will give me an in with the Garotters and a chance to find out what this new regime is all about."

Jachin's gaze narrowed in suspicion. "Give me your cell number. I want to know what you find out."

Landon stared at Jachin for a second before he rattled off his number. When he finished, his gaze slid over Jachin and Ariel. "You both need rest. I don't live with the general pack but on the eastern corner. Follow the stream and you'll find my home."

"We'll manage," Jachin said in a cool tone.

Landon's gaze landed on Jachin's burned hand holding the tarp's edge up. "You saved my life at great pain to yourself."

Ariel gasped at the vicious red-and-black burns bubbling along Jachin's left forearm. His arm had been exposed to sunlight while he'd pulled Landon to the side of the road. She'd been so focused on getting to safety she'd blocked everything else out.

Now the smell of burned, festering flesh swirled around them, making her stomach cramp. She choked down the bile that rose in her throat and looked at Jachin. "He's offering shelter from the sun. Whatever your differences, don't be a fool. Take it."

When Jachin gave a stiff nod, Ariel let out a sigh of relief and stood. "We need to get to the Jeep and try to get it started."

Once Jachin lowered the flap, he joined her. They both moved to stand against the mountain's wall. As they started to follow along the wall's path, Landon called out, "My house key is under the mat."

Ariel paused, glancing back at him in disbelief. "That's so cliché—"

"That it works," he cut in with a wolfish smile.

Shaking her head at his male logic, Ariel continued walking along the wall. She slid around sharp, jutting rocks and avoided prickly shrubs, all the while talking Jachin through the obstacles in his path.

Her heart pumped harder when the wrecked vehicle came into view. Two Garotters were slumped over in the front seats. "There it is. The soldiers might be dead. They aren't moving."

"They're dead. I can't hear heartbeats," Jachin replied in a calm tone.

Ariel stepped away from the rock wall to head toward her goal, but Jachin grabbed her arm. He hissed in pain at the cost to his skin. Unforgiving sunlight singed it further. "If they shot at the Jeep, you might still be in their range."

As he pulled his arm back under the tarp, she acknowledged his point. "What do you suggest?"

"The vehicle veered toward the mountain, so we may still be sheltered by it. Are there any overhangs above us?"

Ariel pushed away from the mountain wall and leaned out to cast her gaze upward. Scanning the area that led toward the vehicle, she said, "Yes, there's a slight overhang, but it cuts short a good twenty feet before the Jeep."

"Let's follow the wall as long as we can, then we'll make a dash for the vehicle."

Ariel jerked her attention to his tarp-covered head. "You can't go. You have to stay out of the sunlight. I'll drive the car to you."

"How do you think you're going to get two men out of that vehicle while covering yourself from gunfire?"

Ariel worried her bottom lip with her teeth. Damn, he was right. She blew out an exasperated breath and gripped the gun tight as her palms began to sweat. The cuffs slid down her wrists when she lifted the weapon in a ready position. "Okay, I'll go first, then you go while I cover you with the pulser gun. Hopefully we'll be out of the vampires' range and I can help you move the men."

She'd barely stepped out from under the rock face when a dark blur zipped past her. Ariel gasped and her insides rocked in concern, but she kept to the plan. Squinting against the bright sunlight, she held the gun trained upward, ready to fire as she began to run backward. There was no reason to fire and draw attention their way unnecessarily.

"Come on," Jachin called to her in a low voice at the same time she heard the vehicle's engine trying to turn over. Ariel tensed at the sudden grinding whir. She glanced behind her to see the Garotters were already on the ground and Jachin sat in the passenger seat, his tarp askew as he leaned toward the steering wheel.

The noise must've given their position away, because gunfire hammered against the vehicle, large BBs dinging the metal frame. Ariel's pulse raced and her adrenaline spiked.

She fired off a rapid round of shots toward the mountains while bolting with all the speed she could muster toward the Jeep. Jachin caught the weapon she tossed his way as she climbed into the doorless military-style vehicle and dropped into the driver's seat.

While Jachin fired the gun to give her cover, she jammed the gear into place, turned the key once more and pushed on the clutch.

The engine chugged, sluggish and slow at first, before roaring to life. A breath of relief rushed through her at the sound. Her entire body trembling, Ariel shifted the gear and edged on the gas, backing the crumpled vehicle away from the rocks.

"Which way?" she yelled over the staccato of gunfire, intuitively keeping her head low.

"Back up the mountain," Jachin croaked in a pained voice.

Ariel shifted the gear once more, then turned the steering wheel all the way around as she punched the gas to the floorboard.

A splintering sound drew her attention and she saw that a bullet had caught the top of the pulser gun in Jachin's hand.

"What the hell?" he asked.

She quickly replied, relief rushing through her he hadn't been hit instead, "A bullet just shattered the gun's barrel. It's useless now."

Once they rounded the curved mountainside road, Jachin dropped the weapon to the car's floor, his groan of agony punctuating the air.

Ariel's heart lurched at the sound. She squared her shoulders and let her sympathy for his pain override the nausea churning her stomach. Reaching under the tarp, she grabbed the top of his left hand and laced her fingers with his. "Hang on. Don't pass out on me."

When he tensed at her touch, she started to pull her hand away. He quickly entwined their fingers, locking her hand to his as he ground out, "Wishful thinking."

Ariel wasn't sure if he was referring to her or himself with his comment. Probably both. "Just tell me what road markers I'm looking for and I'll get us there. Um, I'll need my hand back in a sec to shift gears."

His hand tightened around hers. "Tell me the gear when you need it."

She cast her confused gaze briefly in his direction, but all she saw was camouflage. When she came upon a curve, she began to slow down, needing to shift gears.

"What gear?" Jachin asked.

She waited for the engine to grind in protest. "Second."

When the gear shifted beside her knee, moving to the correct position, Ariel jerked her attention back to the road, amazed and somehow not at all surprised by his show of telekinetic power.

Even in excruciating pain, Jachin exuded confidence.

As she drove, she told him the road signs they came upon and followed his directions. Her heart stuttered a little at the realization Jachin hadn't released his hold on her hand. His tight grip displayed a very human trait: he might be able to withstand high levels of pain, but he seemed to need their physical connection.

"It's just another hundred yards." Ariel had never been more thankful to see shelter in her life. When she glimpsed the outline of a house through the woods ahead of them, all she could think was, *Please let there be running water, an actual flushing toilet and something to eat. Hot water would be heaven!*

Jachin trekked along beside her under his tarp. He'd been strangely quiet, almost broody. He hadn't spoken since they'd stashed the Jeep in the forest along the road and set off into the woods. She was pleased with herself that she'd found the stream Landon mentioned all on her own. They'd been following its soothing gurgle for a half hour when she spied a lone house.

Sunlight filtered through the heavy foliage above them, giving the forest a dappled, cool feel. Two deer lifted their heads, then darted away as she and Jachin approached the one-story log cabin. Ariel pulled back the rattan mat, and the door key gleamed like a gold doubloon waiting to be stolen.

"Men and their simple logic," she mumbled as she grabbed the key and let the mat drop back into place.

Once they walked inside, Ariel shut the door and slid

the dead bolt home. Setting the key on the small round wood table next to the door, she flipped a light switch. Satisfied to see the soft glow coming from a huge lamp hanging from the vaulted ceiling, she moved into the living area and called over her shoulder to Jachin, "Wait until I close the blinds before you take off the canvas."

A quick glance at the winding staircase leading upstairs told her she'd been wrong about the house. From the outside it appeared to be a one-story, but it was actually a loft home built into the hilltop.

She walked the oak wood floors, stepping over casual navy-blue-and-teal country-style throw carpets to close several blinds on the bottom floor. After she'd completed her task in the main room and the kitchen downstairs, she climbed the curved staircase in the far left corner of the great room. As she reached the top, she sucked in her breath at the gorgeous view the huge picture window allowed of the Shawangunk mountain range.

Her gaze lowered to the king-size bed next to the window, and she began to tremble as her heart rate came down. Ariel realized just how hyped-up on adrenaline she'd been. Every part of her body ached, from her head to her feet.

Exhaustion swept over her like ocean waves, rushing around her legs, trying to pull her under. The bed looked so inviting with its black-and-brown patterned down comforter. Framing the huge mattress, a highly polished rustic headboard and footboard of rough-carved oak surrounded the bed. The combination of earthy colors and wood was both masculine and beautiful in its simplicity.

Her arms felt heavy when she lifted her hands to grip the thick canvas curtain material between her fingers. She pulled the khaki curtains closed and let out a sigh once the room dimmed considerably.

As she approached the stairs, she realized she hadn't heard a sound from Jachin. Heart thumping, she started down the carpeted stairs, her fingers tensing around the polished carved-wood railing.

Her pace picked up until she saw him sprawled out on the leather couch in the living room, the tarp thrown in a forgotten heap on the living room floor. His backpack leaned against the couch, and his boots, socks and hand-cuffs were lying next to it on the floor.

Huh! How'd he unlock his cuffs? And then she saw a mangled paper clip lying next to the cuffs. She glanced at the open drawer that had been pulled out from the coffee table next to the couch. It was filled with enve-lopes, loose-leaf paper, a stapler, a box of paper clips, scissors and tape.

Interesting office-supply cabinet, Landon, she thought with a half smile as she leaned over to shut the coffee table's lower drawer. She picked up an unbent paper clip and, after several unsuccessful attempts to unlock her own cuffs, turned to Jachin. "I don't know how you did this…."

His eyes were closed and his bare muscular chest rose and fell in the slow, steady breaths of a deep sleep. She blinked back the rush of tears when her gaze traveled his huge frame and settled on his burned arms. The skin no longer oozed, but it was far from healed. Ariel bit her lip to keep from gasping at the horrific damage the sunlight had inflicted upon him.

She started to turn away, when her mind registered a distinct difference in his left hand, specifically the top.

Placing her hands on her thighs, she leaned closer. The pressure against the cut on her right hand made her wince, but she was too curious to worry about herself at the moment.

Instead, she focused on Jachin. The skin across the top of his hand and between his fingers was perfectly healed, while the flesh around the sides of his hand was still marred and burned.

She knew he'd exposed both his hands to the sunlight, so why was part of his hand healed? When she straightened and started to back away, pain lanced through her palm. Ariel glanced at her right hand. She was surprised to see the wide cut across her entire palm still oozed and dried blood coated her fingers.

Her gaze darted between Jachin's hand and her palm, a hypothesis forming. She'd held that part of his hand. Had her blood healed his skin?

"There's only one way to find out," she murmured as she moved over him and folded her fingers inward, squeezing her cut. The moment she placed her blood-coated fingers and palm across his arm, Jachin flinched.

Deep sympathy welled within her, making her throat tickle and her heart physically ache when his dark gaze met hers, groggy and pained. "Go back to sleep," she whispered, placing her other hand against his forehead.

Before the last word was out of her mouth, his eyelids had closed. His skin felt cool under her palm as Ariel worked quickly, moving her cut hand across his wounds, touching lightly.

By the time she started on his right arm, the skin on his left one had already begun to heal. It also felt warm when she went back and swept trembling fingers across the mending flesh. Unable to comprehend the fact her blood was healing his skin, she mentally justified her actions.

He wasn't the vampire who had taken her family from her. If he hadn't kidnapped her, others like Sethen and Thad probably would have…with different results. Jachin had saved her life several times over. She was just return-ing the favor, healing him as best she could.

She refused to acknowledge the tingling in her breasts, the hardness of her nipples or the definitive jolt of sensual power that flooded her sex at the realization her blood could heal him.

Her breath hitched when her gaze landed on his mouth. Relaxed in sleep, his lips weren't formed into the hard line she was used to seeing. Instead his mouth held a languid sensuality that stole the breath from her lungs, just as his kiss had aroused her more than any man's had. She swiftly removed her hand and backed away.

She didn't want him. She didn't want…a vampire.

After Ariel stepped into a much-needed shower and washed away a day and a half worth of dirt, sweat, blood and grime, she tried to use the soapsuds to remove the handcuffs, but the damn things weren't budging.

Then she remembered something she should've thought of while she'd been the guards' prisoner in the truck.

"Idiot," she mumbled to herself as she bent her left thumb all the way across her palm and downward. This time, with the help of a little more soap, she was able to nudge the cuff off her hand. She quickly did the same thing with her right hand, then set the broken handcuffs in the corner of the shower while she washed her hair.

Standing in front of the mirror, she wrapped some toilet paper around the cut on her palm and began to towel-dry her hair.

One thin cut marred her forehead and another ran along her jawline. A dark bruise had begun to form on her cheekbone under her left eye. She was a mess!

She tapped at her silver hoop earrings that sported a four-leaf clover perched on the bottom curve of each hoop, saying with a smirk, "Lotta luck you've brought me." As her earrings swung back and forth, she leaned closer, frowning at her left earring.

One of the leaves had broken off, leaving her with a three-leaf clover instead. "And now I know why," she said with a sigh, leaning back to survey her overall appearance.

Despite the beat-up look her face sported, the woman who gazed back at her stood with a confident bearing. Her blue eyes probed her reflection with an assessing stare— a look that had more impact and presence than she'd ever projected before. Had her experiences these past thirty-six hours—had it really only been that long?—brought this demeanor on?

As she rolled up the long sleeves on a button-down chambray shirt she'd borrowed from the back of Landon's closet, Ariel acknowledged that Jachin putting her in several life-threatening situations had forced her to gain— or find—a spine of steel.

Who'd have thought that spending time with a *real* vampire would've been more beneficial to her psyche than creating an entire fictional—and controllable—cast of vampire characters in her book?

Nothing could bring back her family. In many ways she

still feared Jachin and loathed all vampires, but she'd also discovered a different side to vampires—a twisted reason for their treatment of humans—she'd never have known if Jachin hadn't told her the truth.

And then there was Landon…whatever he was.

She slid a pair of Landon's thick white socks on her chilled feet before grabbing up her soiled clothes. Once she'd put her stained, torn shirt and bloodied black dress pants and underwear into the washing machine, she walked over to the bed, pulled back the covers and fell onto the blissful mattress with an exhausted sigh. First a nap, then she'd find something to eat, she told herself as she drifted off to sleep.

She ran through the woods, the full moon lighting her path. Her pulse raced and her stomach tensed as she glanced back to see if her pursuer had followed. Hard pounding shook the earth underneath her feet. Leaves crunched and trees rustled in the unseen monster's wake.

He was gaining fast!

Ariel screamed and plunged onward. Her legs trembled and her chest ached as she doubled her efforts to get away.

Jachin stepped out from behind a tree, directly in her path. Relief swept over her and tears streamed down her cheeks as she threw herself into his open arms.

She was safe.

Ariel awoke breathing heavily as if she were still running. It was hard to tell by the drawn drapes how long she'd slept, but the grogginess in her head told her it had probably been most of the day. She trembled at the complete faith and trust she'd shown in Jachin in her dream. It disturbed her on many levels. Why had she dreamed of him in that light—in the form of a protector?

Shaking the fog from her mind, she pulled back the thick covers and climbed out of bed to head to the lower floor.

Jachin still appeared to be sleeping as she passed by the couch and made her way down the short hall to the kitchen. She needed food to clear the cobwebs out of her head.

Whereas Landon's freezer was packed with brown-paper-wrapped meat, his fridge was almost bare except for a couple of blocks of cheese.

Her stomach rumbling, Ariel pulled the sharp cheddar out and set it on the table. While she was rifling through the pantry looking for a carb of some kind, she spied an unopened bottle of Shiraz. Grabbing a box of crackers from a top shelf, she snagged the bottle of wine, found a wineglass, a plate and a knife, then sat down with her stash at the small wooden table, ready for a mini meal.

As she snarfed down the food at a record pace, she considered her dream once more and acknowledged her attraction to Jachin had to be due to their unusual circumstances.

Talk about messing with one's mind! Not in a million years could I have come up with a situation in my book that would hold a candle to these last thirty-six hours, she thought with a half laugh as she took a bite of a cracker.

Once she'd eaten and drunk until she was full, Ariel put the half-empty bottle of wine and the rest of the food away, feeling strangely relaxed.

It was the wine, she thought with a wry smile. After everything she'd been through, she deserved a glass—or ten. But she'd been good and only had two.

Her thoughts returned to Jachin as she turned off the kitchen light and headed into the living room. He never looked her way. Instead he stared at the wall, stoically silent.

"Would you like me to throw your pants in the wash?"

"No." He continued to study the far wall.

She straightened her spine at his cold tone. "Would you like some wine? I found a nice Shiraz."

His jaw ticced. "No."

"Want something to eat?"

His shoulders tensed and his gaze narrowed, but he still didn't look at her.

Duh…he's a vampire. She felt like smacking herself on the forehead. *Why am I trying to draw him into conversation?* she asked herself as she walked away. And yet, since the day he'd kidnapped her Jachin had never hesitated to speak to or glare at her. She much preferred his glacial stare than being completely disregarded as if she didn't exist.

Ariel stood in the hallway between the kitchen and the living room, nibbling at her lip as she wondered how to draw him out. When she caught sight of the stereo system built into the hallway wall, a plan began to form.

Chapter 8

Ariel left behind her inviting peach-and-sugary-almond smell when she walked away, the tempting scent permeating the air all around him. Bunching his hands into fists, he expected a tight, splitting sensation as his slowly healing skin cracked and bled all over again. He glanced down at his arms. His heart thumped in surprise when he found his skin covered in a thin layer of dried blood but otherwise completely healed.

With his body healing faster than expected, he and Ariel would be able to resume the hike to the Sanguinas manor as soon as the sun went down. The sooner, the better. They had a head start on the vamps tracking them, but he didn't want to lose the lead they'd gained.

And yet…he *wanted* more time with her.

Furious at himself for the irrational thought, Jachin

focused on his body and the pain that should have been rolling over him in waves.

He hadn't thought it possible for him to heal such severe burns without an influx of human blood. Raising his arm, he flexed his fingers once more, and the scent of Ariel's blood surrounded him as if he'd bathed in it.

Grinding his teeth in sexual frustration, he ran his hand across his stubbled jaw. Her blood's inviting aroma floated around him, musky and alluring, evoking a sudden dream-like memory of Ariel leaning over him, running her hand down the burns on his arm.

His groin tightened and his cock filled with blood. He ached for her with a ferocity that disturbed him. Closing his eyes briefly, he tried to rid the image of Ariel caring for his wounds from his thoughts.

When she'd asked him if he wanted anything to eat, it had taken all his willpower not to grab her around the waist and yank her into his lap, honor and duty be damned.

She's mine.

Upbeat music began to play throughout the room, inter-rupting his lustful, possessive thoughts. He immediately tensed, preparing to get up.

His limbs refused to work at the sight of Ariel sliding across the wooden floor in front of the coffee table, singing into a wooden cooking spoon. She lip-synched the words from an old Pat Benatar song, her voice full of sass.

His entire body went rock-hard at the sight of her gorgeous bare legs peeking below the shirt she wore. Her thigh muscles flexed while she gyrated to the music, her back to him. As she sang the next line, she cast a gaze through her hair to see if she had his attention.

Undivided, he thought.

His pulse thundered and his groin throbbed. He was thoroughly captivated and jealous all at once. When his gaze drifted down Landon's shirt, territorial resentment made him want to bellow. She should be wearing *his* shirt, bathed in *his* scent.

She turned and faced him, singing the title, "Hit Me With Your Best Shot."

At the sight of the bruise cresting her left cheek, dark, primal instincts knotted his stomach and seized his heart. His hands curled into tight fists as his thoughts and emotions tumbled from banked passion to full-on arousal to dominant protectiveness instantaneously.

The scent of sweet almonds wrapped invisible, sultry tendrils around him, grabbing his throat like a vise, taking his sexual hunger to a much higher, more fundamental craving.

When his gaze drifted past Ariel's tight grip on the makeshift microphone to the trickle of blood sliding down her wrist, Jachin's fangs exploded from his gums.

His iron-fisted control finally snapped.

Ariel opened her eyes, surprised to see an empty couch. She'd only been trying to evoke some kind of response from the man, even if it was laughter. Instead she'd run him off with her horrible singing.

The sensation of muscular arms encircling her waist from behind caused her to gasp and drop the "mike." Her heart hammered as the spoon clattered on the wood floor.

Pinning her body against his hard, naked chest, Jachin

ran his lips up her neck. His warm breath made her skin prickle. "I thought I'd dreamed you touching me."

"I don't know what you're talking about," she denied in a whisper, shocked by the excitement that fluttered in her chest at his nearness and seductive tone.

Jachin lifted his healed hand from her waist and spread his fingers wide in front of her, palm down. "Why did you heal me, Ariel? You could've let me suffer for hours."

Her heart tripped as she stared at his forearm and the back of his hand. Streaks of dried blood coated his arm. Faint handprint patterns were interspersed in the smeared red pattern.

She wasn't ready to admit she'd willingly helped him. It was one thing to act goofy so he couldn't ignore her but another thing entirely to admit she'd consciously healed the man who'd kidnapped her. Hell, she wasn't even sure why she'd done it.

She shook her head. "I—I'm not sure what you're talking about."

Jachin grabbed her hand and lifted her arm so she could see the fresh blood dripping down her wrist from her bandaged wound.

He knows. He wasn't just guessing. She began to tremble all over.

Retaining his hold on her hand, Jachin turned her body around to face him. His expression held intensity and something else—something she'd never seen reflected in his steady gaze—that made her pulse skitter erratically.

Desire.

As she stared in mesmerized fascination, he lifted her

arm and ran his tongue along the rivulet of blood, following it up her wrist. He closed his eyes and groaned as he turned her arm so he could reach her palm. Her belly fluttered at the warm sensation of his tongue on her skin, but she knew this wasn't right, watching him taste her blood and the pleasure they both seemed to derive from it.

She clenched her fist and tried to pull her arm away. "My blood will poison you. Don't."

Jachin's grip tightened on her fingers and his eyes snapped open, tormented and aroused. "It's not enough to hurt me. Let me heal you."

The fact he asked her permission instead of demanding it made her insides shudder in intimate response. She let out an unsteady breath and uncurled her fingers.

Jachin held her gaze as he pulled the bloodstained tissue apart, uncovering her wound. The blood-moistened paper fluttered to the floor and his warm fingers laced with hers. When he ran his tongue over the heel of her hand, making his way toward her cut, her breathing increased and her thighs began to tremble.

Ariel tried to get a grip on herself, to bring some reality back to this dreamlike scenario. She needed to focus on something real, something that reminded her how deadly this man could be. She zeroed in on the long scar that went down the side of his neck.

But instead of thinking about the violent life he'd lived—an aggressive, primal existence that had probably earned him that wound—she wondered if it were possible for her blood to heal this old wound, as well. Before he stopped her bleeding completely, she thought she'd try.

Pulling her hand from his hold, she started to lay her

bloody wound across his scar, but Jachin grabbed her wrist. "No," he said with a firm shake of his head.

Her gaze locked with his and she tried to understand why he'd stopped her. "I was able to heal your other wounds. At least let me try."

He shook his head again and lifted her hand toward his mouth once more. His firm, wet tongue laved across her bloody palm, eliciting the most erotic sensations she'd ever experienced.

The warm pressure, the way he savored her, sent waves of heated tingling down her arm, straight to her breasts and shooting to her core. When her knees started to give way, Jachin caught her, his arm supporting her weight.

He never paused in his tender ministrations as he pulled her close, locking their bodies together. In his firm embrace, heart to heart, hip to hip, the smooth rub of his tongue took a more personal and seductive turn, devastating her senses.

Sharp pain radiated from her cut at the first swipe of his tongue, causing her to wince. Instead of backing off, Jachin flattened his tongue and pressed harder against her wound. The pleasure/pain felt so decadent she found herself sighing and her fingers curling against his cheek in an involuntary caress.

"It should begin to heal now," he rasped right before he pulled her even closer and buried his nose against her neck. Ariel tilted her head back, accepting the heated slide of his tongue up her throat.

He had her so wrapped up, so aroused, she didn't have time to think, to worry. She just experienced and felt... everything—his tight grip on her waist, the soft thickness of his hair as her fingers moved to slide through it, the exhilarating press of his hard erection against her.

When he lifted her in his arms, her whole world tilted off-kilter. Ariel met his hungry gaze, her breathing shallow. "Where are we going?"

"Shower," he said as he started toward the stairs.

His clipped one-word response told her just how on edge he was. "But I've already had one."

Jachin leapt toward the second story. Her stomach pitched and she gasped, gripping his shoulders tight. She didn't have time to adjust to the surreal sensation of flying through the air before he landed past the banister on the soft carpet upstairs.

"Not with me, you haven't," he ground out. He turned toward the bathroom, his fingers pressing her closer.

Ariel's arms tightened around his neck at his sexy, dark tone. With his injuries healed, the strong, dominant Jachin was back.

Full force.

The thrilling zing that rippled down her body scared her more than a little. As soon as they walked into the bathroom, the bright lights turned on and water began to pound on the walk-in shower's slate-gray tiled floor.

Ariel couldn't help but smile in appreciation of Jachin's telekinetic powers. While heat and steam began to fill the room, she toed off the thick, loose socks from her feet. Her belly fluttering, she let out a soft cry of surprise when Jachin stepped right into the shower and under the warm spray with her in his arms.

"What about our clothes?" she started to ask as her light blue shirt turned a darker hue under the water. Instead of answering, he kissed her throat, and all logical, rational thoughts evaporated, rising with the steam to the ceiling.

When he set her feet down on the floor and stared at her with his intense gaze, Ariel's heart thumped as she threaded her fingers with his.

Blue, his eyes were a beautiful shade of steel-blue…so dark she'd mistaken them for black. Until now. Or maybe it was the first time she'd really looked at Jachin as a man instead of a vampire.

A man she wanted.

Gripping his fingers, she lifted his arm to let the shower water sluice over it in pounding, cleansing warmth. Water dripped from her partially wet hair onto his skin. She didn't say a word while she ran her other hand down his arm, helping wash away the remnants of blood that still remained. As her palm slid over his skin, the muscles in his forearm contracted and relaxed.

Once she'd reached the end of his fingers, he grasped her wrists, encircling them with his fingers. "How did you get your cuffs off?"

Her gaze followed his and she saw he was staring at the cuffs she'd left in the corner of the shower. She smiled and pulled her wrists from his grip. Lifting her hands in front of him, she bent her thumbs along her palm and downward the same way she had to remove the cuffs. "I'm double-jointed. You have your talents and I have mine."

Jachin grasped her wrists once more and pulled her arms away from her body.

"Being double-jointed has its benefits," he said in a suggestive tone as his gaze raked over her nipples jutting against the wet shirt.

Ariel's body ignited at his double entendre. While his gaze devoured her body, she slowly inspected his breathtaking physique, observing the long red scar on his waist and the remnants of the earlier deep claw wounds on his shoulder. Both had already started to fade considerably. His muscular chest and rock-hard stomach held her rapt attention until she felt his fingers on her chin. Her line of sight moved up his towering height until her gaze collided with his.

Jachin traced his fingers down her throat, then cupped the back of her neck. Her pulse thundered in her ears as he used his hold to pull her flush against his chest. His broad shoulders blocked the spray from hammering her face, while his arm wrapped around her waist, locking her against him.

He leaned close and paused when his lips were a half inch away from hers. Her stomach tumbled and she waited for him to cross the small distance between them. *I love the way he looks at me, arousal and hunger meshing in his gaze.*

When his lips covered hers, Ariel leaned into his powerful frame. Even though Jachin's wide shoulders blocked the water, his hard body radiated a seductive heat that sent warmth all the way to her toes.

Wrapping her arms around his waist, she moaned against his lips and accepted the slow slide of his tongue exploring her mouth.

Ariel ran her tongue alongside his, teasing him. Jachin groaned and cupped her face with his hands. Slanting his mouth over hers, he thrust deeper and invaded her mouth with a primal passion, demanding an intense response.

He tasted of mint and an elusive erotic flavor that only made her crave more. Ariel gripped his thick biceps and responded to his faster pace, pressing her mouth harder against his with a desperation all her own. Her nipples were tender and sore, her breasts throbbed and tingled and her sex ached for release from the coiled sexual tension clawing within her.

Jachin gently kissed the bruise on her cheek before sliding his lips to her jaw, where he planted tender kisses along the edge. "You're the most stubborn human. You constantly test my patience." His husky tone sounded tortured as he traced his hands down her waist and palmed her rear through her wet shirt.

The water's warm spray hit her face as she tilted her head back. Threading her fingers in his wet hair, she thrilled in his hot mouth worshiping her neck. "You've kidnapped me, thrown me out a window, tossed me in your trunk—twice—dangled me over the edge of the mountain, hauled me for miles up the mountainside and infuriated me beyond my limits," she panted back.

The realization that she wanted him after everything he'd put her through, not to mention the fact she'd handled it all with finesse, fueled his desire. Jachin pushed her back against the cool tile wall.

"Your verve and tenacity astound me." As he ran his lips along her neck, Jachin fought the urge to sink his fangs deep. His canines had fully extended in his arousal, demanding he take her blood.

The hunger clawed at him, relentless and raw. He closed his eyes, fighting the urge. Commanding his fangs to retreat, he muttered, his voice rough with need, "You're more resilient than half the vampires I know."

Her grip tightened on his shoulders as she let out a husky laugh. "Watch it or I'll think that's a complimen—"

It was a compliment, the deepest one he could pay her. Jachin couldn't hold back any longer. Covering her lips with his, he thrust his tongue into the sweet recesses of her mouth at the same time he pressed his erection against her body.

His tight grip on her hips and the hard press of his body against her told Ariel how much he wanted her. She wrapped her arms around his neck and parried her tongue with his, thrilling in his aggressive, dominant kiss.

His hands slid lower. The rough grip of his fingers grasping her rear in a possessive hold made her throb for sexual fulfillment. When he pulled her hips upward slightly and ground his erection against her naked mound, she mentally cursed his jeans separating them. "Not close enough," she whimpered against his mouth and tightened her hold around his neck, trying to press closer.

He growled low in his throat and slid his fingers under the hem of her wet shirt, massaging her bare flesh.

When he lifted her as if she weighed nothing, Ariel's heart hammered in frantic thumps. She moaned an excited "Yes" against his mouth, kissing him deeply as she wrapped her legs around his hips and locked them together.

Jachin leaned her back against the tile at the same time he rammed his denim-covered cock against her throbbing folds. Ariel shivered and keened at the pleasurable friction the rough material caused.

"Let go, Ariel," he said in a husky tone, moving his hips against her, his thrusts turning rougher, almost possessive. Ariel mewled her encouragement at the same time she came to the startling conclusion that taking a shower with one's clothes on was one of the sexiest experiences she'd ever had. But then, she suspected that *any* sexual experience with this particular male would be mind-shattering.

Panting, she canted her hips, seeking release, but with each erotic press of his body against hers, her core began to ache for a fullness only he could fulfill.

"Jachin," she begged, laying her head back against the wall and gasping for breath. Tears formed in her eyes and she began to shake with the need to have him inside her.

In answer, he pressed his hips fully against hers, literally pinning her against the cool wall. Instead of thrusting, he began to rock his erection along her sex with slow, intentional pressure. The constant pleasurable bombardment to her body's sensitive nub, combined with the shower's wet heat and the sensation of his muscular strength holding her up, was the hottest aphrodisiac.

"Jachin…" She dug her nails into his shoulders as her heart stuttered and slight tremors began deep inside her. His lips skimmed her neck, adding to the surreal sensuality of the moment.

"You're irresistible," he said right before two tiny sharp edges slid along her throat.

His fangs.

The sensation reminded her of the beast within him, residing just below the surface, barely in check. She should be frightened at the thought he might bite her at any second. Instead she was shocked that the knowledge only spiked her desire.

The danger, mixed with her trust in him, sent Ariel right over the edge. Rapid body-rocking waves of unparalleled ecstasy slammed through her core, taking her breath with their intensity. She didn't feel the least bit inhibited as she rocked her hips and pressed her body even closer to Jachin. Every contraction deep inside her felt wicked and decadent and so incredibly sexy. She moaned and rode his erection until her limbs began to shake.

Jachin pressed his lips against her neck and palmed her rear, grinding his cock against her until she stopped moving.

Ariel clung to his hard, wet shoulders, her arms trembling as her heart rate began to slow.

Without a word, he lifted her away from the wall and stepped out of the shower.

"Jachin?" she asked when the water stopped hammering the shower floor. His only response was to slide a hand up her back and lock her body against his as he carried her to the bed.

She fell against the soft comforter at the same time his knee depressed the mattress between her thighs and his hands landed on either side of her head. His gaze searched her face, hungry and haunted, while cool droplets of water dripped from his hair onto her cheeks. As he lowered his head to hers, she speared her fingers in the wet mass and her heart ramped up once more.

Jachin's mouth claimed hers at the same time she felt a tugging sensation on her shirt. He ripped her shirt open, exposing her naked body. Buttons pinged off the dresser against the far wall. Ariel gasped at the cool air that puckered her nipples, loving the look of pure predatory hunger in his gaze.

Placing his hands back on the bed, he stared at her. Everywhere his gaze landed, she burned for his touch. She ran her palms along his shoulders and down his muscular chest.

When her fingers grazed his hard nipples, a growl rumbled underneath her hands. He lowered his head and flicked his tongue against one of her taut nipples, returning the favor.

She arched her back and whimpered, hoping he'd take the aching tip into his warm mouth. He splayed his fingers across her hips and pressed her body back against the bed, then dipped his head and captured the sensitive nipple between his lips.

When Jachin rolled his tongue around the tip, then began to suck hard, exquisite pleasure radiated down her breast, spreading to her lower muscles in torturous spasms of renewed arousal.

Ariel pressed his head close and closed her eyes at the blissful sensations splintering through her. She didn't care that they were both soaking wet. All she cared about was having him deep inside her as soon as possible.

Digging her heels into the bed, she began to rock her hips, pleading, "Please, Jachin. I want you so much."

He gripped her hips tight, holding her still as his mouth slid down her body, trailing hot kisses across her belly.

When his fingers tightened around her thighs, Ariel opened her eyes and lifted her head to see he was down on his knees on the floor at the end of the bed.

As he tugged her toward him, the sinful dark expression on his face told her exactly what he intended.

"I want to feel you inside—" she started to say but cut herself off in a gasp of pure decadence when his hot mouth connected with her pulsing sex.

Not as much as I want inside you. He spoke to her

mentally at the same time his tongue dove deep in her channel, penetrating with aggressive, purposeful thrusts.

Ariel's fingers fisted in his hair. She keened her approval, pressing against his mouth, squirming in feverish excitement. When he ran his tongue along her folds, then moved the firm bit of sensitive skin waiting for his attention in tight circles, she lost her ability to think. "Don't stop," she demanded, her skin flushing at the sheer pleasure she derived from his action.

He groaned and flattened his tongue against her, taking a leisurely lick along her sex before she felt a teasing sensation, the flirt of his finger along the edge of her entrance.

Ariel's pulse thundered in her ears and her breathing turned ragged. She tugged hard on his hair. "Jachin, I can't take any more!"

He growled low in his throat right before he slid a finger deep into her core. Ariel's breath hitched at the intense pleasure having a part of him inside her elicited, but he began to suck on her at the same time he added another finger, and her world tilted into a series of heart-pounding tremors.

She canted her hips, bucking against his mouth and hand, so ready for release she wanted to scream.

His mouth moved for a brief instant and he replaced it with the insistent pressure of his thumb. Slowing his thrusts, he turned his fingers to rub on a sweet spot deep within her.

His fangs ran along her upper thigh, and Ariel's excited pants turned to ragged, hitching breaths as heightened sensations built inside her.

"I can't hold back," she started to say.

"Come, Ariel," he said in a raspy voice full of desire

right before he plunged his fangs into the soft-erogenous place where her leg joined her body.

Ariel's scream of pain quickly turned to a wail of blessed euphoria. Her body began to clench around his fingers in amazing climactic spasms of fulfillment. She bucked and moaned, riding the blissful feelings gripping her body in dreamlike pulses of ecstasy.

She dug her nails into his shoulders and wrapped a leg around his back, unwilling to let the indescribable awareness blossoming in her body end.

While her contractions slowed to tiny vibrations, Ariel came back to earth and the sensation of Jachin's fingers stilling inside her. His warm tongue laved at her wounds in a slow, almost reverent adoration of her body.

"Jachin." She lowered her leg from his back and smoothed her hands across his shoulders, enjoying the sinew underneath her palms. The muscles under her hands tightened and flexed before he withdrew his fingers from her and stood.

Without a word, he turned and walked back into the bathroom.

Ariel sat up on her elbows and bit her lip. She glanced down at the bite wounds on her leg that were already almost closed. Her heart jerked at how much she'd enjoyed Jachin's fangs sinking into her skin.

It was the heat of the moment, she rationalized as she got up from the bed and shivered. Pulling the wet shirt around her naked body, she followed Jachin into the bathroom, feeling confused…and oddly bereft, as if something special was slipping through her fingers.

He leaned on the counter, staring at himself through the misty fog on the mirror.

Ariel placed her hand on his arm. "Why did you walk away?" Uncertain why he'd left her, she struggled to get the words out. "Do—don't you want—"

Before she could finish, Jachin had her pinned against the·wall behind her. His intense, dark gaze locked with hers. Grabbing her hand, he cupped her palm over his impressive erection and bit out, "Hell, yes, I want! But you're not mine to have."

Ariel shook her head. "I don't belong to anyone—" She cut herself off and pulled her hand away from his body. A sinking sensation weighed heavily in her stomach. "You're still planning on taking me to your vampire leader, aren't you?"

Jachin placed a hand on the wall above her head. "Remember when I said everyone has an agenda? Mine hasn't changed. I'm not a good person, Ariel. Never forget that."

Her chest burned with betrayal. She'd never felt so hurt in her life. "But…you saved Landon, the man responsible for capturing you. You've rescued me—"

"I saved Landon because I might need him. Period." Jachin stepped away and the shower started up on its own again. Turning his back to her, he began to strip out of his wet jeans.

Ariel closed her eyes against the sight of his gorgeous naked backside. Not because she didn't want to see it but because she couldn't bear to. Her stomach churned as she walked out of the bathroom, hugging the torn shirt against her cold body.

Teeth chattering, she rifled through Landon's drawers until she found an old pair of black sweatpants and a long-sleeved heather-gray T-shirt. Once she tugged off the wet shirt, she trembled all over while she jammed her legs into the pants.

Brushing away the tears stinging her eyes, she told herself the uncontrollable shivering was due to being cold. After she pulled on the dry T-shirt, she tied the sweatpants' drawstring around her waist. Retrieving the torn, wet shirt, she walked down the stairs with heavy footsteps.

What an idiot I was to think anything had changed because I had saved him. I should've left his sorry ass behind while he was sleeping, she berated herself as she shoved the ruined shirt in the trash can in the kitchen.

"What is Landon?"

At Ariel's question, Jachin paused on the top stair. His shower had been cold and bitterly disappointing. Ariel's hurt expression when he'd told her never to forget what kind of person he was lingered in his mind, but he hadn't lied to her. Everything he'd said was true. The one part he didn't express to her was that he would live the rest of his life wishing he were Braeden and able to revel in her sweet body, to challenge her quick mind, as often as he wanted.

The thought of Braeden touching Ariel, let alone sinking his teeth in her delicate skin, made Jachin's stomach churn and possessive anger burn in his chest.

Tension ebbed inside him as he stared down at Ariel sitting on the sofa on the floor below. He'd expected the silent treatment, not for her to ask questions about the Lupreda. But if she was going to live among the Sanguinas and become Braeden's mate, it was probably a good idea for her to go in knowing their history.

"Landon is Lupreda," he replied, continuing down the stairs.

Ariel eyed his navy-blue T-shirt and jeans. "Hopefully Landon won't mind us borrowing his clothes." She pulled her bare feet toward her butt and wrapped her arms around her bent knees, an expectant look on her face. "What is a Lupreda?"

Jachin sat down on the other end of the couch. He met her questioning gaze. "Lupreda are werewolves."

He heard her heart rate ramp up as her eyes widened. "Werewolves? Where did they come from—" she started to ask, then cut herself off. "Don't tell me our government had something to do with them, as well."

Jachin shook his head. "No, they weren't created by the government."

"But they were created, weren't they? Who created them?"

Her probing stare made his chest constrict. He wasn't sure why it mattered to him that she didn't think the Sanguinas as a whole weren't monsters, but it did.

He turned and bent his knee on the cushion between them, facing her. "We created the Lupreda."

Her blond eyebrows rose in surprise. "Why?"

"To hunt."

She let go of her knees and pulled her legs underneath her. Placing her hands on her thighs, she leaned closer, a challenge in her gaze. "What? Humans weren't enough prey for the Sanguinas?"

His eyes narrowed at the sarcasm in her tone. "Humans were food. Weres were worthy adversaries."

"Until the Sanguinas started getting sick." She plunged on, dogged in her questions. "Did you take the Lupredas' blood, too?"

"No, they were created, synthesized. Their blood wasn't pure. It couldn't sustain us like humans' blood could."

She rolled her eyes. "Yes, it's always nice to be reminded that we're part of a healthy diet plan for you."

"Not anymore."

"I'm thrilled to know there's some natural justice in this world," she said with a smirk.

"The humans' blood turning poisonous wasn't a natural occurrence, Ariel," he replied in a cold tone.

"You think we poisoned ourselves on purpose?" she asked, incredulous.

"No, I think the Lupreda did it."

Ariel let out a low whistle. "Well, they'd certainly had a reason to. No wonder Landon appeared to distrust you…." She paused. "So why *did* he help you—us?"

"Because of the prophecy."

She frowned. "But the prophecy has to do with vampires making a comeback. Why would Landon want any part of that?"

Jachin met her confused gaze with a steady one. "Because I believe the prophecy will lead to eventual peace. Landon is of a similar mind. He wants peace between our two races."

"And what about humans, Jachin? Where are we in this peaceful utopia you seek?"

Jachin's defensive hackles rose at the bitter tone in her line of questioning. "You now know better than anyone how pleasurable a vampire's bite can be."

Her blue gaze flashed in anger. She opened her mouth to deny the truth of his comment but instead looked away. "That was an unusual circumstance. I doubt the general public will be clamoring to offer up a donation."

Her words were like a knife twisting in his chest. He'd bitten her while he pleasured her because he'd wanted her to crave the sensation of his fangs digging deep…and, damn it to hell, he'd wanted to brand her as his.

He moved across the couch and turned her chin until her expressive eyes met his. "Would you prefer that I erase what happened between us from your memory?"

Jachin's heart stuttered to a slow, sluggish beat while he awaited her answer.

Ariel's eyes widened in surprise. "You can do that?"

He couldn't stop his fingers from trailing down her neck. Her skin was so soft. "I've studied the art of mental manipulation, but it has to be done soon after the person experiences the event I need to erase, while his or her mind is still in a susceptible state."

His gaze slid down the smooth column of her throat. He ached to plunge his fangs into her sweet skin once more, to hear her moan and call his name. He didn't want to erase her memory, for his would always remain, teasing him in constant erotic torture.

Ariel closed her eyes and took an unsteady breath. He applied gentle pressure against her neck and heard her heartbeat ramp up. The realization that his touch affected her at such an intimate level made his pulse soar.

"What is your wish? Do you want to forget?" he forced himself to ask.

Her breathing turned shallow and her eyes snapped open. A look of resolve crossed her face. She straightened her spine and pushed his hand away from her throat.

"Yes."

Chapter 9

Jachin's heart jerked. He never thought one word could cause him physical pain, but he was wrong. Just as he'd been wrong for allowing his emotions to come into play with Ariel.

She was a means to an end, a human pawn in the Sanguinas' survival. Nothing more.

"As you wish," he said right before he captured her mouth with his.

When she started to pull away, he cupped the back of her head and spoke in her mind. *Relax. I seek nothing more than a distraction so your mind opens to me.*

Ariel's mouth slowly softened under his until her lips parted.

At the same time Jachin's tongue touched hers in a lingering sensual dance, he entered her mind and began to manipulate it. Starting from the moment she sang to him on the couch until right before she watched him get in the shower alone, he pushed every memory of their intimate time together to her subconscious.

As he worked through the delicate intricacies of her mind, Jachin's body tightened in arousal all over again. He felt what she felt—how much she'd enjoyed his hands on her skin, his fingers sliding inside her, his mouth claiming her. He experienced her aching need to be filled, her desire for him to take her fully. His gut clenched, causing him to pause the process.

The deep emotional connection with Ariel surprised him. He'd never experienced the emotions of another during memory erasure before. For a split second his selfish desires demanded he stop the process entirely. Why did she want to forget how good he made her feel? Was it because he was a vampire?

He kissed her harder, slanting his mouth across hers as anger whipped through him, slamming into his chest. Ariel responded to his kiss, moaning against his mouth, spiking his fury.

Denting his pride.

Jachin refocused on the task, but for some reason he couldn't bring himself to wipe the memory of their intimacy from her mind altogether. She might not consciously remember the events, but at least a part of her would feel connected to him, even if she didn't know why.

When she shoved at his chest and made angry muffled sounds, Jachin knew he'd been successful.

With deep regret, he pulled away. "Thank you for healing my wounds."

She stood and quickly glanced down at her shirt and sweatpants in confusion before narrowing her gaze on him. "Considering you still plan on taking me to your vampire leader, I should've let you suffer." Without another word, she turned away.

Even as she walked up the stairs, her footfalls heavy with anger and her spine rigid with resentment, his body instantly reacted to her outward display of inner strength. Her pride made her so much stronger than he'd ever given a human credit for in the past.

His appreciative gaze slid down her back to the curve of her hips outlined by the cinched sweatpants. For the first time in his life Jachin wished he was human and free to indulge in the hunger and desire that raged inside him.

Upstairs in the master bedroom, Ariel paced back and forth on the carpet. Fury festered within her, a bulging wound ready to explode. It bothered her that she didn't know why she'd been wet and cold upstairs earlier. She just knew she'd had to change. Her chest physically ached, she was so tense. She vaguely remembered arguing with Jachin, but she felt as if she'd lost a period of time.

One part of her memory stood out in vivid clarity. After all her efforts to save him, Jachin's unwavering determination to take her to the Sanguinas leader hurt deeply. But as much as that bothered her, what shook her up more was the passionate depth of his kiss. It spoke of emotions she knew the man wasn't capable of.

And what of your own response? It took all your will-power not to respond when you desperately wanted to. Why are you so attracted to this man? Why do you forget he's a self-serving, coldhearted beast with his own twisted agenda whenever his lips touch yours? she berated herself as she nibbled on her fingernail.

Ariel stopped pacing and rubbed her temples, seeking an answer to the mess her life had become. The Garotters hadn't planned to let her go. And she was pretty sure they still had connections to the police, if indirectly. Even if she got away, she couldn't trust law enforcement. Landon was the only person she felt she could go to for help, but, other than remaining at his house until he showed up, she had no idea how to contact him.

Loud bamming at the front door drew her attention. She moved to the banister to peer downstairs in time to see the door splinter off its hinges and slam against the wall as two men rushed inside.

Her heart stuttered and her gaze jerked to Jachin, who was already standing in an attack position.

Get the hell out of here! Jachin spoke in her mind when the two men flew across the room in superhuman speed toward him. At that heart-stopping moment she realized two facts: the men below weren't vampires, since they'd attacked during the day; and if Jachin told her to leave, that meant he wasn't sure he'd win this fight.

She might be furious with the vampire, but she respected his judgment. She turned and ran to the window, pulling back the drapes. Squinting at the sunlight that shined in her eyes, she flipped the lever on the window and lifted the glass up.

Remembering she'd set the Jeep's key on the nightstand, she ran over to get it. Once she grabbed the key, she tied it on the pants' drawstring and quickly jammed her feet into her shoes.

Moving quietly, Ariel walked to the window and hooked her leg over the edge. Before she climbed out, she turned to listen to the fight on the level below, her stomach tensing in fear for Jachin. Downstairs, furniture scraped across wood and glass crashed to the floor amid the sound of fists hitting bodies, male grunts and primal growls of anger.

As if he sensed her hesitation, Jachin's angry voice entered her mind once more. *Now, Ariel, damn it!*

That was all it took.

Ariel gazed out the window to the bushes twenty feet below her and wondered how well the seemingly thick foliage would break her fall.

Time seemed to slow down as she dropped. When she landed, she was sore all over but glad nothing seemed to be broken. Ariel climbed out of the bush and took off in a run toward the front of the house, her heart hammering. She'd take the path along the stream and make her way back to the Jeep. Glancing up through the trees, she knew she had very little time before the sun went down and the vampires came out to hunt.

"Survive, Jachin, and so will I," she whispered before she took off in the direction of the stream.

Ariel ran for two miles through the woods. When she spied the Jeep they'd left on the side of the road, she breathed a thankful sigh of relief and picked up her pace for the last few hundred feet.

Once she reached the banged-up Jeep, Ariel got inside and tried to catch her breath. Saying a silent prayer, she slid the key in the ignition, punched the clutch and turned. The engine whirred stubbornly several times before it finally kicked to life.

She'd only driven about a mile when steam started rolling out of the front of the Jeep's crumpled hood. Glancing at the temperature gauge, her spirits plummeted. The indicator was on "hot." The engine was overheating—and the sun had nearly disappeared.

The Jeep made it another half mile before the engine died completely.

As the vehicle rolled to a dead stop, someone landed in the passenger seat beside her, saying in a smug tone, "Damn, you're having one helluva day."

Ariel gasped at the blond vampire who'd tried to run her car off the road earlier. She had assumed he and the other vampire with him had died when his car went over the mountain. Blood crusted his forehead and scrapes showed through the tears on his clothes, yet he still managed a cold, deadly smile, fangs on full display.

Ariel started to jump out of the Jeep, but a stocky, dark-haired vampire blocked her path. "Think the two weres will kill him, Vlad?" he said to the blond vampire next to her.

Vlad exited the Jeep in one fluid movement. "It doesn't matter. We'll be long gone before he's able to come after us. Grab her and let's go."

As Vlad dragged Ariel through the woods at a fast clip, the evening's full arrival carried her thoughts to Jachin. Had he defeated the weres? Or had they defeated him? Her heart sank at the thought.

Jachin growled like a man crazed, his heart thumping. Landon's living room looked like a war zone already, but Jachin didn't have time for an all-out brawl. Ariel was out there and it was getting dark.

He slashed out a warning with his talons as the last werewolf circled around him. He'd already knocked the first were out. The beast inside him had roared for him to finish this once and for all, but he knew he might need Landon's help. Murdering wolves from the man's pack wouldn't help his cause. If he wanted to create goodwill, he had to extend some himself…and that meant leaving the men breathing.

"I have another pressing engagement. Can we get this over with?" he egged the man on.

The Lupreda snarled at him and clenched his fists by his sides, his breathing growing heavier by the second. His shirt hung from his shoulders in shreds and his chest oozed blood from Jachin's earlier blows. He and the other werewolf had gotten a swipe or two in with their own claws, but Lupredas' claws were no match for Sanguinas' razor-sharp talons.

Right before the stockier Lupreda dove at him, Jachin noted something strange in the man's eyes. They glowed a bright green color.

Jachin slammed into a wall with the force of the man's hit. The impact knocked the wind from his lungs and surprised the hell out of him as he dropped to the wood floor. He could've sworn the man felt heavier and had hit him harder with that blow.

Sheetrock fell around them, giving him a chance to shove the man across the room. Furniture crashed with the were's landing, but the man immediately jumped to his feet and shot toward him.

Jachin blinked in surprise when the werewolf's shoulders began to jerk, his knees bend and his height increase as he grew at least a foot taller. A primordial sound erupted from the were's throat at the same time his jaw started to elongate, tightening his skin and sharpening his features.

How the hell is he shifting outside the full moon's three-day cycle? Jachin wondered, temporarily stunned. Despite his altering form, the were continued forward, slamming his fist into Jachin.

Pain exploded in Jachin's throat and his vision dimmed. He spun away from the Lupreda's blow and for a second he thought he was going to pass out. The werewolf jumped on his shoulders, and Jachin shook his head, letting out a battle cry. He grabbed the werewolf's hands, pinning the man to his back. Once the Lupreda fully shifted to wolf form, he'd be much harder to catch and his claws far more dangerous.

As the werewolf growled in his ear, Jachin flexed his thighs and jumped backward across the room, slamming himself and the were into the brick fireplace.

When the half-morphed man's head slumped against his shoulder, Jachin blew out a heavy breath, grumbling, "It's about damn time."

He walked over to the werewolf lying in the middle of the living room floor and tossed the second werewolf over his shoulder to land with a thump beside his friend. Once he was out cold, the second were began to shift back to his human form.

Jachin rubbed his neck as he considered what the Lupredas' broader shifting freedom would mean to the Sanguinas. Glancing past the open door, tension began rising within him. Dusk had arrived. Ariel was out there alone with vampires hunting her. Tensing, he turned and kicked the overturned couch back over to find his backpack.

Slinging the strap over his shoulder, he gave the two unconscious men one last growl before he took off running out the front door.

Ariel's stomach churned when the vampires set her down at the entrance of what appeared to be an old, abandoned mine. Moonlight shone through the old planks nailed to the outside frame along the mountainside, reflecting on a pile of huge caved-in boulders inside the entrance.

Vlad grabbed her head and made her duck under the planks. Once all three of them stood in front of the crumble of rocks, her throat began to tickle at the realization she'd be going in but never coming out.

She couldn't see in the darkness, but Vlad must've pushed some hidden button. Rocks rubbed against rocks. She pulled back, expecting the mountain to come down on their heads. Vlad gripped her arm to keep her still and Ariel stared in surprise as the entire "wall" of rocks behind the boards began to slide out of the way.

As soon as they ushered her past the threshold, the rock wall slid back into place behind them. The vacuum sound doused the cavern into total blackness, making her throat knot. She froze at the total lack of light.

Vlad's fingers dug into the soft flesh on her arm and he growled in her ear. "This way."

Wings flapped above them. Bats. Heart jerking, Ariel bit back a scream. She stayed right behind Vlad while putting her free hand out to her side to keep from running into a stone wall.

Several minutes passed, drawing them farther into the

confusing maze. With each step they took, her panic mode inched upward.

Vlad suddenly stopped. More rocks rubbed along rocks. Her insides cringed at the horrific noise as dim light filtered through the open rock wall.

Vlad hauled her beside him once more and stepped out of the mine into a small cleared area surrounded by trees. Stars twinkled through the thick foliage, the moon providing much-appreciated light.

Though she was thankful she was finally able to see a little, Ariel knew she'd never be able to find her way back through the maze she'd just walked through on her own, even if she could get past the guards. Sheer helplessness squeezed her chest as she noted the two men standing on either side of the entrance they'd just exited.

Gripping his automatic weapon, the tall, blond-headed guard glanced at her. "I wish I could say it was nice of you to bring us breakfast, Vlad."

"I'm sure bringing this human here is pointless, but by doing so we'll prove once and for all Ezra's prophecy was nothing but sickness ramblings," Vlad snorted.

When they started to walk away, the shorter, dark-haired guard asked, "Is it true Jachin has survived all these years?"

Vlad paused and his laugh sounded bitter. "Stay alert. If he's still alive, he'll head this way."

"For the human?" the blond guard asked.

Vlad glanced at Ariel. "He was trying to bring her here. My guess is he planned to use her to get back in Braeden's good graces."

"He won't get past us." The sharp-featured, dark-haired guard scowled, holding his gun up.

While they followed a path through the woods, Ariel's heart sank at Vlad's last comment. She was a peace offering in Jachin's need for approval with the leader of the vampires? The realization that the man's agenda could be so selfishly personal and not for the good of his race—that she was nothing more than a puzzle piece to be moved to *his* strategic advantage—made her nauseous.

Deep emotional hurt roiled her stomach, doubling her over. Pulling from Vlad's hold, she retched in the thick grass until dry heaves racked her frame.

"Worthless and weak!" Vlad spat, grabbing her arm and hauling her along beside him.

Ariel didn't care what he called her. Nothing could hurt her more than Jachin's sheer betrayal. She must've really come to like the man on some level if his treachery hurt this much.

The smell of puke filled her nostrils and a sharp acidic taste coated her mouth as she lifted her head. She wiped her hand across her lips and pushed her shoulders back, determined to face her enemies with a spine of steel.

They'd only walked through the woods for a little while when a huge castle-style mansion, standing off in another clearing, came into view through the wall of trees in front of her. She began to tremble all over—not from fear but from eerie familiarity. From the high walls to the shadowed outline of the gargoyles gracing the turrets, the mansion was exactly as she'd described in her novel.

Upon entering the castle, they walked into a great-hall-style main room. Hundreds of sconces lining the tall walls, highlighted a petite woman with long, curly dark hair. She separated from the crowd, her long violet dress hugging her curves as she approached them.

"Braeden is with Vivian at the moment." The female vampire's deep blue gaze skimmed over Ariel. She reached out and encircled Ariel's wrist with her small hand. "I'll take her and make sure she's cleaned up for him."

Vlad's fingers tightened around Ariel's arm. "She stays with me."

The woman raised her nose in a regal pose and narrowed her striking gaze. "Would you have him take his anger out on you because she wasn't presentable?"

Vlad glanced disdainfully at Ariel's soiled and crumpled clothes. "Bring her back here when you're done," he said, letting his hold slip from Ariel's arm.

When the woman turned to lead Ariel away, Vlad grabbed the female vampire by the back of the neck and yanked her toward him. Her hold on Ariel's hand slipped away from his rough treatment.

Vlad ran his nose along the column of her throat, then laid his extended fangs against it. "For allowing you this honor, I expect to be amply compensated, Mira."

She pushed away from him, her nostrils flaring. "When he returns, he'll kill you for taking what was never yours to take."

Vlad laughed and clapped the stocky vampire beside him on the shoulder. "Do you hear that, Aaron? Even after ten years of desertion, she defends him."

His dark gaze narrowed on Mira and his voice turned harsh. "After you take her to Braeden, you'll submit to me as my mate. Don't expect the council to challenge my desire to increase the clan's population."

Mira whirled around, her eyes flashing as she grabbed Ariel's hand once more. Stunned by the ruthlessness that seemed prevalent in all vampires, Ariel allowed Mira to lead her from the great hall and down a corridor lined with more sconces and doors along either side.

The entire time she followed the vampire, Ariel looked for places to escape or hide, but she couldn't decipher what doors might lead to another room versus an exit.

When Mira finally stopped, opening a door on their right, Ariel gasped at the opulently decorated room. Persian rugs lined large sections of the stone floor, and tapestries of intricate designs decorated the walls like living murals. A huge crystal chandelier hung from the high ceiling in the middle of the suite. An ornate four-poster bed sat at the opposite side of the room. The place oozed sophisticated elegance.

The female vampire pulled Ariel fully into the room and shut the door. "How is he? Is he well?"

Ariel was confused by the expectant look on the woman's beautiful face. "How is who?"

Mira moved with elegant grace toward a doorway off the main room. Walking into the other room, she called out, "Jachin. It has been ten years since I saw him last."

Chapter 10

Ariel had considered rushing out of the room as soon as the female vampire left her alone, but Mira's question made her pause. Her heart cinched at the woman's question about Jachin. Suddenly all Mira's comments to Vlad started making sense. Mira must be Jachin's lover. The thought fisted Ariel's stomach.

But she had to know the truth. She followed the sound of rushing water and walked into the room Mira had entered.

The woman leaned over a beautiful black porcelain tub. She held her hand under an ornate silver pipe that protruded from the wall, allowing the water to flow across her fingers. Ariel wasn't surprised the Sanguinas didn't have traditional water systems way up in the remote mountains. But there was only one pipe, which meant the water had to be one temperature—freezing cold.

"Um, I took a shower not too long ago."

Mira glanced at her over her shoulder. She gave a knowing smile. "You look like you haven't bathed in days."

Ariel stiffened. Her body sported so many scrapes and bruises she felt like a well-used voodoo doll. "You try being dragged through miles of woods by two vampires with the possibility two werewolves might be hot on your trail."

Mira straightened, her amused expression turning serious. "Two weres?"

Ariel nodded. "They attacked Jachin. He told me to run. Unfortunately, I ran right into Vlad and Aaron."

"And Jachin?" Mira asked, clutching her hands to her chest.

Ariel rolled her eyes at the woman's concern. "Your lover is a hell-bent vampire. I seriously doubt those two weres could defeat him." She realized she spoke the truth. She believed Jachin would defeat them.

Mira's eyes crinkled. She began to laugh so hard tears formed in her eyes.

Ariel didn't appreciate being the brunt of some unknown joke. She crossed her arms. "I'm so glad to be a source of entertainment for you."

Wiping tears from her eyes, the petite woman tried to compose her face, but her blue gaze still held mirth. Reaching out to Ariel, she said, "Take off your clothes, and while you bathe I'll explain my amusement."

Ariel shook her head. "I'll wait until you leave." No way was she stripping in front of Jachin's lover. Even if nothing had happened between Jachin and her, the attraction had been there. She didn't want or need to be scrutinized by a genetically perfect superhuman female.

Mira chuckled as she reached into the tub. When the vampire flung a handful of water toward her, Ariel gasped and lowered her arms at the frigid temperature that splattered her face and neck.

Cupping another handful, Mira held it for a second and said, "If I don't stay, another vampire will take my place. Let me help, Ariel. I'll warm the water so your bath won't be frigid," right before she tossed the water her way. This time the water splattering against her felt wonderfully warm.

Ariel's eyes went wide in surprise.

"Surely Jachin told you we can control our body temperature." Mira sat on the edge of the tub and swirled her fingers in the water. "I've learned to broaden my powers beyond my own body over the years."

I'll just bet you have, Ariel thought, clenching her jaw. No wonder Jachin saw her as inferior to those in his own race. But if she was going to have to take a bath in someone's presence, she'd choose Mira over Vlad or Aaron.

Mira leaned over the tub and swirled her hands through the water several times. After a few minutes she straightened. "It should be warm enough to keep you from shrieking now."

"Can I at least have bubbles or something?" Ariel asked after she quickly removed her soiled clothes, stepped into the tub and sank into the water until it covered her breasts.

Mira sighed and turned her back to Ariel. "There's some soap and a sponge on the shelf next to the tub."

Ariel had just picked up the soap and run it down her shoulder when Mira said, "Don't forget to remove your earring."

"Um, thanks." Ariel removed her right earring and then started to take out the other one only to find her left earlobe empty. She frowned as she thought back to the last time she'd been wearing both her earrings. Her cheeks burned at the possibility she might have lost one of them in Landon's bedroom while putting on his borrowed clothes. And she'd given *him* a hard time about clichés!

"I can see why Jachin would find you intriguing. You show absolutely no fear."

Mira's comment drew her attention. "I do?" Ariel rubbed the soap on the sponge. The warm water felt so good, and the scent of jasmine and roses floating in the air further lulled her.

"He can be a fierce man. He'd like that about you," Mira continued.

Ariel pondered the female vampire's observation about her and doubted Jachin would view her the same way. "What was so funny in what I said about Jachin a minute ago?" Ariel asked as she slid the sponge down her chest, washing away the sweat and dirt.

Mira shrugged. "You were very accurate in your assessment of Jachin. I was laughing because you called him my lover."

Surprised, Ariel dropped the sponge in the water and her gaze locked on the perfect hourglass curves of Mira's petite frame. "You've never been lovers?"

Mira cast her a devilish look over her shoulder right before streams of water dumped on Ariel's head. "No, silly. Jachin is my brother."

Ariel swiped the water away in time to see the bath sponge fall back into the water from above her head. She jerked her gaze to Mira, frowning at the woman's telekinetic mischief with the sponge. Mira snickered and put her back to Ariel once more. "But I thought…well, the things you said to Vlad sounded like you and Jachin—"

"Once my brother left, Vlad took it upon himself to be my protector. Let's just say Vlad's idea of a protector and mine are very different." Deep hurt reflected in Mira's somber tone.

Based on Vlad's earlier comments and now Mira's, Ariel realized the bastard must've violated the woman. She felt like a jerk for inadvertently bringing up a painful subject. "I'm so sorry, Mira. I—"

Mira slid a half smile her way. "It's okay. You meant no harm." Her smile faded and her blue eyes turned to steel as she faced away once more. "Vlad caught me off guard only once. It'll never happen again. After Jachin left, I had to grow up. I blamed my brother at first, but I know he wouldn't have left if he'd had a choice."

Ariel's heart pounded. Finally she could find out what Jachin would never tell her. As she began to massage the soap in her wet hair, she asked, "Why did your brother leave the Sanguinas?"

Mira sighed. "Jachin had an affair with Braeden's girlfriend."

"That got him kicked out of the clan?" Ariel asked in shock.

"You have to know Braeden's ego to understand how this could happen."

"I don't get it. If Braeden wanted this woman, why didn't he just marry her and be done with it?" Ariel gulped before she asked the last question. "Is it because she wanted Jachin instead?"

"All Vivian ever wanted was Braeden. That wasn't the problem. The prophecy was."

"The prophecy?" Now Ariel was completely confused. She quickly dunked her head under the water to wash out the soapsuds.

Mira turned to face her. "My understanding is you wrote a book about vampires. In this book you detail a prophecy where the leader of the vampires mates with a human, right?"

Ariel slowly nodded as every piece of the puzzle started falling in place, even the answer as to why Jachin had kept his distance from her. He'd screwed up once with Vivian, getting himself banished from his clan. "Are you saying that the reason Braeden couldn't mate with Vivian was because, as the leader of the vampires, he was bound to fulfill the prophecy?"

"Enter human author, Ariel Swanson."

As the full impact of Mira's last statement sank in, Ariel began to understand Jachin's dogged belief in the prophecy. In a twisted sort of way, she respected him for never giving up, even when he had to have faced certain death being forced to live among humans with poisoned blood. How *had* he survived?

If only her own life weren't hanging in the balance as part of the package. She hadn't asked to play an integral role in the Sanguinas' survival. She wasn't the human who would mate with the vampire leader. It was just a made-up, fictional prophecy anyway.

"You have to help me, Mira. I'm not the human to fulfill this prophecy. All I did was write a book—a fictional novel."

Sympathetic understanding filled the vampire's gaze. She walked over to a cabinet and opened it. "Did you not write a prophecy that was known only among Sanguinas word for word in your novel?"

According to Jachin, she had. Ariel grudgingly nodded.

"Didn't you also describe our home, our sanctuary, exactly as it stands?"

"But I didn't write about the mine we went through to get here. My vampires just lived deep in the woods," Ariel argued.

When the woman raised a doubtful eyebrow, a sinking sensation bottomed out in Ariel's stomach.

"I'm not tough, Mira. I'm terrified of vampires. I always have been ever since they slaughtered my entire family. I knew the vampires would come for me, too. That's why I wrote that book—to help me conquer my fear."

"I'm sorry about your family, Ariel." Mira turned and retrieved a thick blue towel for her. As she held out the towel, Ariel quickly stepped out of the tub and into the material's warmth. After she wrapped the towel around Ariel, Mira continued, "Since we can't change the past, facing one's fear is usually the best way to overcome it. Becoming Braeden's mate will be a new beginning for all of us."

Ariel dug her toes into the high-piled burgundy bath rug underneath her feet. Despite the towel's warmth, she shivered uncontrollably. Mira ran her warm hands down Ariel's arms, displacing the chill bumps that had formed. "It's going to be all right. My brother lived and breathed the prophecy. I trust him with my life."

"But he left you!" Ariel cried, desperate for the woman to understand from her point of view.

Mira's optimistic expression shifted to one of deep hurt. "That was cruel."

Ariel's heart went out to the one vampire who'd treated

her more like a friend than an inferior. Impulsively she wrapped her arms around the petite woman, hugging her close. Tears filled her eyes at her untenable predicament. "I'm sorry, Mira. I'm just so frightened. I don't want this."

Mira squeezed her tight, then ran a calming hand down Ariel's long wet hair. "Life has a strange way of forcing you down paths you'd never thought you'd have the strength to walk. Despite your claims to the contrary, you radiate a strong inner power. I promise I'll be here for you, always." Setting Ariel away, she sniffed back her own tears. "Now come on, I'll feed you before I get you dressed and ready for Braeden."

"You have food?" Ariel asked, pulling back.

Mira laughed. "Yes, Sanguinas do eat…well, fruits and vegetables anyway. Growing our own produce was the best way to remain completely under the radar these past twenty-five years."

Jachin stood in front of the second fake rock wall inside the abandoned mine. As far as the Sanguinas' guards knew, he was still banished. He hoped at least one of the guards on the other side of the wall still believed in the prophecy. He didn't want to have to kill any more of his kind. As it was, due to malnourishment, very few women had been able to conceive since the sickness. With vampires taking blood from each other, their numbers had to have dwindled even more over the past decade.

Jachin rolled his head from shoulder to shoulder, easing the tension within him. Taking a deep breath, he mentally prepared for the battle ahead and pushed the hidden palm-size rock inward, twisting a quarter turn until the wall began to slide out of his way.

Talek and Darel pointed their machine guns his way.

"I didn't think you'd have the balls to come back here. How the hell did you survive on your own all these years?" Darel demanded with grudging respect.

"Dying wasn't an option." Jachin stepped through the entrance. As the wall closed behind him, he continued, "Which one of you is going to have to be carried out of here tonight?"

The guards glanced at each other and then burst out laughing. While they were distracted, Jachin struck. He pulled the knife tucked in his belt and grabbed Darel, holding the sharp tip next to the guard's jugular.

Tensing his arm muscle, Jachin used his grip on the knife's handle for leverage. He yanked Darel backward until the vampire's spine slammed against the rock wall.

When Jachin faced Talek, the other guard's fingers tightened around his weapon as if he were preparing to fire. "I refused to die after I was banished and I refuse to die now. My belief in the prophecy has never wavered, Talek. Has yours?"

Darel dropped his weapon and his claws extended from his fingertips as he tried to pull Jachin's hand and the knife from his neck. Separating himself from the pain Darel inflicted, Jachin kept his hold tight and his eyes locked with Talek's. The metallic scent of his own blood filled the air while tension ebbed between them.

Darel chose that moment to attack. He hit Jachin's arm holding the knife, managing to lower it but not dislodge it. Instead the recoil buried the blade into Darel's collarbone.

Furious with the vampire for his stupidity, Jachin hissed as the man moaned, "Stay put."

"Things are not as they once were," Talek said.

Talek's inability to look him in the eye knocked Jachin in the gut. Had they all given up? "Don't you want a better life?" Jachin asked, playing on Talek's conscience. "The Sanguinas are barely living, former shadows of their old selves. All I want is to ensure Braeden follows through with the prophecy for the sake of our future."

"Our future? You are no longer a part of this clan," Talek snarled.

Jachin narrowed his gaze. "I've lived separate from my people for ten years and yet I still held on to my beliefs. Won't you consider the possibility that I only have the best interests of the Sanguinas at heart?"

Talek's blond eyebrows rose in skepticism. "You say this while you have a knife buried in Darel."

Warm blood dripped over Jachin's hand, stinging the gashes Darel had caused. The guard's hands had fallen away. Even though he hadn't intended to stab Darel, Jachin wasn't going to allow Talek to distract him from his goal. "He'll live, but will you be able to live with yourself if you don't allow me a chance to convince Braeden that the human woman *will* play a role in our destiny?"

"She's here. Braeden…will follow through."

Jachin jumped on the hesitation. "You're not convinced. I hear it in your voice. Has Braeden moved away from the prophecy these past ten years?"

"He never speaks of it. Many who believed in the past have given up."

Jachin's concern for Ariel spiked. His gaze narrowed. "I must speak to Braeden."

Talek gave him a firm nod, but he didn't lower his gun. "Bring Darel."

Jachin turned his attention to the guard he had pinned to the wall. Darel had passed out, and only Jachin's strength and the knife held him up.

Withdrawing the blade from the man's flesh, Jachin caught the vampire's limp body before he fell to the ground. Sliding the bloody blade behind his belt, he lowered Darel to the ground and squatted, assessing the gaping wound.

He gripped the back of Darel's neck to support him as he lowered his mouth to the man's wound.

"Don't take his blood!" the tense guard ordered behind him.

"Shut up, Talek!" he grumbled before he swiped his tongue along the bloody hole.

When he sat back on his haunches and watched with satisfaction as the wound began to close, awe filled Talek's voice. "How'd you do that? We haven't been able to heal wounds that fast for several years now."

His clan's situation was worse than Jachin thought. While it was true, going without food these past couple of days had weakened his powers, he didn't realize just how much Roach's synthesized blood had kept his abilities from diluting overall until that very moment. The old man's disappearance knotted his stomach. Had Roach died because he'd helped Jachin?

Jachin lifted Darel's limp body in his arms and met Talek's curious gaze. "Let's go."

As Jachin exited the woods and approached his old home, Darel's weight suddenly felt heavier in his arms.

Jachin's heart constricted at the Sanguina manor's run-down appearance. Thick ivy crept along the castle's walls, while moss covered several of the gargoyles, giving the place a sinister, evil ambience instead of the powerful, rich presence it had once held. Along with their loss of hope for a brighter future, did his people no longer take pride in their home?

He felt the weight of condemning gazes staring down at him from the windows above, sensed the resentment at his return, but he refused to look up. Fury seethed inside him. They didn't need to see bitterness and anger reflected in his gaze. As the heavy wood door opened, Jachin swallowed his disappointment.

What the Sanguinas needed was someone willing to fight for their future, and he damned well planned to make sure Braeden followed through with the prophecy.

Thoughts of Ariel tugged at his conscience. Was she frightened? Had the Sanguinas who'd taken her treated her with the respect she deserved as their leader's destined mate?

His gut twisted when he thought of Ariel with Braeden, but he shoved the guilt and his own selfish desires to the back of his mind. His clan needed hope. The beautiful human, with her unflappable inner strength, her unfailing willfulness in the face of adversity, and her admirable capacity for compassion, was the perfect role model.

Ariel had written about vampires with lives and hopes and dreams. Once she spent some time with them, she'd realize her fictional story represented a future for the Sanguinas—a future she had the power to shape. More than just a new beginning for the Sanguinas, Ariel's qualities represented everything the vampires had secretly wished for but had never truly attained.

Humanity.

Ariel walked beside Mira, trying not to visibly shake even though she trembled inside. As she headed down a long, wide hall toward a set of heavy wooden doors, her new soft-soled shoes made no sound on the stone floor. Men and women lined the walls on either side of the hall, openly staring at her. Some gazes spewed hatred while others were full of open curiosity.

What were they all thinking? What did their leader, Braeden, plan to do to her? Her chest tightened and many questions flew through her mind.

Ariel was wearing a red chiffon floor-length skirt made of several separate panels that swirled in and around her legs as she walked. Over the skirt she wore a gold long-sleeved hip-length jacket that buttoned tight at her waist and under her breasts. Red silk thread created an intricate border pattern along the deep vee neckline, while cutouts exposed fair skin at the curve of her shoulders. Mira had spent considerable time on Ariel's hair, pinning the bulk of it up. Once she'd curled tendrils around Ariel's neck, she'd placed an intricately designed ruby-and-diamond circlet on top of her hair as a final touch.

As guards opened the heavy wooden doors, Ariel's resolve faltered at the indrawn, sucking noise the movement created. She was being sucked into the one place she feared the most—a den of vampires ready to drain the life out of her. Mira's hand touched the small of Ariel's back and she ushered her forward into a huge room with marble columns lining either side.

Even though Ariel trembled deep inside, she refused to let anyone see the depth of her turmoil. Squaring her shoulders, she put one foot in front of the other. A man with short, dark hair and assessing eyes stood in a formal black suit in the middle of the room, his hands folded behind his back.

By the deferential way the other vampires lined the edges of the hall, giving him space, he had to be Braeden. Ariel swallowed her growing panic with a painful gulp as she headed toward him.

A tall, narrow-faced woman with long, straight black hair separated from the crowd and stepped in front of her, blocking her path. Her dark brown eyes slitted in hatred right before she backhanded Ariel.

Pain exploded across Ariel's mouth and dizziness roared through her head from the woman's vicious attack. If it weren't for Mira's hand suddenly supporting her upper back, she'd have slammed to the floor from the power of the woman's blow.

"Keep your distance, Vivian," Mira barked right before the tall woman flew into the crowd of people as if an invisible force had knocked her backward.

Once several vampires set her on her feet, Vivian smoothed her long, formal black dress and zeroed her gaze on Mira. "Stay out of this."

Ariel wiped the trickle of blood that spread across her throbbing lip. She was about to tell the bitch she could have the man when Vivian snarled and leapt across the room toward her, deadly claws and fangs extended.

Right before the woman reached her, a dark blur came from behind Ariel. A man grabbed Vivian in midair, gripping the vampire's upper arms. Jachin spoke in a harsh tone as he set her on the ground. "Would you destroy the Sanguinas' chance for a future for your own selfish gains, Vivian?"

"The prophecy is a farce, ramblings of a delusional man meant to give us hope during bleak times." She peered around his broad shoulder at Ariel, her gaze narrowed in anger. "She's nothing more than spoiled food."

Murmurs spread through the group of vampires and Ariel's heart thudded. The female vampire would've shredded her to pieces, yet Braeden hadn't tried to stop her.

His inaction spoke volumes to her.

"You were wrong, Jachin. Your leader doesn't want this." Every eye in the room turned to Ariel, and the crowd quieted down until she heard her own rapid breathing.

"Don't you dare speak for me," a man's voice snarled in her ear. Braeden had moved so fast she never saw him coming. He grabbed Ariel's arm and hauled her to his side as he addressed Jachin, scowling his displeasure.

"What are you doing back here? How did you get past the guards?"

Jachin set Vivian away and faced Braeden, his gray T-shirt covered in blood. His jaw ticced when his gaze locked on the man's hand around Ariel's arm. Ariel noted the bloody wounds on his hand. Was all that blood his?

"He insisted on an audience." A tall, blond vampire stepped forward, carrying an unconscious dark-haired man whose neck and clothes were smeared with blood. Ariel recognized both men as the guards from the mine entrance.

As the limp man moaned and began to stir, the tall man set the other down on the floor and continued. "Jachin wants to make sure the prophecy is fulfilled."

While the blond man had Braeden's attention, Jachin spoke in Ariel's mind. *Are you unharmed?*

Rage made her chest burn. She wanted to scream at him, to slam her fist against his jaw for dragging her into his world, but right now Jachin was the lesser of many evils around her.

"You were wrong," she repeated through clenched teeth, glancing his way.

The grip around her arm tightened. "Quiet," Braeden ordered before he met Jachin's gaze. "I think it's best if you see this with your own eyes." Nodding to the three vampires who'd moved behind Jachin, he finished, "Before we put you to death."

As he spoke, the vampires rushed forward. Two men grabbed Jachin's arms while one stood behind him, ready if he broke free.

Braeden raised his voice and addressed the whole room of vampires. "This human doesn't believe I'll fulfill my duties as your leader. What do the Sanguinas say?"

"You'll do your duty."

"We know better, Braeden."

"Prove her wrong," several shouts called over the general murmur.

"Behold…" Braeden grabbed Ariel's arm. Her heart jerked and her stomach pitched as he walked her in a circle in front of his people like a piece of meat about to be slaughtered.

Chapter 11

While Braeden worked the Sanguinas into a frenzy, Jachin stared at Ariel's bravado-filled expression. In the short time he'd known her he'd learned to read her. Sharp pain stabbed at his heart and gut in jealous, possessive jabs. Even in her fear, her ethereal beauty and core strength reflected outward, making him feel, for the first time in his life, inferior to a human.

His duty to his people warred within him as he scanned the Sanguinas' faces around him. Hope welled in several of them, but most gazes held bloodthirst, not expectant looks for salvation.

Jachin's eyes locked with Ariel's, and the look of sheer betrayal in their beautiful blue depths hit him as if he'd been slammed by a battering ram. Sharp guilt and remorse tore through his body, slicing through his heart and lungs, stealing his soul.

"Let's prove once and for all the validity of the prophecy," Braeden grabbed Ariel's other arm and turned her to face him. His dark gaze locked with hers. "Ready to be my mate and all that entails, Ariel Swanson?"

Ariel shook her head in frantic jerks. She struggled, trying to tug away from his hold. "No! Let me go."

"Too late." Braeden's fanged smile, both devious and gleeful, made Jachin want to pound his face to mush.

In her heart, Ariel knew the Sanguinas leader cared nothing for the vampires around him. Why couldn't Jachin see that? she wondered as a sense of hopelessness plunged to her stomach.

When Braeden yanked her forward and lowered his fangs toward her neck, her heart rate quadrupled. She let out a scream of sheer terror and shoved at his powerful shoulders while trying to mentally brace herself for the pain she knew he'd inflict.

Before his teeth connected, she was jerked sideways and slammed to the floor by a forceful hit. Ariel gasped for air, and her hip throbbed from the impact with the stone floor. She stared in surprise at the sight a few feet away from her.

Jachin had Braeden pinned to the floor. He sat on the vampire leader's chest, his fingers around the man's throat. "Don't touch her. She is all that is good and pure. I wanted to believe in you, Braeden—for the sake of the clan—but you'll only destroy her."

Several vampires rushed forward. While one removed

Jachin's knife from his belt, others hauled him off Braeden's chest. The vampire leader stood up and brushed at his suit with unhurried motions. His gaze filled with loathing as he approached Jachin, now held back by four male vampires.

"That's what this is about, isn't it? You want this human. You always want my women—and yet you'll never have them," he sneered.

Extending his claws, he ripped one side of Jachin's face and then the other. Deep furrows welled with blood down Jachin's cheeks while Braeden slammed him in the gut with several punches.

Ariel's heart died a little with each blow. Tears filled her eyes and she bit her lower lip. She'd never been more frightened for Jachin than she was at this moment. How he withstood the pummeling without yelling in pain, she had no idea.

After Braeden gave the final insult by spitting on Jachin, he walked over to Ariel. He hauled her to her feet by her arm. "I will fulfill this prophecy once and for all."

Before Ariel could prepare herself once more, Braeden yanked her forward and plunged his teeth deep into her neck.

The pain shooting down her throat was so unbearable her knees buckled. Braeden gripped her arms tight to keep her from falling to the floor. As she screamed at the all-consuming fire tearing at her neck, he closed his bottom teeth against her skin, as well, taking her level of pain to new depths. A vicious growl erupted from his throat right before he began to suck.

Once he took his first swallow, Braeden withdrew his fangs and spat her blood on the floor. He turned in fury toward Jachin, eyes blazing, canines coated bright red. "Her blood is tainted like all the others." His icy gaze narrowed as he grabbed the back of Ariel's hair pinned atop her head and turned her toward Jachin like a throwaway trophy. "Was that your plan? To poison me so you could to take my place?"

Ariel winced at the sharp pain radiating from her head. She trembled when Braeden confirmed that her blood was poisonous. She'd be worth nothing to the vampires now. She might not want to be the vampire leader's mate, but she didn't want to die, either.

Her situation was dire, yet in the darkness surrounding her one tiny light shone. Jachin had tried to save her. He *did* care.

Braeden jerked her around in a circle once more, this time by her hair. Sharp pinpricks shot through her skull. Her eyes watered as he displayed her to all the vampires looking on. "You have before you another tainted human—"

She was surprised when Braeden cut himself off and sucked in his breath as if shocked. He drew her hair up tighter, forcing her to bend her head forward to keep from passing out from the pain. Tears rolled down her face from the stabbing agony his action caused.

"You are wrong!" Jachin ground out through his own pain.

Braeden turned her around so her back faced the crowd and Jachin. "Jachin is not only a traitor but he brings an enemy in our midst. See this crescent shape on her neck? Tell them your name." Ariel tried to turn and look at him, but he kept his hold tight and growled, "Tell them!"

"Arianna Lee," Ariel screeched out in pain as a sick, twisted realization settled in her mind. There was only one way this vampire could know Ariel Swanson wasn't her real name.

"Does that last name sound familiar, anyone? She bears the same mark as the man who ordered the destruction of the Scions project. My father took care of the human responsible and his wife, and I made sure his other descendents paid the ultimate price—until the sickness caused us to withdraw from their world. I never could find one female. She's the last in his line." He turned her back around so she faced the crowd. "George Marvin Lee tried to eradicate our family, and now we can finally destroy his."

Ariel felt Jachin's heavy gaze on her, the question in his eyes. She was just as surprised at the news that her grandfather was the man responsible for the government project's demise, but now the systematic murders of her family members made a kind of morbid sense.

Fury for her family's murders rose from deep within her, spreading like a disease through her lungs, filling her chest with black revenge.

"Take her," Braeden demanded to a vampire nearby. When the man tried to grab Ariel's arm, she shrugged free and dove for Braeden, ready to dig her nails into his hateful face. "You murdering bastard! You killed my entire family."

Braeden grabbed her wrists before she connected. A satisfied smile spread across his face. "Why, yes, I did. And I enjoyed every minute stalking the weak humans who thought it was acceptable to destroy *my* family. Even your pathetic brother."

Peter hadn't committed suicide? Ariel growled her wrath, enraged that the man stood there mocking her as if he enjoyed every second of her pain. "You'll never teach your people humanity or help them find happiness with such blackness in your heart."

Braeden backhanded her straight into another vampire's waiting arms.

"Hold her," he barked, then turned to the men holding Jachin. "Let him go. I have a score to settle first."

Jachin broke free of the vampires' hold and sprang across the room toward Braeden, fangs displayed and claws extended. Watching the bastard bite Ariel, purposefully inflicting pain, took him over the edge.

The force of his impact sent both men skidding across the floor. While they were still moving, both sliding on their shoulders, Jachin slammed his fist into Braeden's jaw and throat before shredding Braeden's jacket with his extended claws.

When they came to a halting stop, bright red blood appeared, seeping into Braeden's white shirt underneath. The Sanguinas leader roared in pain and rammed his hand into Jachin's chest, sending him across the room to slam against the far wall.

Disoriented from the blow, Jachin slid down the stone wall, then shook his head and stood.

The crowd spread, allowing Braeden room. He let out a combat roar and launched himself across the twenty-foot distance toward Jachin.

They collided midair, both men striking out at one another, each landing damaging blows. Braeden caught Jachin's left bicep with his claws, while Jachin sliced at Braeden's neck.

When they landed, Jachin folded his fingers in a beckoning motion. "Come and get it. You and I both know this is going to end with me digging your sadistic black heart out of your chest—"

Braeden's face twisted with fury. He dove at Jachin, ramming his head right into his gut. Jachin's breath whooshed from his lungs and he slammed into a solid marble column. Excruciating pain splintered down his spine, but Jachin shoved the pain away, focusing on one thing.

Ending this.

Grabbing the back of Braeden's coat, Jachin quickly flipped the man over. With a bloodcurdling yell, he gripped Braeden's lapel and extended his claws once more—

"Jachin!"

Ariel's terrified scream stopped Jachin cold.

Aaron held a knife to Ariel's throat, a determined look in his eyes. "Let him go."

Jachin's heart thumped hard, his muscles tense. Revenge for his people and for Ariel flowed through him with such a palpable thrum, he had a hard time letting go of Braeden's coat. Finally his fingers listened to his brain and they began to ease.

Braeden scrambled to his feet and backed several feet away from Jachin.

Ariel's fear ricocheted throughout her body. The sharp knife pressed against her neck told her just how close to death she was.

Braeden swayed slightly and straightened his torn lapels. A cold, deadly smile tilted his lips as he glanced over Jachin's injuries.

"You've lost a lot of blood. How long has it been since you've fed? I hear your stomach rumbling." Jerking his chin toward Ariel, Braeden continued, "Her family tried to kill us. I think it would be the perfect revenge for her last breath in this life to be at the hands of the voracious beast within you."

Jachin snarled in disgust. "Have the guts to finish the job yourself, you spineless bastard."

Braeden closed the distance between them and slammed his fist hard into Jachin's face, knocking him out.

Once Jachin was out of commission, the vampire holding Ariel removed the knife from her throat. Ariel shook, and her stomach roiled at the sight of Jachin lying there bleeding and unconscious. As two men picked him up by his arms and began to drag his limp, bleeding body out of the room, she wept for Jachin and for herself. She couldn't believe that he'd risked the Sanguinas' future to save her from Braeden and, by doing so, had sealed his own fate.

The look on Jachin's face when Braeden had told him that her grandfather was the man who'd shut down the program had been heart-wrenching. Fury, anger and betrayal had burned in his eyes. Not only were they both about to die, but any sympathy he might have felt for her, any emotion, had disappeared from his gaze before he'd looked away.

Now he would spare her no mercy.

The man grasping her arm began to pull her along, following the men who now carried Jachin. Vivian's cold smile held triumph as Ariel walked past her, while unshed tears glittered in Mira's sad blue eyes. Many in the crowd turned their backs to her, and others stared at her with hatred.

Led by Braeden, the vampires carried Jachin down a hall on the opposite side of the castle and began to descend a set of narrow curved stone stairs. Ariel stumbled when the man holding her shoved her forward, indicating she should follow them downward.

One of the men hit a button on the wall, and sconces lit up ahead of them, lighting their way as they spiraled down several stories of stairs. Once they reached the bottom, a man pulled open the heavy wooden door.

Cooler air rushed forth when they passed through the doorway and entered a long hall full of heavy wood doors. *It's a dungeon,* she thought at the same time a groan of pain escaped Jachin.

A guard used his key to open a door and then both men tossed Jachin into the room with satisfied laughs.

"Wait here," Braeden said to her guard before he went inside the room, pulling the door closed behind him.

When Ariel heard a loud thump as if someone had been thrown against one of the walls in the dungeon, she winced and worried for Jachin.

A few minutes later, Braeden walked out with a satisfied smile on his face. He gripped her face as the guards pushed her forward.

"Maybe you'll get lucky and he won't drain you dry before the sunlight takes care of him." He let out a vindictive laugh. "Either way, you'll rot in this prison." He moved to the side and the guards shoved her inside the room so hard she fell to the floor, gasping in pain.

Her circlet askew, her eyes wide with apprehension, Ariel met Jachin's gaze. The heavy door shut behind her, sealing their fates with a resounding thunk.

The air grew thick with tension and the sweet smell of her blood around them. Even the tiny bit of blood at the corner of her mouth was enough to incite his hunger. The sconces' light reflected off her white-blond hair, making it appear to shimmer.

She looked so beautiful and fragile with her red skirt swirled around her on the hard, cold floor. He knew her blood would revive him, but he also knew the primal survival instinct inside him would bloom into a ravaging beast. He wouldn't be able to stop until she was completely dead.

His fangs elongated at his traitorous thoughts. Jachin clamped his lips shut and closed his eyes, lying perfectly still on his back. As long as she didn't move, didn't stir the air, he might be able to keep the thirst inside him under control.

Ariel spoke in a rush, her voice shaking with regret. "I didn't know about my grandfather's connection. I never knew what his job was, just that he worked for the government before he retired. After my brother died, my family was gone. I changed my name to try to stay one step ahead of the vampire I feared would come looking for me next. I've had this identity so long Ariel is my name now. I'm so sorry, Jachin."

Jachin didn't want her to apologize. He didn't want her to be completely innocent. He was fighting his need for blood with every ounce of willpower left inside him. Eventually he wouldn't be able to contain the bloodlust raging throughout his body. He wanted to blame her—but he knew he couldn't.

Concern etched her words. "You need to get up, use your strength to fight your way out of here," she continued, digging deeper…making him want her even more.

* * *

Ariel stared at Jachin's tense jaw. The man was awake, but he was completely ignoring her. She glanced up at the circular window covered with cross-bars in the corner of the room. It was too small to crawl through, yet it was large enough to let in plenty of sunlight. She was pretty sure it went all the way up to outside ground level. In the bare, stone-walled room, there wasn't anywhere Jachin could hide from the sun. Fury swept through her, making her chest ache. He was their only chance out of this dungeon, and yet he lay there on that mesh bed hanging from the wall by chains as if he planned to accept his death with open arms.

"Damn it, get up, Jachin!" She literally shook in her anger. "Where is that survival instinct that kept you alive during your banishment?"

His dark gaze narrowed on her, his voice low and deadly. "Do you know what I did to survive? I killed humans for money and I never once felt an ounce of guilt."

When he finished, he closed his eyes again. She clenched her fists in frustration that he was trying to alienate her…as if he wanted her to hate him. She realized that was exactly what he was trying to do.

Squaring her shoulders, she strengthened her tone. "It's not going to work. You saved me today when you had everything to lose by doing so. There is humanity stirring in that heart of yours."

Nothing, not a flicker of acknowledgment.

"Where's your will to live?" Ariel stood and walked over to stand next to the bed. Hitting his shoulder, she demanded, "Survive, Jachin! Survive for both of us!"

Jachin turned to face her so fast she jumped back. Ariel

tripped on her gown's hem and fell to the floor, bruising her rear in the process.

He sat up on his elbow and roared, "All I hear is your warm blood rushing in your veins. Stay away!"

The feral look on his face, his eyes glazed with blood-lust and the sight of his fangs fully extended told her he *would* drain her. She didn't think her death would be a quick one. Ariel had never been more frightened in her life.

How could she have been so wrong about Jachin? She'd never seen this side to him—hungry, angry and on the edge of losing control. Her throat seized and her heart threatened to ram a hole right through her chest.

Ariel stumbled to her feet and rushed to the door. She knew no one would come to her rescue, but self-preservation was a powerful if not always a logical force. She began to hammer at the thick wood with her fists, screaming at the top of her lungs. "Help me! Someone, please! Mirrrra! Help me!"

Two big hands landed on top of hers, pinning her fists to the door. The sight of Jachin's fingers burrowed deep into the wood, displaying how easily he could shred her thin skin to bits, cut her scream off in a strangled gulp.

His hard body pressed against her back as his warm breath brushed across her neck. "I was bred to survive at all costs. I *will* take your blood," he rasped next to her ear.

Ariel began to pant in short, frightened gasps of air.

"The question remains, Ariel…will it be with your consent or without?"

Chapter 12

As Jachin's question echoed in her head, Ariel struggled for breath. Turning to face him, she searched his harsh features and remembered his promise that he would never hurt her.

But somewhere underneath the haze of bloodlust reflected in his eyes she saw compassion. She knew he cared for her.

In the midst of all this chaos, despite her fear of vampires, she'd come to care for Jachin, too. More than anything, she appreciated his heroic effort to protect her from himself.

The fact that her family had played a role in the Sanguinas' past and ultimately their current circumstances allowed her to shed some of the guilt that had been building around her heart, placing a barrier between them. They both had reasons to hate—did those reasons cancel each other out?

Her blood had healed his wounds in the past. Maybe her blood wouldn't be his death warrant. She was well aware she was playing with a fire on the verge of an out-of-control inferno, but if she was going to die, then let her death come in the arms of a man who seemed to care enough to fight his programmed primal instincts as long as he could.

Her heart beat at a rapid pace as she kissed one of the wounds on his chest. Swiping the bit of blood from her lips with her tongue, she placed her trembling hands on the torn fabric over his hard pectorals and met his tortured, haunted gaze, answering his question. "Make me beg for it."

A sense of relief rushed through Jachin at her consent, but he couldn't let down his guard or he would lose total control. He yanked his claws from the door, and as his talons retracted, he ran his knuckles across her cheek. His hunger raged within him, turning his attraction to Ariel to full-fledged, overwhelming lust.

She didn't remember their time together, but it was all he could think about. Amid the dark, ravenous animal clawing inside him, he held on to the memory, the beautiful sight of her complete, passionate surrender.

He didn't know how to recover her memory, but he hadn't completely erased it. He hoped like hell he could help her come back to it. The look of tentative trust mingled with fear in her eyes stabbed at his heart. He needed her to rediscover their passion.

"You lay naked on the bed, completely open to me,

while I tasted your body." His fingers trailed down her neck, barely touching her skin.

Her brow wrinkled in confusion, her voice a bare whisper when she said, "I don't understand."

"In Landon's cabin. There was a period of time you don't remember." Jachin traced his fingers down her throat until he touched the swell of her breast right above the jacket's collar. Extending his talon, he popped the first button off her jacket.

Her breath hitched as his action exposed her cleavage, but her gaze never left his. "I remember wondering when I had changed clothes and why you were kissing me."

Jachin's body tensed with his need to rip the jacket open. He fought back the voracious creature battling in his mind. "We took a shower together." He popped open another button.

"No." Ariel closed her eyes for a second and shook her head.

Another button fell to the stone floor, spinning until it fell over on its side with a quiet plink. "Your hair was wet."

Her gaze flew to his as the truth of his statement sank in. "I—I don't remember." Her lips trembled and she moved her hands to his shoulders.

A generous show of beautiful fair skin was now exposed, and her sweet, firm breasts were barely covered by the jacket. His body throbbed for hers in painful anticipation while his thirst grew in exponential proportions.

Jachin severed the last button holding the fabric together, a dark grunt of male satisfaction echoing in his head. "You asked me to erase your memory."

Unshed tears glittered in her beautiful blue eyes, acknowledging the first signs she believed he might be speaking the truth. "Why?"

"Only you can tell me your reasons." Jachin gingerly cupped her neck with both hands, rubbing his thumbs along her collarbone.

Her head moved back and forth in an adamant motion. "I don't remember any of it. How can you expect me to tell you what my reasons were?"

His fangs seemed to elongate even more with the need to clamp down on her neck. Sliding his palms down her chest, he spoke in a low tone full of pent-up need. "I remember every sweet, erotic detail, from your wet body grinding against mine to your sweet, musky flavor as you begged me to take you."

Ariel's body stiffened. "I did not!"

"You will remember!" he demanded as he palmed her breasts, then ran his thumbs across her hard nipples. Despite her mortified tone, she gasped at the brush of his fingers against her sensitive skin.

He gripped her waist and pulled her against his chest. "I've overcome many obstacles and unbeatable odds in my life, but holding back from filling your body with mine was the hardest temptation I've ever faced."

"So we didn't...?" Confusion and frustration flitted across her face as she trailed off. She cupped his jaw, tears sliding down her cheeks. Her glittering eyes searched his face for answers. "I wish I remembered."

With sheer willpower Jachin forced his fangs to retreat. Lowering his mouth to hers, he spoke in her mind. *We'll just have to make a new memory together.*

* * *

Ariel welcomed the deep thrust of his tongue against hers, the blissful obliteration of every emotion except exquisite pleasure. When he cupped the back of her head and slanted his mouth across hers, his kiss consumed her, taking her fear and turning it into an all-out adrenaline rush.

Ariel's breasts tingled from his touch, her belly fluttered and her sex ached. How could his kiss elicit such a deep response? Did her body remember and crave what her mind couldn't recall?

She moaned against his mouth and blocked out the cool stone chamber, her dire situation and the fact the man seducing her might very well take every single drop of blood that pumped in her veins. She just wanted to feel alive for what could be the last day of her life.

As Jachin's tongue explored every crevice of her mouth, flashes of memories scanned through her mind: Jachin standing behind her, his arm around her waist while he asked why she'd saved him; his lips grazing her neck as his hand cupped her breast over Landon's button-down shirt. She'd wanted him desperately.

When Jachin gripped her waist tight and his lips skimmed down her neck, she began to tremble. It was as if he sensed his current seduction was spurring her lost memory to return.

He backed her against the door and lifted her slightly in the air. Grinding his hard erection against her mound, he groaned alongside her neck as he swiped his tongue over the wounds Braeden had inflicted. His body held her pressed against the door, his hands palming her hips before sliding lower until he cupped her rear through the skirt's fabric in a tight, possessive hold.

How can you forget this, Ariel? he whispered in her mind. *What we share is indescribable.*

His husky mental words coupled with his aggressive action made her heartbeat ramp up to an erratic pace and her pulse thunder in her ears. She felt his barely controlled tension knotting his shoulders underneath her hands and reveled in it. Ariel had never been more sexually wound up in her life.

I couldn't bring myself to fully erase your memory...just to push it to your subconscious. Jachin's warm tongue ran along the other side of her neck as he lowered her to the floor and slid his hand past the panels in her skirt.

The sconces' light appeared to dance in the dungeon's small space, moving in time to their heavy breathing. She didn't have time to ponder the cool air hitting her bared skin before his warm hand slid up the inside of her thigh.

Jachin lifted his head and captured her gaze at the same time his fingers traced through the curls between her legs. "I might've erased your memory, but I'll never forget the way you felt, the way you smelled or how you tasted."

As he slid his finger deep in her channel, his nostrils flared and his chest lifted and fell as if he'd lost control of his ability to slow his breathing. Ariel whimpered at the erotic sensations his invasion caused. Her heart hammered out of control, and she clenched her walls around his fingers, wanting more...wanting his body ramming deep inside, stretching her tight and making her scream with the need to come.

"I've never wanted this much—Ariel...both your blood and your moans of pleasure."

When he added another finger, déjà vu flashed more patches of buried memories through her mind, while the lustful, haunted look in his eyes made her belly tumble and her knees threaten to give way. Witnessing his need for her on so many levels finally brought all the memories flooding back, completely freeing her heart and mind.

"I remember." Ariel breathed hard as she began to tug at his jeans' button and zipper.

Jachin slammed his fingers deep inside her channel and cupped his palm against her mound. "Tell me why."

She gasped at his aggressive action, feeling both filled and frustrated by him. Ariel tried to move her hips, to continue the pleasurable build blossoming inside her, but he held her pinned against the door, his expression hard and unreadable.

The pressure of his palm against her sensitive nub was almost unbearable, a mixture of oh-so-good and almost too much at the same time. She let go of his jeans and grabbed his hand to try to relieve some of the friction, but he refused to budge.

"Tell me why you wanted me to erase your memory," he repeated in a voice of steel.

Her stomach flipped back and forth between flutters and cramps, she was so on the edge. "I—I don't know."

His gaze narrowed and his jaw tightened. He moved the heel of his hand and replaced it with his thumb, sliding the rough pad back and forth along her sex. "I need to know, Ariel."

Ariel's frantic panting hitched with each brush of his thumb against the firm, sensitive skin and the brief sight of his fangs when he spoke. She wanted to climax with those fangs staking a claim, just the way he'd done to her in Landon's cabin.

"Because I didn't want to care for a vampire. I—I

didn't want to fall for a man who would throw me away so easily—"

He didn't let her finish. Instead he kissed her hard, with a fierceness that surprised her…as if he were trying to absorb every part of her heart, body and soul.

Jachin spoke in her mind as he kissed her jaw and then her neck. *I couldn't let him have you. No matter my duty to my people. It felt wrong on so many levels. You're mine!*

When he moved his lips to her neck and she felt the sharp points of his fangs gliding along her skin, Ariel's pulse skittered while her heart swelled. He'd finally admitted what she already knew—he'd come to care for her. She tugged his jeans down, so ready to join with him that her body ached.

Jachin gripped her hips and lifted her body against his. Ariel clutched his shoulders, and her heart thudded out of control as he slid the head of his erection inside her. His cock was so much larger than his fingers, but the tight fit only made her moan more. She gyrated her hips, wanting to take all of him at once.

Setting her back against the door, Jachin plunged deep inside her, filling her completely as his voice whispered in her mind, *I want to be the only man to make you scream.*

Ariel let out a keening cry at the glorious sensation of her body stretching to accommodate his girth and deep penetration. "You're well on your way," she responded with a half-hysterical laugh.

He buried his nose against her throat as he withdrew and thrust hard, slamming her against the door again and again.

Tight coils of intense pleasure flooded through her sex, making her even wetter. His teeth grazed her neck several times, but he never bit her, even though she felt the warm air exhaling from his nose in heavy puffs.

She wanted to feel his teeth sliding inside her body. Ariel shuddered as she felt her climax approaching with each of his aggressive thrusts.

She speared her fingers in his hair and used her hold to press his mouth against her neck, telling him what she wanted.

Jachin slowed his hard thrusts to one last deep penetration until he stayed buried completely. His fangs clamped on her throat, pinning her still.

The sharp pinpoints made her insides quake in rippling desire. Ariel's body hummed with the need for release. He was rock-hard inside her.

"Bite me," she rasped, clutching her legs even tighter around his waist.

Beg.

She gripped his hair and demanded in tiny huffs, "Bite me!"

Jachin's negative response was a low growl in his throat. He pressed his body fully against her, applying pressure to her sensitive nub.

Ariel's breathing turned rampant and her body began to shake. Her heart melted when she realized he was holding back for her, giving her exactly what she'd asked for. "I want to feel your fangs deep inside me. Make me scream, damn it!"

His fangs sank deep at the same time he rolled his hips against her body.

Ariel's vision blurred at the sheer combination of pleasure and ecstasy he caused. She didn't even feel pain. Instead she screamed and gripped him close, sobbing in satisfaction as wave after wave of erotic shudders rippled through her core, splintering along her body in a shock wave of indescribable bliss. She clenched her body tight, moving with him to absorb every single thrust of his aggressive possession.

When he groaned against her neck and kept drinking as if he savored every drop, she knew in her heart that at least to the only vampire who mattered, she wasn't poison.

Digging her nails into his tattered T-shirt, she rode the sensations as long and as hard as she could until her body quit moving out of complete exhaustion.

Jachin was in a fog of sheer lust and gluttony. He'd never tasted blood as rich and sweet as Ariel's or felt so sexually satiated. He was so bewitched he could drown in her blood, her flavor, her alluring smell, and die a happy man.

Ariel's muffled voice entered his mind. "Jachin?" *Why does she sound so far away?* he wondered as he swallowed with fervor once more.

Something landed on his shoulder, like an annoying fly. He grunted and shrugged the insect away. But it persisted, trying to draw him out of his euphoric state. A haze of irritated anger flashed before his eyes so primal he saw nothing but black.

"Jach…in." Ariel sounded even farther away, her voice strangled and weak.

The change in her tone knocked him out of the high he'd fallen into. Jachin squeezed his eyes shut in order to focus, to pull himself back. The sensation of Ariel's body going limp in his arms made his eyes snap open. His heart jerked and his gut clenched as he withdrew his fangs and quickly laved at her wounds to close them. Carrying her over to the bed, he gently laid her down on it. He cupped her pale face, alarm and fear rushing through him.

She gave him a wan smile. "For a few seconds I actually saw stars."

When her eyes fluttered closed, Jachin set his jaw and touched the pulse on her neck. Its slow, sluggish thump sent his own pulse thundering in his ears. He'd never felt more alive or stronger than he did at this moment. With that realization, swift, gut-wrenching guilt knotted his stomach. *Selfish bastard. You failed to keep a lid on your thirst and now you've taken too much blood from the woman who would help save your clan.*

His heart swelled as he gazed down at Ariel's face. She was the human the prophecy spoke of. He admired and respected her more than life itself. If she died due to his reckless feeding, he'd walk right into the sunlight. It would be a fitting punishment for the monster he was…and would always be.

He sat on the bed, his jeans around his ankles, and gathered her lifeless body in his arms. His eyes stung with tears as he ran his nose through her hair. "I'm so sorry I couldn't control my bloodthirsty instincts, Ariel. I don't expect you to forgive me. I'll never forgive myself."

"You'd better…" She sounded tired but gave him a smile. "If we ever get out of here, I'll be demanding an encore performance."

Jachin clenched his teeth and looked away, shaking his head. "No."

She cupped his jaw and applied pressure until his eyes met hers once more. "You snapped out of it as soon as you heard my voice. Your heart has more capacity than you give yourself credit for."

Her eyes widened as she stared at him, searching his entire frame in wonder. "It's amazing. The wounds on your face and chest are already healed. Even the old scar on your neck—it's gone."

"I was happy to finally let that bastard's scar heal."

Realization dawned on her face. "Did Braeden give you that scar?"

He nodded. "The day he banished me."

"Is that why you didn't want me to heal it—because you thought you deserved it?"

"Yes." Jachin's tortured gaze swept over her. "You've given me everything, and here you lay, weak and drained."

"I kind of like the idea you were so out of it you couldn't think straight while you took my blood." A hint of a smirk crossed her face. "It was like you couldn't get enough of me—hey, I guess that makes me your drug of choice, you junkie."

Jachin frowned at her attempt at levity. "I could've killed you, Ariel." He ran a frustrated hand through his hair. "Damn it! I can't trust myself around you."

"Yes, you can, because you're an honorable man."

Jachin's gaze locked with hers. "You've been a complete surprise to me in so many ways."

"Do you mean because I'm a weak human?" she asked, raising her eyebrow.

"No, in spite that fact. You taught me that strength and humanity are a state of mind."

Her lips tilted upward. "That's okay. I still think you're stubborn, arrogant and hard-nosed, vampire."

"Your compliments really get me right here," he said in a dry tone, tapping his heart. When her smile broadened, relief swept through him. She was going to be okay.

Silence descended between them and Jachin lowered his forehead to hers. They sat there holding each other for several minutes. Neither of them seemed to want to break the peace-filled moment between them.

After a few minutes, a scraping sound came from the window. Jachin frowned and laid Ariel back on the bed before he stood and pulled up his pants. Buttoning his jeans, he walked over to investigate.

A scrolled piece of paper lay against the inside curve of the stone.

His heart raced as he withdrew the scroll and pulled off the ribbon holding it closed. A small key dangled from the ribbon while he read the note.

If you've killed Ariel, I hope the sunlight crisps you before her poisoned blood gets to you. If you've managed to stave off your hunger so far, I've included a key to a dumbwaiter we never use. It's at the end of the hall, past the last dungeon chamber. You'll have to figure out how to get out of the chamber on your own. There are two guards posted at the bottom of the stairs at the opposite end of the hall. I'll be waiting. Luck, brother.

Jachin took a deep breath, his lungs filling with air as elation rushed through him. He owed his little sister for this one. Once he'd untied the key from the ribbon, Jachin slid it in his jeans' pocket and turned to Ariel.

She sat up on her elbow and glanced from the note to him, her expression expectant. "What is that?"

"Mira has given us a way out. We'll still have to figure out how to get out of this room. Are you up to helping me?"

Ariel's eyebrow rose. "Do you promise never to hold back with me?"

Jachin set his jaw at her request. He knew she was referring to his vow never to take her blood again. Despite her faith in him, short of being knocked unconscious, he sure as hell didn't trust himself to stop the next time his fangs sank into her sweet skin, especially during sex. The combination was addictive beyond words. "I promise never to be dull."

She frowned. "That's not what I asked."

"It's the best answer you'll get," he countered, scowling at her.

"My powers of persuasion are greater than you give me credit for," she said with a confident smile and stood up.

When she swayed a little, Jachin was by her side in a millisecond, steadying her. "You rest and I'll figure out how to get the guards to open the door."

Her gaze narrowed on him. "Your lack of confidence in me is insulting." Stepping away from his steadying hand, she tilted her chin up and squared her shoulders. "What do you need me to do?"

He rubbed his jaw for a couple of seconds, then met her gaze. "Do you think you can convince the guards to unlock the door?"

Ariel glanced down at the swell of her breasts and cleavage exposed by the gaping jacket. She gave him a siren's smile as she pulled him toward her. "I need you to bite me again—and this time don't close my wound."

He balled his hands into fists. "Hell, no!"

She tilted her head, exposing her neck. "Bite me."

His fangs descended despite his mental resistance. Jachin's fingers dug into her skin. The need to take what she offered burned in his throat.

His entire body tensed, his cock filling instantly as her fingers slowly slid up his thigh. Even through his jeans her tantalizing touch set him on fire.

"Bite me, Jachin."

When her hand suddenly cupped his package in an aggressive hold, Jachin's hips jerked forward as if his body had a mind of its own. He bit back the groan of pleasure that rumbled up his chest even as he lowered his mouth to her sweet skin.

Jachin kissed the column of her throat, marveling at her complete trust in him. When he slid his tongue up her throat and she moaned, her fingers curling tighter around him, he braced himself and plunged his fangs deep.

Ariel gasped and her body tensed in his arms...and all he could think was, *Sweet hell, I'll never get enough of her blood!* But he tightened his chest and forced himself to slowly withdraw his fangs so he wouldn't hurt her.

When he pulled back, Ariel's languorous gaze locked with his. "Was it good for you?"

Her witty comment made him grit his teeth and step away from her hold before he could follow his desires and throw her on the bed. "Call the guards," he said in a curt tone. "I'll pretend to be dead."

"I need to see Braeden. Now!" Ariel yelled and hammered on the door with as much gusto as she could muster.

Thirty seconds later, the small three-inch square of wood in the middle of the heavy wooden door slid open. A man's dark eyes narrowed. "What do you need to see Braeden about?"

Ariel's heart raced as she stepped back and pointed to Jachin's limp frame crumpled on the stone floor. "He passed out a few minutes after he swallowed my blood."

Keep those beautiful breasts covered, Jachin spoke in a possessive tone in her mind.

Ariel coughed at his audacity considering their dire circumstances. When she returned her beseeching gaze to the guard's, the man's eyes were fixated on the trickle of blood that ran down between her cleavage. "I have something to tell Braeden about the Garotters. I need to see him."

The vampire turned and spoke to someone. "Trace. Jachin's poisoned. The human says she has something to tell Braeden about the vampire hunters. Come and stand guard while I open the door." The guard slid the little door shut at the same time boots shuffled across the stone floor toward her door.

"Move away from the door," the guard ordered.

Jachin jumped up at the sound of the key scraping in the lock.

When he quickly levitated and lay in a horizontal position directly over the door, Ariel's heart thumped in surprise. She had to force a composed look on her face as the door opened. Cool air rushed in, displacing the body warmth she and Jachin must've created in the small room.

The guard walked in, gun held at the ready. When he saw Jachin was missing, he only got out the word "Shit!" before Jachin fell on top of him.

Ariel's breath caught at the sight of the other guard lifting his gun. She started to warn Jachin, but he must've sensed the danger.

Jumping up, Jachin grabbed the guard underneath him and tossed the man into the hall. The guard's flying body slammed into the other guard, knocking both men against the wall outside the door. Grunts of pain and the sound of shoes scraping against the stone made her chest constrict. Ariel bit her lip, hoping no one had heard the scuffle.

Before the guards could recover, Jachin rushed forward. He gripped the men by their necks and held them off the ground, squeezing hard. "Drop your guns."

The sound of the guards wheezing for breath, punctuated by the clatter of their weapons hitting the stone floor, made her heart pump at a frantic pace.

Don't kill them, she thought right before Jachin clunked the men's heads together like two cartoon characters. The impact knocked both men out instantly.

After the guards' bodies dropped to the floor, he grabbed one of the automatic rifles and said, "Let's go. We have maybe ten minutes before they come to."

Ariel stepped over the guards, her slippers making no sound on the stone floor. She couldn't help but stare at their necks that were turned at strange angles. "Are you sure they aren't dead?"

"They'll have headaches from hell, but they'll survive," Jachin said in a gruff tone before he grabbed her hand and pulled her down the hall behind him.

Jachin's shoes made quiet shuffling sounds as they approached a three-by-three-foot-square hip-high wooden panel at the end of the hall. He pulled a key from his pocket and inserted it into the lock at the bottom. When he lifted the door, Ariel's eyebrows rose at the thick ropes in front of a dumbwaiter.

"We'll have to go one at a time. Get in. Once you're out, Mira can help you lift me up."

Ariel took a deep breath and climbed into the tight, enclosed space. Bent over with her cheek crammed against her knees, her pulse thudded in her ears as she met Jachin's gaze.

"You're smaller—take this." He started to hand her the weapon, but the gun knocked against the outer edges, obviously too long to fit in the small space with her. "Guess we're leaving this behind," he said with regret and set the gun against the stone wall.

He gave her a reassuring nod and grabbed hold of the rope pulley in front of the dumbwaiter, ready to lift her up.

"Hurry!" she said, her stomach knotting at having to leave him.

"I'll be right behind you," he said as he began to tug on the rope.

Ariel's apprehension hitched with each jerk of the pulley. What if Mira wasn't there when she reached the top? Her blood might've restored Jachin's powers, maybe even boosted them some if the speed with which he'd taken out those vampire guards was any indication, but Jachin couldn't fight a hundred vampires.

She let out a breath of relief when Mira's beautiful blue gaze stared at her as Jachin made the final tug on the pulley. Ariel quickly scrambled out of the dumbwaiter and stepped into what appeared to be a deserted kitchen. Without a word, she turned to help Mira lower the dumbwaiter back down to Jachin's dungeon level.

As they began to pull Jachin up, Mira spoke. "I'm so glad you're well, Ariel."

"What happened to that unflappable faith in your brother?" Ariel put her hands above Mira's and tugged.

Mira glanced at the blood drying on Ariel's exposed chest and the wound on the side of her neck. "I see my concerns weren't unfounded."

Ariel met her gaze, needing Mira to understand. "He took my blood, Mira, a lot of it. He was right about me."

"I was also right about the fact she *is* the Sanguina leader's mate."

They both stared at Jachin in shock as they made the final tug to get the dumbwaiter to the right level.

"I can't believe after we've…" Ariel stuttered, her heart breaking at his statement. He wanted her to be with Braeden after everything they'd shared?

Jachin stepped down and gripped her waist, pulling her close. Once he ran his tongue across her wound to seal it, he met her confused gaze. "The prophecy hasn't changed. The difference is, *I'm* going to be the Sanguinas leader."

"Her blood has made you insane," Mira whispered. As she pushed a messenger-style bag hanging on her shoulder behind her back, her blue eyes darted between Jachin and Ariel.

Jachin's gaze narrowed. "Ariel's blood is untainted. Braeden knows this."

Ariel gasped at his comment. "What do you mean he knows?"

Jachin nodded. "When he was alone with me in the dungeon, he admitted your blood tasted different. He gloated about how he'd never believed in the prophecy. Basically...he always saw me as a threat. Even Vivian was a setup. Braeden didn't want me around, messing up his domain. He enjoyed telling me that my banishment was planned right before he left me in the dungeon."

Mira's garbled low scream drew his attention. His sister held a shaking hand against her mouth for several seconds, then her gaze narrowed in fury. "I'm going to kill the deceitful bastard."

Jachin pulled her close and hugged her tight. "Not if I get to him first. Thank you for helping us. I know you were angry with me for leaving you."

Mira hugged him back, then met his gaze. "Your leaving forced me to grow up. Now I get to ask the tough question—how do you plan on convincing a hundred vampires you're the Sanguinas' new leader?"

Jachin stepped away and met both women's curious stares with a resolute look. "The same way each Sanguina leader has taken his position in the past."

Mira's eyes went wide. "It's a direct-descendent position. I've always assumed the ceremony was just for show." She shook her head. "I risked everything to save you. You and Ariel need to leave while you still can."

"And I'll risk everything to save our people from a self-serving leader like Braeden."

"Going back to our old land will be suicide!" his sister argued.

Hearing the word *suicide* inserted in the heated conversation made Ariel's stomach pitch. "Where are we going?"

His intense blue-black gaze met hers. "To the heart of what is now Lupreda territory."

Chapter 13

"If you insist on this insanity, let's go," Mira said finally, turning away.

They followed the younger vampire down a back hall off the kitchen and through a door that led to the outside. Mira continued forward, heading toward the woods. Jachin paused and cast a curious gaze his sister's way. She must've sensed his hesitation, because she turned and beckoned them to follow, whispering, "Trust me," right before she disappeared into the moonlit woods.

"I took your blood. You're going to be weak for a bit," Jachin said before he lifted Ariel up on his shoulder.

Ariel landed with a tiny "oomph!" "I see *nothing* has changed," she mumbled as he began to run at his vampire's rapid pace after his sister. But she quickly found a benefit she hadn't considered in that Jachin's body heat seeped into her skin, warming her considerably against the cool night air.

Trees rushed by in a blur of pine scents and dark, eerie shapes. All of a sudden Jachin came to a halt and set Ariel down as Mira stood in front of a mountain wall.

In the dim night shadows, lit only by the moon's light, Ariel watched in complete fascination as the female vampire moved her hand in front of her. A huge rock that jutted out from the tall mountainside wall began to move sideways until an opening was revealed.

"I never knew this was here." Jachin glanced at his sister, surprise reflected in his gaze.

Mira disappeared into the dark entrance and popped her head back out to wave them inside with her. After Ariel and Jachin followed her through the opening, she moved her hand in front of the wall again and the rock scraped back into place, cutting the moonlight off completely.

After a few minutes of walking in the dark, they paused, and there was another scraping sound as if a rock wall was moving out of the way. As they continued forward and the rock-scraping sound occurred behind them, Jachin said, "I recognize this part. You've used the same mine, just via another offshoot. Does anyone else know about this other access to the Sanguinas manor?"

"No," she called behind her in a low voice. "With our home surrounded on all sides by tall mountains, I find it…confining at times. I needed to be able to get away for a while."

"Where do you go?" he asked.

"To the edge of the old land," she responded. "I miss the open expanse of it all."

Jachin gripped Ariel's shoulder and tugged to let her know he was making a sharp right turn. She felt so out of sorts not being able to see. Her stomach was a ball of knots, and despite her trust in Jachin to keep her safe, she still put her hand out to protect her head from any rocky surprises.

"It sounds like you put your own safety at risk as well as the other Sanguinas'. If the Lupreda had discovered you, they could've followed your fresh tracks back to our home," Jachin said with a bit of censure in his tone.

Mira's footsteps stopped and her voice sounded more direct, as if she were looking right at them. "I'm not a child, Jachin. I've been very careful."

Jachin took a few more steps and stopped, too. "I want to know why you felt the need to leave so often. You've always loved everything about the Sanguinas in the past. What's wrong?"

"Things aren't the same. Vlad…" Mira paused then let out a heavy sigh. "Like I said, I had to take responsibility for myself."

Ariel felt Jachin's rage well inside him with the tightening of his arm around her. "Did Vlad touch you without your permission?" he snarled.

Mira's exotic scent invaded Ariel's senses and her voice sounded closer. "Vlad thought he could stake his claim. After the initial shock wore off, I've kept him at bay ever since."

"Tell me the council punished him for his actions," Jachin demanded in a low, deadly tone.

"Our numbers are dwindling," Mira responded calmly. "None of the women have been able to get pregnant in five years."

Jachin's anger radiated from him in his stiff stance and tight tone. "I'm going to shred the rapist sonofabitch!" Ariel felt Jachin's movement as he pulled his sister close with his free arm. "I wish I'd been here for you."

Mira made a tsking sound, and Ariel felt Jachin move back slightly as if he'd been pushed. "Let's get you out of here in one piece. Survival first, revenge later."

Ariel and Jachin followed his sister's lead for a few more minutes until they heard her stop walking. The sound of rocks rubbing against rocks grated in Ariel's ears, and dim moonlight began to filter into the dark recesses as another wall opened.

Mira ducked underneath the wood planks to the outside and Jachin and Ariel followed. Outside the mine, Mira stood on her toes and hugged her brother tight for a few seconds before she stepped back and lifted the messenger bag off her shoulders.

She began to pull a set of new clothes for them out of the pack. "Put these on and give me your bloodied ones. You'll have to backtrack a little to lose them." Pointing toward the east, she said, "You go that way. I'll head south."

Jachin and Ariel quickly changed into jeans and T-shirts. As Ariel stepped back into her slipper shoes, Mira handed her a cable-knit sweater, saying with a half smile, "I couldn't find better shoes your size, but this should help keep you warm."

"Mira, I—" Jachin began to say as his sister gathered their clothes and shoved them in the messenger bag.

Mira pulled an automatic handgun from a pocket in the messenger bag and put it in his palm, interrupting him. "You know this can only do so much damage. Now go, run like hell. I can only hold them off for so long with your clothes as scent decoys." She sniffed back tears. "It's good to see you again after all this time. Be safe, brother."

Jachin tucked the gun in his jeans' waistline at his back, then pulled his sister close once more. Releasing her, he promised, "We'll make it right," before he grabbed Ariel's hand. "Let's go. We have a helluva hike ahead of us."

Ariel's heart raced as she ran behind Jachin in the woods. Thankfully they were heading down the mountain, which helped her keep up with Jachin's rapid movements. She knew he was going slower than he would have if she wasn't with him, but she refused to tell him how tired she felt. Their lives depended on them getting far away from the Sanguinas hunting them.

Trees and scents of pine and rich earth sped past. She followed Jachin's steps over logs, rocks and hidden tree roots to make sure she avoided unseen obstacles in the darkened woods. *Man, it would be nice to have night vision,* she thought as her lungs began to burn with the need for more oxygen.

After a few minutes, Jachin slowed and finally stopped.

"Why are we stopping?" She was barely able to get out the question, her need for air was so great.

Jachin hitched his foot on a knot jutting from a thick oak tree and then began to climb up its branches. Ariel craned her neck to watch him climb higher and higher. "What are you do—" she started to ask, until she saw him tug something out from between two branches. Trusting he had a reason for this delay, she began to take deep, calming breaths so her racing pulse would steady out.

Jachin dropped to the ground with a heavy thump, set

his backpack at his feet and quickly unzipped a small front pocket.

How the hell did his backpack get here? she wondered.

As he pulled a cell phone from the tight pocket, she thought she saw something fall to the ground. While Jachin dialed a number, she bent down to retrieve whatever he'd dropped. The moonlight filtered through the trees, reflecting on the shiny metal lying among the leaves.

Ariel picked up the thin circle of silver and instantly recognized the broken clover perched inside the bottom curve of the hoop. "There you are." She clasped her hoop earring in her hand and quickly stood to listen as Jachin spoke into the phone.

"It's me." He paused and listened for a second. "You can blame your pack mates for the condition of your home. I left them breathing, didn't I?"

It was Landon, Ariel realized as Jachin continued. "I need your help. I'm heading to the circle."

"Are you on lukin weed?" Landon's furious voice shouted through the phone, echoing around them.

"Shut the hell up and listen," Jachin gritted out. "I want to take over the clan, to lead my people and fulfill the prophecy, but I need safe passage into Lupreda territory."

Landon's voice rumbled across the line. Jachin's lips thinned. "Got it. Did you learn anything about the Garotters?"

A few seconds later Jachin closed the cell phone. Ariel tensed in anticipation. "Did Landon agree to help?"

Jachin met her gaze, his expression serious. "Landon was on his way to Lupreda land when I called, but two very pissed off pack members are already back home, raising a stink, cursing all Sanguinas. He doesn't know if he'll get there in time to help us…or even if he can."

She didn't like that answer. "What about the Garotters? Did he learn anything?"

Jachin shook his head. "The men he saved disappeared from the hospital before he had a chance to talk with them."

When he slid his cell phone into his pocket, she glanced at his backpack and then up in the tree and asked the question that had been nagging her since he'd stopped to retrieve the bag. "How did your backpack get up there?"

A muscle in Jachin's jaw tensed and relaxed several times. The nonverbal clue told her she wasn't going to like his answer.

His steady gaze met hers. "I planted it here in the event I wasn't welcomed back into the clan, in case things went wrong. If the Sanguinas decided to hunt me down, I knew my best chance to shake them would be to go through Lupreda territory."

Even though she knew what had played out, knew that the man cared for her on some level, she couldn't help the fact his answer made her chest ache as if she'd been hit by a baseball bat. "And what about me? You really *had* planned to leave me behind?"

Jachin gripped her arms in a tight hold, his intense gaze searching hers. "Don't do this, Ariel! I've been burying my feelings for you from the moment I first kissed you in the woods. To have to stand there and watch Braeden touch you made my stomach burn in raging jealousy." His fangs unsheathed and his hands cinched harder around her muscles as he continued, speaking in her mind. *Even before I discovered his treachery, I wanted to kill him because of you. I'm a survivor. Having a contingency plan is what I've been programmed to do. Don't condemn me for that.*

Despite the heavy feeling in her chest, Ariel looked past the anger in his gaze to the vulnerability simmering just beneath the surface and tried to see the situation from Jachin's point of view. If she had cared for the person who she believed was destined to play a role in helping her people, would she have been as selfless? Would she have walked away? Her heart ached for the sacrifice he'd been prepared to pay.

Nodding her head in understanding, she spoke in a firm tone, "There's a reason I described the Sanguinas manor as it stands, as well as your prophecy word for word in my novel. I'm meant to be involved somehow."

Jachin pulled her close and kissed her brow. His hold tightened around her shoulders. "You're the toughest adversary I've ever faced."

His roughly spoken words, underlined with emotion, warmed her heart. Ariel squeezed his waist and kissed his jaw. "Never forget it. Now let's go. We've wasted enough time."

She started to walk away but stopped when she realized Jachin hadn't followed. When she turned, she saw him holding his backpack, digging into the same pocket he'd retrieved the cell phone from.

"What is it?" she asked, curious at the look of determination on his face while he turned the bag upside down and shook it hard.

Jachin briefly glanced at her. "Just a sec." He dug into

the pocket once more before he growled in frustration and dropped the backpack on the ground.

"What were you looking for?" she asked as he approached her, frown lines creasing his brow.

Jachin clasped her hand and murmured, "Just something I wanted to keep. We'd better get going."

When he avoided meeting her gaze, Ariel's heart skipped a beat. Had he been looking for her earring?

His fingers started to loosen around hers, and she knew that signal meant he was getting ready to release her hand and take off running. She tightened her grip, needing to know. "Is this what you were looking for?" she asked, opening her other hand to show him the earring.

Jachin picked up the hoop and rubbed his thumb where the clover's fourth leaf should've been. "Call me superstitious," he said in a gruff tone as he slid the piece of jewelry into his front pocket.

Her heart melted, turning to putty at the realization he'd stowed away a little part of her in his "contingency plan."

As he took off running at a faster-than-normal pace, she followed, calling out with a knowing laugh, "I think you're pretty special, too."

After they'd traveled the rest of the way down the mountain and the woods had finally started to flatten out, Ariel's running slowed to a fast walk. Her lungs burned and her head felt full of stuffing.

Jachin ran up to her and grabbed her arm, forcing her to stop. "You need to tell me when you need a break."

She swallowed and kept her breathing shallow, trying to hide how tired she was. "I'm fine. Let's go."

His penetrating gaze searched hers. "I hear your heart racing. You've lost blood, and if you don't take it easy, you'll collapse. I can't lose you."

She finally took several deep breaths, thankful for the brief reprieve. "I know this is important. I don't want to slow you down."

Jachin pulled her close and buried his nose against her neck for several seconds. Kissing her jaw, he met her gaze. "You've given so much. I don't want anything to happen to you."

Ariel placed her hand on his stubbled jaw and met his intense gaze. "The situation with your race is bleak. A family member of mine had a hand in that…at least initially. I want to help if I can."

A grim look crossed his features. "My people have been led down a path of hopelessness. I'm going to do my best to bring them back to the ideals my father tried to instill in them before his death."

Realization suddenly dawned, and Jachin's quest, his refusal to give up finally made perfect sense. "Ezra—the man who spoke the prophecy. He was your father, wasn't he?"

Jachin nodded. "I believed my father would've helped direct and guide the future of our people. His death devastated me. I felt the need to pick up the mantle, to carry on his beliefs and ideals. To give our people hope."

"And what of your mother?"

A sad expression crossed his face. "She perished in the first wave of the sickness."

Just as she had lost her family, Jachin had also endured so much. Her heart ached for him. "Then we'll both do what we can to make it right."

His grip tightened around her and the look of appreciation in his eyes made her heart swell. "I've waited for this all my life. I'm not going to give up. We'll be victorious."

His declaration bloomed in her heart, giving her a second wind.

Ariel kissed him on his jaw. "I'm okay to go forward now."

Jachin pulled back and gripped her hands. He glanced at the sky through the thick trees overhead. "We have a little over an hour before the sun rises."

"How much farther to Lupreda territory?" she asked in a hushed voice.

"Another fifteen minutes. When we get there, we need to get to the sacrificial grounds as quickly as possible."

Ariel's heart jerked at his comment. "Sacrificial grounds?"

His lips thinned. "There are things the Sanguinas have done in our past that you won't approve of."

Ariel gripped his fingers tight. "Tell me. I need to know what I'm walking into."

His gaze searched hers for a couple seconds before he spoke. "I told you the Lupreda were bred for hunting. What I didn't mention was what happened once they were caught. We used to perform sacrificial ceremonies, kind of a celebration of a successful hunt…and a kill."

Her heart lurched. "Are you saying that the Lupredas who were caught were killed as part of a sacrificial ceremony?"

When Jachin nodded, her throat constricted. No wonder the Lupreda hated the Sanguinas so much. "Are you insane? If we go there, we'll be the ones sacrificed!"

Jachin's jaw clenched. "I'm well aware of the risks, but this is also the same place where the Sanguinas leader takes his rightful position. There's a pedestal right next to the sacrificial slab called the ascendancy chalice. The way the ceremony worked, the next leader-to-be put his hand on the ascendancy chalice, and his blood would cause the flat stone across the surface of the pedestal to lower into a cone shape, draining his blood into the center of the chalice. In the past, only those in Braeden's lineage have been able to move the stone."

"How do you expect Landon to help you get anywhere near this chalice?" Her chest burned at this incredibly risky plan. "Is he the Lupredas' leader?"

Jachin shook his head. "No, he's kind of an outcast."

Disbelief made her light-headed. "Then what makes you think the Lupreda will listen to him, especially after you just kicked two of the werewolves' butts? They'll tear you—us—to shreds."

Jachin shook his head. "I don't know if they will or not. But for the Sanguinas' survival, all I can do is try."

The risk outweighed the possibility of success. She shook her head, fear rising in her belly like a swelling river ready to overflow. "Jachin, Mira's right. It's suicide."

He tugged his hands from her hold and cupped her face, his serious gaze searching hers. "Your blood healed me, Ariel. Do you realize the significance of that? You *fulfilled* part of the prophecy. And now it's my turn to carry out the rest. I believe I was meant to be the Sanguinas leader, to lead them on the right path. If there is any hope of taking over that role, there's only one way I can prove that to my people. Do you understand?"

"That means you'll have to perform this 'miracle' in your people's presence, without being killed by vengeful Lupreda or outraged Sanguinas first," she said, her voice rising.

He nodded. Yet the look of sheer determination in his

gaze, and his willingness to risk his life to gain his people's trust were attributes a true leader needed to possess in order to change the course of the Sanguinas' future.

She placed her hands around his wrists, accepting his dedication as her own. If anyone could beat the over-whelming odds against them, she had every faith her vampire could. "I'll be with you every step of the way."

He hauled her against his chest and hugged her tight, his voice husky and thick with emotion when he said, "Thank you for believing in me."

When they got closer to the sacrificial land, Jachin knew he was running out of time. He didn't even break his stride as he yanked Ariel's hand and grabbed her waist.

As she landed on his shoulder, she gritted out, "When this is over, if you ever toss me on your shoulder like this again, I'll shoot you. Got it?"

Amidst the danger closing in around them, Ariel kept him grounded and whole. Jachin held her tight and broke into the speed his vampire body was engineered to endure.

His heart raced as he entered the ceremonial area. Stone gargoyles surrounded the cleared-out circular arena. At the far edge of the fifty-foot circle there was a flat rectangular slab supported by a slightly smaller thick rectangular stone riser underneath it. Behind the plate stood a pedestal with a smooth granitelike surface and a crude gray stone as the supporting column—the chalice.

Lupreda were closing in fast. A quick scan told him Landon wasn't among the angry men bearing down on them. They had to reach the chalice before anyone else.

Damn it to hell! He just needed a few minutes.

At that moment, a loud boom sounded—an explosion.

"I don't like this kind of déjà vu!" Ariel screamed, her voice frantic as a gunshot zinged past them.

Jachin was still a good thirty feet away from the chalice. He flexed his thigh muscles and leapt in the air with every ounce of strength in his body as the Lupreda and the Sanguinas raced toward them, Braeden heading up the clan.

He landed with a heavy thud behind the stone chalice and quickly swiveled to face both his brethren as well as the angry were who'd converged in the circular arena. Both groups of men stopped and stared at him in momentary shock. He knew what they were all thinking: only a vampire with a belly full of untainted human blood could've performed that feat.

A thick-boned blond Lupreda yelled out, "You're trespassing. Get the hell off my land!"

"Your land? This land is Sanguinas' property. You're the trespassers!" Braeden sneered. "Get Jachin," he ordered his men right before he launched his body in the air toward the male werewolf who'd dared to challenge him.

When several Sanguinas started in Jachin's direction, the Lupredas weren't about to let a vampire attack one of their own without fighting back. As one, the Lupreda engaged the Sanguinas in an all-out hand-to-hand battle. In the midst of sounds of claws ripping flesh and sinew, cries of pain and snarls of fury, Ariel began to squirm on Jachin's shoulder.

"Put me down so you can do what you need to do."

Setting her feet on the ground, he took a deep breath and stepped up on the stone square that jutted out from the pedestal's base. Jachin cut a slit in his wrist with an elongated fingernail, then placed his hand in the carved hand-shaped indention on the pedestal's flat charcoal-gray stone surface.

A couple of Sanguinas broke free from the fray and rushed toward the sacrificial plate.

Jachin's gut tensed.

He reached to the base of his spine and gripped the gun's handle, ready to pull it from its tucked position in his pants.

Two Lupreda beat him to the punch. They attacked the approaching Sanguinas with a vengeance.

One werewolf tossed the first vampire through the air, literally throwing him back into the fight, while the other were grabbed the second vampire by the neck and wrestled him to the ground.

Jachin relaxed his grip and released his hold on the hidden gun. His heart raced, making blood pump faster from his wound. The red liquid seeped quickly into the carved-out circular path that split off the base of the "hand" and curved into the continuous circular groove that continued its spiral pattern for twenty bands around the hand imprint.

When his blood filled all twenty grooves until they began to overflow, sweat beaded Jachin's brow. His insides rocked, threatening to explode from his chest. *Come on,* he mentally willed the stone grooved surface to descend. *Move, damn you! Prove I'm the next San-guinas leader.*

"What's wrong?" Ariel whispered, her tone tense.

"It's not moving." At the same time he spoke, the sac-rificial plate a few feet away from the chalice shook as the blond were who'd challenged Braeden earlier landed on it. He snarled and crouched low, his throat and white button-down shirt shredded and bloodied, his ripped flesh oozing.

"I'm alpha of the Lupreda pack." The man's eyes blazed, ready for a fight as he balled his hands into fists. "I'm going to enjoy laying you out and splitting you open on this plate," he continued in a savage tone right before he leapt toward Jachin.

As the Lupreda flew through the air toward him, Jachin pulled out the gun he'd tucked in his pants waistline. Rage bloomed in his chest while he thumbed back the hammer, ready to empty the entire clip into the were. Before his finger fully pinched the trigger, a blur sped past, knocking the alpha to the ground.

Landon, his lip bleeding and his left eye swollen shut, wrestled the alpha were onto his back. Lodging his elbow into the man's throat, Landon pinned him to the ground and growled, "Let him try, Nathan!"

All the fighting and yelling, snarls and growls faded into the background when Ariel put her hand on Jachin's arm, drawing his attention. "I have an idea. Do you trust me?"

Jachin nodded, tension making his chest ache and his stomach knot.

She held up her wrist and her gaze locked with his. "Bite me."

He shook his head. "I don't understand."

"Just do it!" she demanded and pushed her right wrist under his nose.

Her sweet feminine smell invaded his senses. He didn't have to make his fangs extend. The sharp points exploded from his gums on their own in recognition of the offer in front of him.

Leaning toward her wrist, he plunged his fangs deep. It took all his willpower to withdraw his fangs without taking her blood, but he managed.

Barely.

Ariel moved in front of him. Placing her feet on top of his, she laid her right hand over his in the chalice's hand imprint. She gripped her right forearm with her left hand and squeezed tight.

Jachin realized her intent when her action caused her blood to rush out of her vein and down across his hand. As her blood entwined with his, mixing along the carved-out circular trail surrounding the palm imprint, the stone circle maze began to shift, elongating, deepening.

The stone moving, creating a cylindrical cone out of the circular maze, caused their combined blood to follow the path down inside the pedestal. Jachin's heart raced and hope swelled within his chest.

When the pedestal began to glow, every man stopped fighting and stared at Jachin and Ariel standing at the chalice.

Another ear-popping explosion ricocheted in the forest right before tremendous pain slammed into Jachin. He locked his body, tensing his muscles and baring his fangs as the gunshot wound burned in his shoulder.

Jachin jerked his narrowed gaze toward the crowd to see Braeden holding a gun, fury etched in his bleeding face. Without a moment's hesitation Jachin aimed and pulled the trigger of his own weapon.

Braeden turned at the last second, taking Jachin's bullet in his arm. Growling his outrage, Braeden started to raise his gun again when one of the Sanguinas knocked him back and wrestled the gun from his hand.

Jachin tucked his weapon away, pent-up tension releasing from his shoulders. He'd have to thank Saul for the vampire's swift intervention. If all went well, Braeden would be judged for his many crimes against the clan when they got back to Sanguinas manor.

When the cone reached its final destination, descending deep inside the pedestal, the whole chalice began to hum and light up, glowing a bright white color.

Chapter 14

Jachin's eyes stung from the brilliance. He'd never seen the chalice glow before. He wasn't sure it ever had.

The humming's pitch grew higher and higher, winding Jachin's body tight. Just when he thought he couldn't take the noise and the power any longer, a bolt of lightning shot out from the pedestal, striking the sacrificial plate. A sonic boom quickly followed, reverberating throughout the woods. The force sent every single Sanguina and Lupreda standing in the arena slamming to the ground.

A streak of fire veined across the middle of the sacrificial plate right where the lightning had struck. Jachin and Ariel stepped back from the chalice at the same time the thick slab cracked completely in half. As soon as the sacrificial plate's two halves hit the ground, the chalice began to dim and shake until it also split right down the middle, spilling their blood onto the ground.

Awed and a little taken aback by the sight he'd just witnessed, Jachin faced the crowd, conviction in his steady gaze. "I, Jachin Black, as deemed by the ascendancy chalice, take over the Sanguinas as their rightful leader. I promise to lead my people out of the darkness they've fallen into these past twenty-five years."

"You can't take my place!" Braeden shook off Saul's hold, his face contorted with rage. "Only my family line—the Raptours—can lead the Sanguinas."

"Then Jachin has exactly what he needs," Ariel said.

Surprised as hell by Ariel's comment, Jachin glanced at her. Her eyes were glazed over as if she were in some kind of trance.

"Ariel?" he asked right before her eyelids fluttered closed and her knees gave way.

Jachin's heart raced in fear. When he lifted her limp body in his arms, he saw the wound on her chest. The bullet that had hit his shoulder must've gone right through her first. She'd held so still he hadn't known she was even hit.

He faced the crowd of men staring at him and addressed the Sanguinas in an authoritative tone. "We're done here. Leave the Lupredas' land immediately."

Braeden tried to regain control. "Don't listen to his lies!" He pointed to Ariel in Jachin's arms. "Her blood has poisoned him."

"I haven't seen a vampire jump like that since before the sickness," one vampire said.

"He emptied the chalice, Braeden. Accept the truth," another Sanguina joined in.

Jachin narrowed his gaze on Braeden, anger burning in his chest. "Take him into custody to be judged for crimes against his people. I will explain all when we get back to our home."

His gaze swiveled to Landon. "We'll leave your land the way we found it…with the exception of the sacrificial plate that should've been destroyed years ago."

"Agreed," Landon nodded.

Nathan let out a growl and slammed his fist into Landon's side.

As Landon tried to catch his breath, the Alpha stood up and faced Jachin, his fists clenched by his sides. "Only I can speak for the Lupreda."

"Not today," Landon said through gritted teeth as he swiped his booted foot out, cracking Nathan's leg. Nathan went down, howling in pain. Before he could recover, Landon jumped on the man's chest and slammed his fist hard into Nathan's face, knocking him out.

"Go now!" Landon growled at Jachin.

Jachin watched as the Sanguinas left Lupreda land, hauling a fighting, irate Braeden deep into the woods. Once his people were out of harm's way, the tension in his shoulders lessened. He acknowledged his appreciation to Landon with a curt nod.

Landon stood up and his gaze lowered to Ariel's limp body and her blood staining Jachin's arm. "Is she going to be okay?"

Jachin gathered Ariel close and set his jaw to keep his expression neutral and his emotions at bay. "She has to be." He wouldn't accept anything else. He couldn't.

Without a word, he turned his back on an entire pack of werewolves and carried Ariel into the woods.

His body tensed when he heard rumblings of hatred whispered behind him and low growls emitting from the crowd of weres, but Landon's heavy, authoritative bark silenced the men.

Jachin knew he had very little time to get back to the safety of the Sanguinas manor. As soon as he was out of eyesight, he ran a zigzag, confusing path for a while in case some Lupreda tried to track them.

After he felt he'd muddied their scent enough, he took off for home as if the spawns of hell were clawing at his back…and in truth they were. If Ariel didn't survive, he'd have to go on for his people. But his soul would die with her.

As soon as he entered the manor carrying Ariel, the group of Sanguinas waiting for him parted, allowing him space.

"I hear a faint heartbeat. She's not dead."

"She fulfilled the prophecy, helped Jachin claim Braeden's position."

"You should've seen it. The ascendancy chalice and the sacrificial plate cracked…."

Jachin heard the whispers but ignored them all as he turned away and headed down the hall toward Mira's room. He had no doubt that his old rooms had been taken over the very same day he was exiled.

Mira broke through the crowd, running to catch up with her brother. She cast her worried gaze over Ariel's slack, pale features. His sister's concern echoed in his own heart with each step he took. He couldn't lose Ariel. He didn't deserve her, but he needed her.

"You're bleeding," Mira commented as she opened the door for him to enter her room.

Jachin walked over to her bed and laid Ariel down on it as gently as he could. Ripping her shirt and sweater open with a quick yank, he stared at her gaping wound. The bullet had gone straight through her upper chest, near her shoulder, but the wound it left behind had bled profusely. She couldn't afford to lose any more blood.

His sister's hand on his shoulder drew his attention. She had pulled the torn fabric away from his own chest and was examining his wound. He'd seen that look in her eyes before. He knew the physician in her couldn't resist.

"You're lucky it missed your heart. Even with her blood running through your veins you know your wound isn't going to heal completely until I get that bullet out."

Jachin set his jaw. Right now he needed the pain radiating from his shoulder. It kept his mind sharp, focused, kept him from falling on his knees and begging whatever god might be listening to spare Ariel.

Ignoring his sister's concern, he sat down on the bed and carefully lifted Ariel in his arms. When he ran his tongue over the gaping hole across her chest, then carefully turned her and did the same to her back, his heart clenched at the bittersweetness of the act. As her skin began to mend, he closed his eyes briefly, hoping he wasn't too late.

Laying her limp form back down on the bed, he stared at her pale face with a heavy heart. He'd never known what it felt like to not be able to catch his breath…until now. The squeezing sensation around his lungs felt like a vise cinching tight, burning all the way to his stomach. *I can't lose you, my love. Live. For us,* he whispered in her mind.

Yelling echoed from the main atrium room, the sounds growing louder as they flowed down the hall.

Mira moved toward her door and opened it right as Talek was about to knock. His gaze jerked from hers to Jachin's. "The Sanguinas are splintering. Some still support Braeden. They need your guidance."

Guilt tore at Jachin's heart. "She's lost so much blood," he murmured as he glanced at Ariel's wan features.

Mira grabbed his hand and pushed him in the cushioned chair next to her nightstand. "You're not going anywhere until I get that bullet out. Now hold still."

Before he could stand up, she leaned over him and jammed her finger in the bullet hole, digging deep.

Jachin's vision blurred and he gritted his teeth to stay conscious, growling out, "I was better off *with* the bullet."

"Hush—" she started to say when he felt a sharp tug. "Got it!" she said, pulling her fingers free of his body, a bloody bullet plug clamped between them.

Jachin stood and glanced over at Ariel, his heart aching. Mira shoved him toward the door using her clean hand. "I'll watch over her. If our clan ever needed a true leader, it's now. Go."

Ariel sat at a small café table in a coffee shop she'd never visited before, a cup of coffee in front of her. Bright sunbeams flooded through the big picture window and spilled across the room to warm her body, giving the room a cozy feeling conducive to intimate conversation.

Crisp fall air swirled in the room, drawing her attention to the door. A distinguished-looking man in his early fifties walked in the room. He smiled at her, then took off his heavy black overcoat and hung it on the wrought-iron rack beside the door.

"May I join you?" he asked as he approached her table.

Ariel took in the other ten or so unoccupied tables in the room. Maybe he wanted a little company, too. She smiled, nodding.

He settled in the seat across from her and unbuttoned his black suit jacket. "Your coffee smells good. I might have a cup myself."

She liked this stranger. He had an open face with a genuine smile. He reminded her of someone, but she wasn't sure who. "Yes, you should. It's delicious."

He winked at her. "I understand you're a librarian. And an author," he added.

She tilted her head to the side, knowing she should probably be alarmed this total stranger knew information about her, but something about this place felt so warm and safe that curiosity was all she felt.

"And an author," she conceded with a smile, noticing that he now had a cup of coffee, too. How strange. She didn't see anyone bring it.

"You know more than your mind is allowing."

"Really?" His comment seemed out of place but oddly she didn't mind.

He nodded, a knowing smile tugging at his lips. "Braeden's family line is genetically connected to yours. You subconsciously realized this as soon as you heard Braeden say his last name—Raptour. His father was your grandfather's half brother."

His mention of Braeden made her frown. She felt as if she should be somewhere, as if she was missing some big piece of the puzzle, but she couldn't remember where or why. "Who are you?"

He lifted his cup and took a sip before he answered. "Don't you miss Jachin?"

As soon as Jachin's name came out of his mouth, everything came flooding back: her kidnapping, the Lupreda and the Sanguinas, Jachin and her standing with their hands on the ascendancy chalice. She should be wigged out that she wasn't with Jachin…yet, contrary to the confusing thoughts zinging in her head, her body just felt too relaxed to get worked up about anything. She sighed and picked up her coffee. "Why does all that feel like a lifetime ago to me?"

"You're dying," the older man replied in a casual tone, his deep blue gaze locking with hers.

She wondered why his eyes seemed familiar. Strangely, his comment didn't scare her. She felt blissfully sublime. "That's why you're here? To take me home?"

He shook his head. "No, I'm here to convince you to go back."

The sun's rays had moved up her body, warming her all over. It felt so good she closed her eyes. If only there were a bed or a couch here, she'd take a nap, curled up in the pool of bright light.

"Jachin needs you."

Her eyes snapped open at his comment and a tiny place in her heart constricted. "You seem familiar to me. Who are you?"

"My name is Ezra."

Understanding dawned, and her heart kicked up a bit as she reached over to grab his wrist in excitement. "You're Jachin's father."

He turned his hand over and clasped hers, a warm smile lighting his steady gaze. "Indeed I am."

Someone entered the coffee shop through the exit at the back of the store, drawing Ariel's attention.

Mira walked through the shop, dressed in her turtleneck and jeans. She approached their table, a serene smile on her face. Bending over, she hugged Ezra and said, "Hello, father. It's wonderful to see you again." As Mira sat down in the chair next to her, a sense of wrongness shifted inside Ariel.

Ezra met Ariel's gaze, sadness in his eyes. "You know this isn't right."

Ariel's gaze slipped from Ezra to Mira's face. The serene look remained on his daughter's features. She closed her eyes and rubbed her arms with a shiver. "It's cold out there."

Ariel was dying. Ezra was dead. Mira shouldn't be here. She was alive and well at the Sanguinas manor. The three of them together in this café nagged at Ariel's brain until Mira spoke again. "The sunlight feels so good on my skin."

Ariel's eyes widened and her heart jerked in fear for her friend. Mira was a vampire. She grabbed Mira's arm and shook her. "Sunlight will kill you, Mira! Move away!"

Mira glanced at her skin, then met Ariel's gaze with a smile. "Look at me. I'm fine. I've always wanted to know what the sun felt like on my skin." She closed her eyes once more and sighed her contentment.

When Mira's body began to sway, Ezra reached over and gripped her shoulder to keep her from falling out of the chair. "She shouldn't be here."

The frown on Ezra's face, coupled with the harshness and worry in his tone, snapped Ariel out of her trance-like euphoria.

Mira was dying. She had to help her.

Deep concern for her friend obliterated Ariel's peacefulness, shoving her back into her painful reality. Ariel's heart raced, her chest burned like hell and a strange soreness radiated at the bend in her right arm.

"Can I help her?" Ariel asked, jerking her gaze to Ezra's.

Ezra nodded, his expression solemn. "If you go back."

She jumped up and shook the woman's shoulder. "Come on, Mira. We have to get you home."

Mira mumbled, her words slurred and incoherent. Pain shot through Ariel's shoulder as she bent and lifted Mira's lethargic form up from the chair. Wrapping the other woman's arm around her neck, Ariel grasped Mira around the waist and faced Ezra, breathing heavily from her efforts.

"Thank you."

He smiled. "You are everything I knew you would be."

Turning away from the bright light at the front of the café, Ariel headed toward the Exit sign at the back of the store. Right as she reached the door, Ezra stepped in line beside her, placing his hand on the door handle.

"Tell my son the prophecy was meant for more than the Sanguinas."

Her gaze met his and a strong sense of failure made a lump form in her throat. "Are you saying Jachin didn't fulfill the prophecy?"

Ezra shook his head. "He fulfilled his part."

At that moment Mira lost complete consciousness and her body turned limp in Ariel's arms. Ariel's heart raced and she tightened her arm around Mira's form, her muscles straining to keep the unconscious woman upright. She knew she was running out of time. "Help me help Jachin."

Her voiced hitched with her need to know what part of the prophecy they hadn't fulfilled.

Ezra cupped her cheek, his gaze calm and wise. "My son seeks the rest of the prophecy. Relay it to him for me. 'A leader is needed, you know this is true. Look not to one but two. A lesson was the goal you sought. You, too, must learn from what you taught. Layers of deception must be unveiled for three to become one and peace to prevail.'"

"Is this the part we haven't fulfilled?" she asked, confused by his words.

He gave her a warm smile. "As I said, you know more than you've allowed your mind to realize." Pushing the door open, he said in a gentle tone, "You need to go now."

Ariel stared into total darkness and her heart thudded at the sense of nothingness she faced. Taking a deep breath, she hoisted Mira's body tight against her and stepped across the threshold.

Chapter 15

Jachin entered the atrium to face a group of divided vampires brimming with tension. The smell of sweat hung in air, while the heat level felt twenty degrees higher than it had when he'd passed through the huge room a half hour ago.

Thirty or so vampires railed at the rest. "Braeden is the true leader," one of them shouted. "He didn't leave us for ten years like Jachin did."

"And where is he now?" another sneered.

The man's question made the hair on Jachin's neck rise and his jaw to tighten. "Where *is* Braeden?" Jachin's deadly tone silenced the room. Every vampire turned to stare at him.

"Several of us didn't believe he deserved punishment. We let him go," Tomias said as the tall, dark-haired vampire stepped out from the crowd. "He was fighting the weres, while you have apparently made friends with them." He looked down his narrow nose at Jachin, disdain reflected in his brown eyes.

Jachin cleared the distance between himself and the mocking vampire in a split second. "Know your enemy, Tomias," Jachin growled. "It's a tenet we're taught from day one." Scanning the crowd of vampires and finding certain key Sanguinas missing, Jachin barked, "Where are the council members?"

"They spend most of their days in their rooms," Talek answered in an even tone.

Frustration tightened Jachin's chest. "Get them—now!" he said through clenched teeth.

Talek gave Jachin a quick nod, then strode out of the room toward the living quarters.

Jachin saw Vivian's willowy frame separate from the crowd as if she were going to leave the room. Her role in his banishment thumped like an incessant drumbeat in his mind, making his head pound. "Vivian, I would like you to stay."

She stopped and slowly turned his way. "Dawn is upon us. I'm tired. I'm going to bed."

"You. Will. Stay," he ordered in a cold tone.

Talek entered the great hall with three males and one female vampire following in his wake.

Jachin addressed the group of older vampires who came to stand in front of him. "Are you not the council for the Sanguinas?"

Each of them gave him a perplexed look. "You know we

four make up the council," the oldest council member, Liam, spoke up.

Jachin scanned his gaze down the line of council members. "You are the oldest members of this clan, bringing with you knowledge of your past lives as humans before the Scions project. As the clan's leader, I will look to you to help counsel me, to make sure I'm just, to temper my decisions with sound arguments if you disagree, and together we will vote. The majority rules. Understand?"

The three men and lone woman glanced back and forth at each other in confusion before Elin, the female, finally answered, spreading her hands wide. "Our roles have been in name only for many years. Needless to say, we are surprised by this change."

Jachin focused on them as a group and hardened his penetrating stare. "If you don't think you're up to the challenge of fulfilling the responsibilities of your positions, the clan can elect new council members."

"No!" every single member of the council said in unison.

"Good," Jachin nodded, turning back to the Sanguinas population of nearly a hundred vampires. "I will lead you, but every single one of you is responsible for this clan's survival. Know this now—you *will* be judged for any action you take that puts our lives as a whole in jeopardy."

"We didn't ask for your leadership," a vampire called out from the back of the room.

Jachin set his jaw, knowing he would face some opposition. "Vivian, come forward," Jachin said, waving to her.

The female vampire approached, her movements unhurried. She stopped a few feet in front of him, defiance reflected in her gaze.

"Tell them," Jachin demanded, tension coiling in his chest.

She raised her chin in a haughty pose. "I don't know what you're talking about."

Jachin gritted his teeth and demanded, "Tell them why I was banished."

"Because you tried to take Braeden's woman," she answered with a satisfied smirk.

Rage brewed inside him like a storm on the verge of shifting to a full-blown hurricane. He closed the distance between them in one long stride. Gripping her arm, he turned her to face the Sanguinas.

"Braeden left you to fend for yourself. Look them in the eye and tell the truth, Vivian. They are the ones you have to answer to."

Silence descended on the crowd for several seconds, to the point Jachin thought Vivian wasn't going to speak. Then something broke inside her, and she squared her shoulders and cleared her throat.

"Braeden told me to seduce Jachin. He planned to discover Jachin and me together. He wanted Jachin and his ridiculous ideas about the prophecy gone from our presence."

Gasps of disbelief and rumbles of angry surprise rippled through the crowd.

"Finish!" Jachin demanded, his temper on a short fuse.

The group quieted down as Vivian glanced over her shoulder to glare at him. "I don't know what you're talking about."

"Ariel." He said the one word with such conviction Vivian physically flinched.

When she didn't speak, Jachin tightened his hold on her arm. "Don't deny your race their future for your own selfish reasons, Vivian. Tell them or you'll be judged as a traitor."

She pulled out of his hold and tossed her long black hair over her shoulder as her gaze locked with the rapt attention of her clan. "The human's blood is viable."

While a collective gasp of outrage reverberated throughout the clan, a thick-boned female vampire howled and rushed forth, slamming her fist into Vivian's face.

As Vivian fell to the ground, the woman straddled her stomach and grasped her neck, trying to choke her. "You deceitful bitch! I want to have children."

Jachin gripped the woman's arm and hauled her off Vivian. She bared her fangs at Vivian and tried to pull out of his hold, causing Vivian, her face and neck already swelling, to scramble to her feet to get out of the woman's reach.

Jachin held fast to the enraged female's arm, forcing her to meet his gaze. "Fighting amongst ourselves isn't the answer, Paiden."

After a couple more struggles, the fight left her. Jachin wrapped his arm around Paiden's shoulders and faced the Sanguinas. "I can't say what was in Braeden's mind, but I can tell you what's in mine. The prophecy has always ruled me because I want us to flourish. My ultimate goal is not to hide but to eventually live among humans."

His words stirred worried comments from the crowd. "They deserve the punishment, Jachin."

Jachin met the speaker's defiant gaze. "Don't you think we've all suffered enough for our past mistakes? Before the sickness there were many who believed as I did; desiring a life where humanity was something we all sought, not this hunting and vengeance against humans."

"Maybe your human is the only one," another woman said, her tone doubtful.

Jachin shook his head. "She's not. It wasn't until I took her blood that I realized the difference. I have a theory as to how to determine which humans are viable. I will test this theory myself to make sure no more vampires will be poisoned, then I'll share how to tell the difference."

Jachin scanned his sincere gaze to each and every Sanguina in the crowd as he continued, "We need them. But we need to live in harmony, to live without violence. I will establish guidelines and rules for the safety of our clan. All of you will follow them or you'll be brought before the council and me for judgment."

Speaking of judgment, Jachin thought, his blood beginning to boil as he strode toward the group of vampires. Scanning the crowd as he walked, he finally stopped in front of the blond vampire he sought. Jachin stared Vlad down as his entire body flushed with heat. Rage built to explosive levels within Jachin at the thought of the spineless bastard violating his sister.

"What the hell are you looking at?" Vlad glared at him.

"A condemned man," Jachin growled at the same time he slammed his hand around Vlad's throat.

The man had the gall to stare at him with innocent eyes, as if he hadn't done a damn thing wrong.

Yanking Vlad along, he dragged the man through the group and then pulled him around to stand before the council members.

"What punishment would you hand down to this man for violating my sister?" he demanded of the council.

"Castration," Elin hissed without hesitation, her gaze narrowed.

"Banishment," two men responded with conviction.

Jachin was shocked. He'd expected something more. "And you, Liam? What is your vote?" Jachin's gaze snapped to the last council member.

"Banishment," Liam replied with satisfaction.

"No!" Vlad's garbled plea came out in a high-pitched squeal, making him sound like the pig he was.

Suppressing the savage need for revenge that railed through him, tensing every muscle in his body, Jachin took a deep breath and tightened his hold around Vlad's neck, his claws slowly extending from his fingers. "I would like more options, but I'll follow the majority's wishes. You are hereby banished. You are not allowed to speak to or be in the vicinity of another vampire. If you are caught breaking these laws, then the punishment will be death."

After he asked Talek to escort Vlad out of the manor, Jachin left the Sanguinas to check on Ariel. He was thankful his sister hadn't been in the room when he'd dealt with Vlad. She didn't need to relive any part of what the sadistic man had done to her. His blood boiled that he was forced merely to banish the man rather than meting out the kind of punishment he felt Vlad deserved. At least the man would be gone from Mira's presence.

When Jachin neared Mira's room, a sense of panic overtook him. Something wasn't right. He heard Ariel's heart beating at a sluggish rate, while her breathing came out in frantic pants.

He took the last couple of steps in one big stride.

As he jerked the door open, Jachin saw Ariel try to yank something off her arm. He took in the sight of Mira levitating beside her bed a few feet higher than Ariel, her head, feet and arms drooped, her back arched as a tube filled with blood led to Ariel's arm.

Ariel glanced his way. She rolled to her side and tried to rise up in an effort to get to the tube on Mira's arm, her words slurring as she said, "Heelp me get it ouuuut. She's dying!"

A cold chill ran down his spine and Jachin's throat seized in fear. He rushed to the bed, his heart thudding. Gripping Ariel by the shoulders, he pushed her back on the bed. "Lie back," he commanded as he pulled the tape off the needle that had been in Ariel's arm. Running his tongue across her wound, he pushed her arm up in the air. "Hold it there."

He turned to his sister. She was mumbling and delirious, her features gaunt. He quickly removed the needle from her arm and closed her wound with another swipe of his tongue.

Tossing the tube to the floor, he wrapped his arms around his sister's petite form in the air and whispered in her mind, hoping like hell she heard him. *Relax, Mira. Allow yourself to float to the ground.*

Ever so slowly, his sister's body began to lower into his arms. When he felt her slight weight push at his arms, Jachin carried her to the other side of the bed. As he gently laid her down, Ariel's glazed eyes met his.

"Mira tried to save my life. She can't die," Ariel said right before her arm fell to her side and her eyes fluttered closed. Despite her unconscious state, his mate's heartbeat sounded stronger than it had an hour before. She was going to be okay.

When his gaze returned to his sister, tears stung his eyelids and Jachin began to shake as anger, guilt and fear battled within him. He bit down on his own wrist and pressed the open wounds to Mira's mouth, demanding, "Drink! Don't you die on me, damn you."

She managed a few swallows before her lips went slack and her heartbeat completely stopped.

"No!" Jachin yelled, slamming his fist into the wall above the bed so hard it went right through the thick cement block.

He fell to his knees and gripped her wrist, pressing it against his face as anguish racked his body. "Come back, little sister. Please don't leave us."

Memories of a dream his sister had shared with him when she was a little girl flashed through his mind. "I want to be a doctor," she'd said, her blue eyes bright. "Live in the city and care for those in need of help." He squeezed her hand. She had accomplished her goal and far surpassed it. His heart ached at the loss. "Please don't leave us," he repeated in a hoarse voice.

As if in answer to his plea, a faint tremor tapped at his cheek like fingers caressing his face. His throat tightened at the phantom sensation, and he pressed her wrist closer to his skin, waiting, willing a response. The tremor happened again as the sluggish rush of blood pumped through her veins. Jachin closed his eyes, his heart soaring that his sister's life had been spared.

Ariel sat on the top of Sanguinas manor in her favorite spot—in the indentation between two tall walls, overlooking the beautiful view of the Shawangunk mountain range. It was a great place to think. She'd been doing a lot of that, especially about her next book. The sun sank low in the sky, painting the horizon in gorgeous hues of streaked purples, pinks and oranges. She adjusted the sunglasses Jachin had given her, pulling them down to see the colors in their full bloom, but the evening sun caused her eyes to water and burn. Sighing, she shoved the shades back up on her nose.

When the last bit of sunlight gave over to the night sky, Jachin appeared behind her, lifting her off the battlement. His approach had been so silent she jumped at the sensation of his arms encircling her waist.

"Sheesh, you're entirely too good at sneaking up on me," she said, snuggling into the warmth of his embrace.

He kissed her neck, then whispered in her ear, "I really don't like you coming out here by yourself."

She chuckled. "Ah, but if I'm going to live among a bunch of superhumans, at least I'll have one advantage—being able to walk in the sunlight."

Turning in his arms, she slid the glasses up into her hair and met his gaze. "How's Mira?"

Jachin set his jaw and shook his head. "No change. I told her about Vlad's punishment and even that didn't seem to faze her. It's almost as if she doesn't want to wake up."

Guilt swept through Ariel that Mira had risked her life to save hers. "I'm so sorry, Jachin. I wish there was something I could do."

He cupped her face, his gaze searching hers. "To do what she did for you, my sister had to have come to care for you a great deal. She'd be very upset if she knew you felt responsible. She'll come out of her coma when she's ready. We have to believe that."

Ariel gripped his hands and planted a kiss on his palm, then met his gaze with a steady one. "There's something

I've been meaning to tell you, but I'd wanted to wait for Mira to awaken."

He glanced at the dark sconce on the wall. "Do you wish for some light?"

She shook her head, smiling. "I don't know if it's the thinner air up here or what. Not only are my eyes more sensitive to the sunlight, but I can see every expression on your face as if it were daylight. Odd, eh?"

Jachin regarded her with a penetrating gaze. "Very," he said as he laced his fingers with hers and pulled her over to sit down beside him on a wooden bench. "What have you been waiting to tell me?"

She took a deep breath. "I saw your father."

Jachin frowned in confusion. "My father has been dead for more than two decades."

"I know. While I was lying there dying, Ezra visited my dreams and talked to me about the prophecy."

His shoulders tensed and his fingers tightened on hers. "What did my father say? Word for word."

She took a steadying breath. She knew Jachin wasn't going to like the answer. "He said that you fulfilled your part of the prophecy, but that the prophecy wasn't just about the Sanguinas."

"What?" Jachin stood and ran his hands through his hair as he paced in front of her.

"There's more. Your father told me the rest of the prophecy." Once Jachin stopped pacing and gave her his undivided attention, she took a breath and recited the words Ezra had spoken.

"Peace," Jachin whispered, closing his eyes briefly. Opening his eyes, he spoke earnestly. "In my heart I knew that had to be my father's goal."

When he stared off into the distance for several seconds, Ariel knew he was going over the entire prophecy in his mind. "I think part of the prophecy is about the Lupreda," she said.

Jachin frowned, his expression hard, unyielding. "During my battle with the two Lupreda, I saw one of them start to shift outside the moon's cycle. In the past, they could only shift to wolf form during the three days when the moon was at its fullest."

Ariel nodded. "I think it would help if you spoke to Landon."

Jachin locked his gaze with her unwavering one for a couple seconds. Finally he nodded. "I have to meet with the council to discuss the fate of the Sanguinas who have deserted our clan. We're forming our own Sweeper unit. After we figure out the details, we will leave to hunt down Braeden and the others. After things settle, I'll get in touch with Landon."

Her heart jerked at his casual mention of a Sweeper unit. "Do I get one guess who'll be heading up this unit?"

His white teeth flashed in the night. "The unit has to be trained. Who better to lead them than a man who made a living hunting down and eliminating people for ten years?"

Ariel sighed and wrapped her arms around his trim waist, hugging him tight. His masculine scent wrapped around her, both arousing her and making her feel safe all at once. "I don't want anything to happen to you."

"Having you waiting for me to return home safe is a huge incentive to stay alert." Jachin embraced her and kissed her forehead. "Are you happy here?"

She met his concerned gaze and fell even more in love with him. He had an entire clan's future to plan and yet he took the time to ask about her. "Your world is different than mine in many ways, but isn't that why I'm here?"

A stern look hardened his features. "That's not what I asked, Ariel."

She stood on her toes and wrapped her arms around his neck, her lips close to his. "Wherever you are is where I want to be."

Jachin gripped her waist tight and his lips covered hers, his kiss hard and full of need. She kissed him back, enjoying the possessive thrust of his tongue against hers. It was the first time he'd touched her since their time in the dungeon, four days ago. She'd begun to wonder how long it would be before he kissed her again, and held her as if he never wanted to let her go.

His lips never left hers as he gripped her rear and pressed her against a tall rampart wall, jamming his muscular thigh between her legs.

Ariel's breasts tingled and her sex ached at his primal response. She ground her body against his leg and clutched him close, moaning against his mouth.

When her tongue encountered the point of his fangs, she ran her tongue along the sharp tips and relished in the shudder that passed across his shoulders at the taste of her blood.

He groaned and twined his tongue with hers while he fit his erection against her body. His mouth slanted over hers and his hips moved against her.

Her breath hitched as her body ignited with his aggressive thrusts, but it was the way he sucked on her tongue that made her wish no clothes separated their bodies. She slid her fingers in his hair and pulled him even closer, whispering his name.

Jachin suddenly set her down and stepped away. She shivered in confusion as he took deep, ragged breaths, the look on his face full of lust.

"What's wrong?"

His hand shook as he ran it through his hair. "I can't— I have to go."

When he turned to leave, she grabbed his arm, her chest constricting and her stomach pitching. "You're going to leave me like this?"

He grabbed her shoulders and set her against the stone wall, his face a mask of anger. "If I don't go now, I'll take everything you have to offer…every sigh, every tremor and every damned last drop!"

Her gaze searched his, begging him. "I trust you to stop."

"I don't," he growled in response before he walked away.

After Jachin left her wanting and angry, Ariel needed someone to talk to. She entered Mira's quiet chamber and flipped a switch on the wall to light up several of the sconces, giving the room a warm glow. She'd learned that the Sanguinas did use some power, ironically mostly from solar sources, but they utilized very little so they wouldn't draw attention to themselves.

Sitting down in the chair next to the petite vampire, she picked up Mira's small-boned hand and held it between hers. "We're so worried about you. You should see your brother. As stubborn and arrogant and pigheaded as he can be, he's turning out to be exactly what your clan needs in a leader."

Silence greeted her comments as her gaze traveled over

Mira's face. Even in full repose, the female vampire was beautiful. Ariel's heart ached with guilt. She pressed on Mira's hand and leaned closer. "I know Jachin told you about Vlad's punishment. He doesn't like it, but he knows Vlad will break the rules and meet up with Braeden, Vivian and the few other vampires who deserted yesterday while Jachin was in chambers with the council. Jachin and the council are forming a Sweeper unit to hunt them down."

Ariel watched Mira's face for a reaction to her words. Nothing.

She sighed.

"Jachin refuses to touch me, Mira." Tears filled her eyes as she poured out her heart. "Ever since he took my blood in the dungeon he doesn't trust himself. He thinks he'll drain me completely." She gave a sobbing laugh as she wiped her eyes with the back of her hand. "Isn't that the silliest thing you've ever heard? I know the man cares for me. What kind of relationship is that—to be with the person you've come to care for but never trust yourself to touch them?" In truth, she'd fallen in love with Jachin, but he'd held himself at such a distance the past several days…she didn't trust herself to tell him for fear that it would never really be returned. Could he ever truly love a human?

Laying her forehead on Mira's lax hand, she continued, "I need your guidance. You promised me you'd never leave me!"

Fingers stroked her hair at the same time she heard, "You just have to make him want it."

Ariel gasped and jerked her gaze to the vampire's tired one. Squeezing Mira's hand, she smiled through the tears streaking down her face. "I'm so glad to see those beautiful blue eyes staring back at me."

Mira returned her smile and rolled on her side, her gaze locking with Ariel's as she squeezed her hand. "I've always wanted a sister."

Ariel gave a thankful laugh. "I take it you heard everything I said. Do you have any sisterly advice?"

Even though her face appeared ashen and drawn, Mira's eyes crinkled in amusement. "I have faith in your ability to show Jachin the idiocy of his ways."

Ariel chuckled, her heart soaring at Mira's recovery. "For the record, you scared the crap out of me. Don't ever do that again."

Mira rolled to stare at the ceiling. She let out a heavy sigh. "I didn't want to come back, but I had you whispering in my ear and father scowling at me."

"Why didn't you want to come—" Ariel started to ask when the answer dawned on her. Despite her bravado, Mira had never really gotten over what Vlad did to her. Her heart heavy, Ariel scooted over to sit on the bed. Lifting Mira's hand, she hooked her pinky finger around Mira's and said, "You made me a promise and now it's my turn to make you one. We'll call it a sisterly pact. I'll never leave you. I'll be by your side always."

Mira curled her finger tight around Ariel's and tears filled her blue gaze. She sat up and hugged her tight. "Thank you for coming into our lives."

"I couldn't have said it better myself," Jachin said from across the room as he closed the open door.

Mira sniffed and waved for him to join them.

Once her brother sat down on the other side of her, she

cupped his cheek and smiled, glancing back and forth between them. "It's good to be back and see my two favorite people by my side."

After they talked for a while, Ariel slipped out of Mira's room so Mira could talk with Jachin alone. She headed back to her bedroom to brainstorm her next book.

Be careful what you create, it might come back to bite you.

Ariel sat at the banker-style desk in her bedroom, frowning at the lone sentence she'd written an hour ago on the otherwise blank sheet of paper in front of her. She had been flooded with ideas, but now that she had to actually get them down on paper, she was stuck. She tapped her pen on the smooth walnut surface, wondering where to take that one sentence.

Glancing past her bed to the annoying pendulum clock on the fireplace mantel, she glared at it, then sighed and returned her gaze to the sentence, twirling the pen between her fingers absently. In her dream, Ezra told her she knew more than her mind allowed. Even though she knew she wouldn't publish this next book for the general public, she still felt the need to tell the next story. Maybe it would help unravel the meaning behind the rest of the prophecy.

Ezra's last comment about the prophecy echoed in her head to the slow beat of the pendulum's swing. *Tell my son the prophecy was meant for more than the Sanguinas.*

She straightened her shoulders as a thought popped into her mind. *What if the werewolves have other secrets?*

A knock at her door startled Ariel, making her jump as her pulse raced.

It's me, Jachin spoke in her mind. *I'm heading out with the Sweeper team in a bit. Can I come in?*

Even though she was still pissed at Jachin for the way he'd left her earlier, aching and needy, Ariel's chest tightened at the idea of her mate leaving to hunt vampires—and she had come to think of him that way. She didn't want to think about Jachin getting hurt or, God forbid, killed. When he got back, she intended to take Mira's advice and make the man want her so bad he wouldn't be able to resist her.

For now, she wanted them to part on good terms. She blew out a steadying breath to calm her suddenly tense nerves and stood, calling out, "Come in."

She'd just rounded the desk and was starting toward the door when Jachin walked in. Ariel halted her steps and her heart skipped several beats at the devastating sight before her. *Dear God, is the man trying to torture me?*

Chapter 16

Ariel's heart leapt as she took in his dark hair and stubbled jaw, black T-shirt stretched across his shoulders and defined biceps, tight black jeans and matching combat boots. But what yanked at her throat, drawing a straight line to the yearning within her, was the automatic gun strapped to his thigh and the thick leather vest loaded with knives and other sharp weapons buckled over his broad chest.

The entire dangerous package conjured a fantasy, tapping into her deepest desires—for a dark warrior dressed in battle gear to pull her into his arms and seduce her with his body.

And his fangs.

As her arousal grew, her jeans rubbed annoyingly against her throbbing sex while her thin sweater chafed her tight, sensitive nipples. Despite her reaction, she straightened her spine and tried to sound casual as he strode across the room toward her. "I see you're ready for battle."

Jachin walked right into her personal space, his dominant presence towering and seductively appealing. "I wanted to say goodbye." He ran his thumb along her jaw in a gentle caress, his blue-black gaze following his finger's wake.

Jachin's nostrils flared and his gaze searched hers as if he were trying to see into her soul. Curling his hand into a fist, he lowered it to his side. "As part of this trip, I'm going to head into town and test my theory." He gave her a wry smile. "Wish me luck."

Ariel frowned in confusion. "What theory?"

Jachin's eyebrows rose. "I'm convinced there are more humans like you whose blood isn't poisoned. Whenever I was around you, I detected the scent of almonds. I'd noticed an almondlike smell other times, too, when I was in the city, but it was random enough and mixed with so many other scents that I didn't make the connection until I took your blood."

He nodded, warming to the subject. "When I thought back to the times I'd noticed the sweet, nutty scent, the humans who were in the vicinity were all younger. My theory…my belief is that whatever caused humans' blood to become tainted in the past is being bred out of them with each new generation while leaving a way for us to detect viable humans in the process."

Ariel's chest felt as if someone were squeezing it tighter and tighter. Jachin touched her shoulders. "Don't you see? If I'm right, I plan to establish rules and guidelines for the Sanguinas. There won't be any more violence against humans."

Ariel nodded mutely at the significance of what Jachin

was saying. She knew it was a big deal for the Sanguinas if his theory was right, but her heart was aching. Instead of feeling closer to him, she felt as if they were drifting apart.

Jachin trailed his fingers down her cheek. He stared at her with both sadness and desire in his gaze. "Once I take care of the rogue vampires and the city is safe, I'll take you home."

Her eyes widened and her heart plummeted at his last comment. "What?"

He ran his hands down her shoulders, regret in his gaze. "I never gave you a choice. You've done so much to help me and my clan. I don't know how to repay that other than to let you go, to give you your freedom."

But I'm your mate, she wanted to rail at him. He'd made her care about him, cherish his sister, believe in helping his race…yet he didn't want her. She put trembling fingers to her lips as all the pent-up fury and feelings of rejection she'd been trying to suppress rose to the surface, twisting her stomach into tight knots.

Jachin gripped her arms and pulled her close, his expression intense. "Why are you shaking?"

With her hands trapped between them, she shoved at Jachin's face and neck, pushing him away. "You won't touch me or take my blood, but now that you think there are others out there to supply you with what you need, you're sending me away?"

Jachin dabbed at the blood welling on his chin where her nails must've caught him by accident. His eyes narrowed a split second before he had her flat on her back across the double bed, her arms stretched over her head. "I want you so much I ache," he growled, his face mere inches from hers. His grip tightened on her wrists as his full weight and heavy weapons pressed her body into the mattress. "Yours is the *only* blood I crave, with a need that gnaws in my gut until I feel I'm going insane. As much as it tears me up inside to think of life without you, I was trying to give you your freedom, Ariel…freedom from *me*."

His confession combined with the hungry desire in his gaze swiftly dissipated her anger. Sheer determination took its place. She wanted his body pressed against hers, flesh to flesh, his fangs digging deep. "I don't want my freedom. I only want you. I love you, Jachin. Take what you want."

His eyes searched hers, hunger, regret, guilt and lust mingling in their deep blue depths. "I don't trust myself around you, Ariel. I love you too much."

His fingers loosened around her wrists and she realized he was going to pull away. Ariel's heart jerked. He'd just professed his love, making her heart sing. She couldn't lose this chance to share with him. "I have enough faith for both of us," she said right before she ran her tongue along his chin and upward toward his mouth, swiping away the streak of blood.

Jachin's entire body tensed at her action. When she reached the corner of his lips, cleansing the last drop away, his fingers cinched around her wrists and he turned his mouth with a primal groan, capturing her lips in a possessive kiss.

Ariel's heart raced at the hard pressure of his mouth, the deep thrust of his tongue alongside hers. Her breasts swelled and her nipples tingled, while her body throbbed, ready to feel him plunging inside her, taking her in every way. She craved his dominant, erotic possession. She'd never get enough of this primal side of Jachin.

Ever.

She began to tug at the buckles on his vest as he unbuttoned her jeans. Feverish hands moved with a speed she didn't think possible, dumping weapons, boots and clothes until they both were completely naked.

Jachin leaned on his elbow over her, his muscular arm and warm, hard chest pressing against her side as he trailed his fingers along her bare skin, across her breasts and down her abdomen. "Nothing terrifies me but the thought of losing you."

"As you've found, I'm stronger than you first thought." Ariel gave him a sexy smile as she captured his hand and brought it to her lips. She sucked on the tip of his index finger, then slid her lips down the length until Jachin groaned and pressed his hard erection against her thigh.

Tugging his finger from her mouth, he thrust his fingers in her hair and rolled on top of her, his mouth claiming hers once more.

Ariel moaned at the feel of his hot skin covering hers, the fine hairs on his chest rasping her sensitive nipples and his heavy cock pressing against the inside of her thigh. She wrapped her arms around his neck and arched into him, welcoming his weight.

He kissed her jaw and her neck, his hands running over her breasts and down her sides to grip her hips. His mouth moved across her jaw and she felt his teeth sliding along her skin. While her belly tightened and her channel flooded with moisture in her need for sexual release, her emotions whirled within her.

Her love for Jachin swirled and built in her mind, her complete dedication to this man taking hold of her psyche until all she sensed was his heavy heartbeat, the coiled sexual tension spiking within him and the need to take her blood clawing in his gut.

His cock touched her entrance and she surged against him as understanding of his hunger took hold of her. She gasped at the sheer intensity and almost insatiable need to feed that made his gums tingle right before his fangs descended.

The sensation burned in her chest…his chest…no, it was her own body that burned, *her* hunger that cried out for fulfillment.

Something was happening, something beautiful as she finally understood.

Fire raged within her, starting in her sex and splintering to every pulse point in her body.

She had to make him take her blood, to get him past his fear he would kill her. Breathing heavily, her body aching to be filled, she rocked against him as she moved her lips up the veined column of his throat. Laving his skin with her tongue, she teased him with her warm breath, sliding her hands down his muscular back, until he tensed and gripped the back of her head.

"Ariel…" he said in a hoarse voice as he began to slide inside her.

Ariel's heart thumped and her entire body vibrated with need. Following the primal instincts driving her, she bit down on his neck.

Jachin let out a low groan and moved into her. With her teeth locked on his neck, Ariel realized he'd gone very still against her. Had she bitten him too hard? But the sudden rush of his blood flooding her mouth, the erotic taste, sent her into a euphoric state beyond anything she'd ever thought possible.

When Jachin let out an animalistic sound of sheer ecstasy, she swallowed his blood and the world around her ceased to exist. The only thing that mattered was Jachin providing the most powerful and elemental aphrodisiac.

He began to move inside her, his thrusts increasing with each swallow she took. Groaning, he gripped her hair and rambled like a man drugged half out of his mind. "Damn, I'm… Ariel!"

His hard penetrations sent her body spiraling out of control. Ariel released her hold on his neck and panted at the pleasure radiating within her. He filled her completely, rubbing every crevice, taking total possession. Her pulse hammered and she gripped his shoulders tight. "Feels so good," she gasped.

With each downward thrust, he pressed her harder against the mattress, making her want him even more. She was lost in their lovemaking, drugged by his taste and so close to her climax she began to breathe in short, choppy huffs.

His fingers tightened in her hair and his other hand gripped her thigh, pulling her tight against him as he sank his fangs deep in her neck. Ariel cried out from the pleasure/pain and the euphoric sensations slamming through her. She clenched her throbbing sex around his cock, reveling in the explosive orgasm that rippled though her with hammering crests of sheer unadulterated passionate pulses.

A deep primordial growl erupted from Jachin as he sucked hard on her throat, swallowing like a man who'd been without sustenance for weeks. Her breath hitched each time his lips pulled at her throat. Each draw he took felt as though his tongue were rasping at her sensitive nub, urging it to arousing attention.

Ariel keened and rocked her hips as the sensation continued its relentless pressure. When Jachin slammed his erection deep and ground his body against her mound, she whimpered, then sobbed in relief. Her body gave way to another round of climactic tremors shattering through her, zapping her strength and claiming her breath.

Jachin grunted and surged against her, riding his own climax until they both collapsed in a tangle of arms and legs, pounding heartbeats and glistening skin.

When he laved at the wound on her neck, then placed a gentle kiss on the same spot, she ran her hands over his shoulders, loving how tender this strong man could be. Adrenaline still pumped through her veins, and she'd never felt more sexually satiated.

Jachin lay on his side and turned her face toward his. Running his thumb along her lips, he pushed her upper lip back. Her pulse skipped and her gums tingled as he stared at her teeth.

His gaze jerked to hers, full of wonder. "I thought I'd imagined the sensation of fangs sliding inside my skin. How is this possible?"

Ariel ran her tongue along her teeth. Slight disappointment twinged within her when she encountered normal-size canines. "You did imagine it."

Jachin frowned and cupped her neck. He ran his fingers down her throat in a slow caress. "I just watched your fangs retract. You don't want this?"

Having him confirm what she suspected had happened made her stomach knot. The whole time she'd been experiencing what she thought was *his* hunger and the tingling in *his* gums; she now realized the sensations must've truly been her own.

She laid her hand over his. "I don't know how I feel about this change in me, but I can tell you I now understand the torture you've felt these past few days. It's almost overwhelming, this need for your blood."

He gripped her hand and raised it to his lips, kissing her palm. "As far as I know, no human has tasted a vampire's blood. Your change could be a result of that." His serious gaze locked with hers as he continued. "I won't lie to you and tell you I'm sorry. When you bit me…" He paused and the vulnerable look in his eyes shocked her all the way to her toes. "I've never felt anything more erotic."

Ariel's heart thumped at his comment and her spirits rose. Their attraction was already electric. Her new ability to take his blood gave a whole other perspective—a very positive one. When they made love, he wouldn't have to hold back. He could follow his natural instincts, be as primal and aggressive as he wanted, and for that she was incredibly thankful.

She gave him a brilliant smile and wrapped her arms around his neck. "I'm thrilled to be able to take your breath away when we make love."

Jachin wrapped his arm around her waist and rolled over, pulling her on top of him. His intense gaze locked with hers. "You must go forward with caution. We have no idea the level of changes you've undergone." Concern etched his expression. "You must not walk out into the sunlight like you have in the past. Test your limits carefully first. Understand?"

"I love you, too." She smiled, adoring the worried look on his handsome face. She knew firsthand how fierce and deadly he could be. Being the recipient of his tender, protective side made her feel all the more cherished.

"Ariel! Come inside, sweetie. I want to show you something."

Ariel sighed as she moved away from her favorite place on the top of the manor and the sun's warm late-afternoon rays to respond to Mira's call.

The gorgeous cream-and-gold floor-length dress Mira had given her fit perfectly. The silk material felt so good against her skin. Her "sister" had given her the present a couple of hours before, saying, "I was so excited to finally have a little sister to fuss over I couldn't resist. I spent so many hours on it. Please wear it for an hour and then you can take it off and put it away."

So Ariel had shown her appreciation by sliding into the gown, but she couldn't resist venturing to the roof. Jachin and the Sweepers had gone looking for the renegade vampires two days ago, and her nerves were shot waiting for him to return.

"Come on, Ariel," Mira called once more, drawing her attention.

"I could use the distraction," she mumbled and walked inside the castle's arched wooden door.

Mira smiled and grabbed Ariel's hand. Tugging her along, the vampire preceded Ariel down the spiral stairs that led away from the top of the castle. Excitement bubbled up from her friend in an almost auralike glow, making Ariel smile. Mira was wearing a long royal-blue dress, so maybe she had more gowns to show her. Ariel was glad to see her friend so enthused about…well, whatever it was she was excited about.

Mira was moving so fast Ariel had to grab her skirt and lift it off the ground to keep up with the woman's pace. The chill inside the castle stairway made her wish she could control her body temperature the way Jachin could. In the past couple of days since Jachin had left, Ariel had discovered her ability to see better at night. The sunlight stinging her eyes was a permanent adjustment she'd have to get used to, but other than her fangs extending and her craving for Jachin's blood while he made love to her, she remained mostly human. Only time would tell what other changes, if any, she might undergo as a vampire's mate.

Mira opened the door that led to the main hall and tugged Ariel in front of her.

Ariel stopped short at the sight of all the vampires gathered as if they were waiting for them.

"Um, hi," she said, her stomach fluttering with nerves at their welcoming, anticipatory expressions. What was going on?

The group of vampires began to back away, parting like a wave slicing through the ocean. Mira hooked her arm in Ariel's and walked her forward right down the middle.

When Ariel saw Jachin standing at the end of the hall, looking handsome in a black suit, she started to pick up her skirt and run, but Mira kept a tight hold on her arm.

"Calm and cool, my dear."

"Huh?" Ariel glanced at Mira, then remembered they had an audience—the entire Sanguinas clan.

Elin stood beside Jachin, looking regal in her long teal-blue robe with gold piping. Ariel's heart raced and her entire frame shook with the need to rush to Jachin, to find out if he'd found the rogue vampires, if he had discovered untainted humans.

Mira walked her right up to Jachin and then kissed Ariel on the cheek before she unhooked her arm and stepped back a few feet.

Ariel stepped close to Jachin and asked, "How'd it go?"

Jachin's loving gaze searched her face as he took her hand and wrapped her fingers around the crook of his arm. "I've missed you."

When Jachin turned her toward Elin and said, "We're ready to begin, Elin," Ariel glanced at him, her fingers digging into the expensive black material.

"Is this a Sanguina ritual I wasn't aware of?"

Jachin glanced down at her and smiled. "No, my love, this is a very human ritual known as a wedding ceremony."

Ariel swayed at his calm delivery. Jachin's arm came around her. He chuckled, then whispered in her ear, "Let's save the swooning for after the ceremony. Then I'll have an excuse to whisk you away to our wing instead of sticking around socializing at the party afterward."

"Humans don't do *surprise* wedding ceremonies," she shot back in a low tone, trying her best to compose herself.

He spoke in her mind, *You might not be fully human any longer, but your heart still is. I want you to know I've pledged myself to you in both my world and yours. Elin is waiting.*

As Elin recited the traditional wedding vows and then she and Jachin repeated them, Ariel's chest tightened as she stared at Jachin. *I love him so much it hurts.*

While Jachin slid a beautiful diamond eternity ring on her finger, he said aloud for the entire clan to hear, "I pledge my life, my love, my eternity to you."

When Elin said, "I now pronounce you husband and wife," thunderous applause resounded behind them.

Jachin turned Ariel around to the crowd of Sanguinas and lifted her left land in the air. "I present to you, Mrs. Jachin Black."

After Jachin finished speaking, the entire clan applauded and converged around them to offer well-wishes. Ariel's heart raced and butterflies exploded in her stomach at the Sanguinas' overwhelming offerings of approval.

Jachin carried Ariel over the threshold of their new suite. Unbeknownst to them both, several of the Sanguinas had cleared out Braeden's things and redecorated the room. As he set her feet on the gorgeous thick carpet that now took up most of the entry chamber, he asked, "What do you think?"

Ariel scanned the room for that damned pendulum clock and let out a sigh of relief when she didn't see it anywhere. Through another doorway, a huge four-poster bed with a thick navy comforter filled another room. Between the couches and the wall hangings, the living space was decorated in shades of dark and ice blues with ivory mixed in. She loved the contrast in colors.

"The next time we go to the city we'll retrieve some of your things to add to our home."

Ariel smiled, appreciating his effort to try to make her feel at home. When her gaze landed on a family portrait that hung over an ornate stone fireplace, she walked closer.

Ezra, younger and handsome, was dressed in a dark suit and seated in a leather chair. A regal-looking woman with auburn hair and a young teenage boy stood behind the chair. They both had their hands on the chair's back, while a girl with stark black hair and vivid blue eyes stood on the side of the chair, close to Ezra.

"I haven't seen that picture in more than a decade," Jachin said in a low tone behind her.

"Your mother was beautiful," Ariel said, her heart tugging for his losses.

"She was a good soul. I miss her."

Ariel turned sad eyes his way. "I'm sorry you lost your parents."

Jachin put his hands on her shoulders and gave them a gentle squeeze. "You lost everyone you loved, too, due to Braeden and his father. We will find him."

The old hurt returned when she thought of her family, but this time fear wasn't its constant companion. Remembering her earlier fear for Jachin's safe return, she glanced up at him. "What happened with the Sweepers?"

His dark eyebrows drew downward. "We discovered two vampires and hunted them almost to town. But Vivian, Vlad, Braeden and the other three weren't with them. We can only presume they've made it to the city, and without other means for food, it'll only be a matter of time before they start hunting humans. My theory about other viable humans was correct. I'll have to get the Sanguinas trained so they can help find Braeden and the others." His gaze locked with hers as his arms encircled her waist. Pulling her against his chest, he asked, "How's the book coming?"

"Okay at first. Now…it's slow," she said with a grimace.

Jachin kissed her forehead. "I remember reading somewhere that authors sometimes read when they're stuck on a story. You do know we have a library, right?"

Her entire body tensed in excitement. "Library? No. I didn't."

He smiled. "Then I'll take you there tomorrow so you can read to your heart's content."

"Ah, I'll be in heaven," she said with a smile. "A stint of reading will do me good, I'm sure."

His gaze turned serious as he ran his hands along her upper back. Jachin reached into his suit pocket and uncurled his fingers in front of her. A single platinum ring lay across his palm. "You really didn't think I'd forget this, did you?"

Ariel's heart leapt and she lifted the heavy ring. As she slid the band down his left ring finger, she said, "I pledge my life, my love and my eternity to you…." Lacing her fingers with his, she kissed the ring and met his loving gaze as she finished, "My Sanguinas mate."

* * * * *

You can lead a horse to water...

When Alyssa Barkley and Clint Westmoreland
found out that their "fake" marriage was never
rendered void, they are forced to live together
for thirty days. However, Clint loves the single
life and has no intention of being tamed, but
when Alyssa moves in, the sizzling attraction
between them is ignited and neither wants the
thirty days to end.

Look for
TAMING CLINT WESTMORELAND
by
BRENDA JACKSON

Available February wherever you buy books

Visit Silhouette Books at www.eHarlequin.com   SD76850

Romantic
SUSPENSE

**Sparked by Danger,
Fueled by Passion.**

When Tech Sergeant Jacob "Mako" Stone opens
his door to a mysterious woman without a past,
he knows his time off is over. As threats to Dee's
life bring her and Jacob together, she must set
aside her pride and accept the help of the military
hero with too many secrets of his own.

Out of Uniform
by Catherine Mann

Available February wherever you buy books.

Visit Silhouette Books at www.eHarlequin.com   SRS27571

REQUEST YOUR FREE BOOKS!

2 FREE NOVELS PLUS 2 FREE GIFTS!

Silhouette®

nocturne™

Dramatic and Sensual Tales of Paranormal Romance.

YES! Please send me 2 FREE Silhouette® Nocturne™ novels and my 2 FREE gifts. After receiving them, if I don't wish to receive any more books, I can return the shipping statement marked "cancel." If I don't cancel, I will receive 4 brand-new novels every other month and be billed just $4.47 per book in the U.S. or $4.99 per book in Canada, plus 25¢ shipping and handling per book plus applicable taxes, if any*. That's a savings of about 15% off the cover price! I understand that accepting the 2 free books and gifts places me under no obligation to buy anything. I can always return a shipment and cancel at any time. Even if I never buy another book from Silhouette, the two free books and gifts are mine to keep forever.

238 SDN ELS4 338 SDN ELXG

Name   (PLEASE PRINT)

Address   Apt. #

City   State/Prov.   Zip/Postal Code

Signature (if under 18, a parent or guardian must sign)

Mail to the **Silhouette Reader Service™:**
IN U.S.A.: P.O. Box 1867, Buffalo, NY 14240-1867
IN CANADA: P.O. Box 609, Fort Erie, Ontario L2A 5X3

Not valid to current Silhouette Nocturne subscribers.

Want to try two free books from another line?
Call 1-800-873-8635 or visit www.morefreebooks.com.

* Terms and prices subject to change without notice. NY residents add applicable sales tax. Canadian residents will be charged applicable provincial taxes and GST. This offer is limited to one order per household. All orders subject to approval. Credit or debit balances in a customer's account(s) may be offset by any other outstanding balance owed by or to the customer. Please allow 4 to 6 weeks for delivery.

Your Privacy: Silhouette is committed to protecting your privacy. Our Privacy Policy is available online at www.eHarlequin.com or upon request from the Reader Service. From time to time we make our lists of customers available to reputable firms who may have a product or service of interest to you. If you would prefer we not share your name and address, please check here. ☐

SN07

HARLEQUIN®

INTRIGUE®

BREATHTAKING ROMANTIC SUSPENSE

Look for

UNDER
HIS SKIN

BY RITA HERRON

Nurse Grace Gardener brought
Detective Parker Kilpatrick back from
the brink of death, only to seek his
protection. On a collision course with
two killers who want to keep their
secrets, she's recruited the one detective
with the brass to stop them.

Available February wherever you buy books.

BECAUSE THE BEST PART
OF A GREAT ROMANCE
IS THE MYSTERY.

www.eHarlequin.com

HI69310

nocturne™

COMING NEXT MONTH

#33 THE QUEST • Lindsay McKenna
Warriors for the Light

Pursued by the Dark Lord and his dire knights, Nolan Galloway must put aside his tragic past with Kendra Johnson to journey through death and redemption—and a love renewed.

#34 DARK SEDUCTION • Kathleen Korbel
Daughters of Myth

A great war is brewing. Only Sorcha, daughter of the fairy queen, can prevent it by enchanting Harry Wyatt. But this handsome man, who has the very faerie stone she seeks, trusts her the least. And now she must make Harry believe in the impossible…and in the power of love to stop this faerie war.

SNCNM0108